THE MACKENZIE CHRONICLES

A GUIDE TO THE MACKENZIES / MCBRIDE SERIES BY JENNIFER ASHLEY

MACKENZIES / MCBRIDES

JENNIFER ASHLEY

JA / AG PUBLISHING

CONTENTS

Introduction   v

THE MADNESS OF LORD IAN MACKENZIE   1
LADY ISABELLA'S SCANDALOUS MARRIAGE   25
THE MANY SINS OF LORD CAMERON   47
THE DUKE'S PERFECT WIFE   63
A MACKENZIE FAMILY CHRISTMAS: THE
PERFECT GIFT   83
THE UNTAMED MACKENZIE   95
THE SEDUCTION OF ELLIOT MCBRIDE   109
THE WICKED DEEDS OF DANIEL MACKENZIE   121
SCANDAL AND THE DUCHESS   137
RULES FOR A PROPER GOVERNESS   153
A MACKENZIE CLAN GATHERING   183
THE STOLEN MACKENZIE BRIDE   197
ALEC MACKENZIE'S ART OF SEDUCTION   217
FIONA AND THE THREE WISE HIGHLANDERS   239
THE DEVILISH LORD WILL   255
A ROGUE MEETS A SCANDALOUS LADY   273
A MACKENZIE YULETIDE   291
THE SINFUL WAYS OF JAMIE MACKENZIE   307
Final Note   327
Mackenzies / McBrides Series Timeline   329
Mackenzie Family Tree   334
Series ISBNs   339

A Note on Availability   343
Other books by Jennifer Ashley   347
About the Author   349

INTRODUCTION

Welcome to the *Mackenzie Chronicles*!

What follows is a guide to the Mackenzie / McBride series by Jennifer Ashley, which began with *The Madness of Lord Ian Mackenzie.*

In this guide, you'll find character sketches of the main couple of each book, a brief synopsis of each story, an excerpt for that book, and my notes and thoughts about the story and the characters—including why I wrote that particular book, challenges I faced, and what I enjoyed most.

I have included a family tree at the end to keep all the characters straight, and a timeline for the stories, which does not not necessarily follow publication order.

I also have the entire series listed in publication order with links to where you can find them.

Note that the Mackenzies series is ongoing. I will begin a second volume when new books come out, and alert my mailing list as well as my FB group, plus I will post such news on my website (www.jenniferashley.com) and blog.

I hope you enjoy the guide and the series.

Best wishes,
   Jennifer Ashley

THE MADNESS OF LORD IAN MACKENZIE

CHARACTERS

Main Characters

Lord Ian Mackenzie

THE YOUNGEST SON IN THE SCANDALOUS MACKENZIE FAMILY, brother of the current Duke of Kilmorgan, Ian has been considered "mad" for most of his life, or at least, very odd. He can be quiet, almost broody, but then will break out with something extraordinary. He remembers everything he sees, hears, reads. He learns languages with flawless ease in a few days. He can play something on the piano after hearing it once, no matter how complicated. He remembers complex things like every entry on a ledger after seeing it once, or knowing the position of every card in a deck after looking at it once.

Ian doesn't believe he can connect to people like his brothers can. He holds himself apart, thinking he has nothing to give but his strange talents for memorizing things. He can obsess over things, like Ming pottery, which he collects—but it has to be certain kinds of bowls within a very narrow period. Anything else just isn't right.

Ian enjoys pleasures of the flesh (food, wine, women) because he thinks they give him the substitute for emotion, which he believes he can't feel (because it's difficult for him to articulate it).

On the other hand, he's kind, generous, and incredibly loyal. He befriends and helps people though he doesn't talk to them much. He looks out for the weak because he learned in the asylum in which he spend most of his boyhood that the meek mostly inherited beatings.

He survived and he's still surviving at the beginning of the book, not thinking anything will change for him, until he instructs Curry to secure him tickets for the opera and to find out everything he can about one Beth Ackerley.

Beth Ackerley, nee Villiers

BETH ACKERLEY, born Beth Villiers, was born to a gentlewoman and a French confidence trickster. Her father, drunk most of his days, died when Beth was young, leaving her and her mother penniless. Because her mother's family, country gentry, disapproved of the marriage, Beth and her mother are forced into poverty, living in and out of workhouses in the East End of London. When Beth's mother passes away, she becomes a typist in a workhouse in Bethnal Green, where she meets and marries the local vicar, Thomas Ackerley. After a brief but happy marriage, her husband dies, leaving her grieving, and again penniless. Fortunately, Beth has been introduced to a wealthy, elderly woman who takes Beth as her companion. When the elderly woman dies, Beth finds, to her surprise, that she has been left much of the woman's fortune, and her large house in Belgravia.

Beth decides to use the money to better herself—learn new skills, make new friends, and soon becomes engaged to the son of her benefactor's friend. She's happy with the engagement, preparing to settle down to a quiet life.

Then she meets Ian Mackenzie.

———

IMPORTANT SECONDARY CHARACTERS
Mac Mackenzie
Cameron Mackenzie
Hart Mackenzie
Daniel Mackenzie (Cameron's son)
Isabella Mackenzie (nee) Scranton (wife to Mac)
Mrs. Palmer
Inspector Lloyd Fellows
Lyndon Mather

AUTHOR'S NOTES

THE QUESTION I AM MOST ASKED ABOUT THE MADNESS OF LORD Ian Mackenzie is "Is Ian on the spectrum?" The answer is yes. I never say the words autism or AS in the book, because both these conditions weren't recognized until the twentieth century.

At the same time, there must have been plenty of people on the spectrum in the Victorian age, and I wondered how a person would deal with such a thing at a time when such disorders were not understood.

I did not set out to write a book with an AS hero. Ian Mackenzie came first. I watched him in my head for a long time, trying to decide just what his character was telling me. After a lot of research, I realized he was on the spectrum.

Regardless of how he gets labeled, Ian is Ian. He behaves as he does because that is who he is. Those who love him, love him for himself.

I also wanted to explore how the support and love of another person can open one who has folded in on himself. Ian can function in the world, but only because he copies "normal" behavior. Once he meets Beth, he starts to understand the why of what he does—and cares to understand it.

As for the rest of the family—I had all four brothers and their stories in mind before I developed and wrote the first book.

The Mackenzies—Ian, Mac, Cam, Hart—are decadent, wealthy, Scotsmen. I saw a family of men who lived hard and didn't care what the world thought of them. Raised by an abusive father, they are now free to do as they please, with family money doled out equally to them—though Hart controls the dukedom and the main property.

The Mackenzies love intensely, but at the same time are very bad at relationships.

Mac, the artist, eloped with Lady Isabella Scranton the night he met her, but they separated a few years later.

Cameron, a genius with his horses, married very young to a volatile woman who died, leaving him with an infant son, Daniel, to raise on his own.

Hart pursues power with ruthless obsession. He was once engaged to Lady Eleanor Ramsay, a Scotswoman, but she broke things off with him after a turbulent courtship. Hart married a quieter woman who passed away giving birth to his son, who also passed that night. Hart will do anything to protect his family, and often drives them to exasperation, but Hart, who remembers their father best, vows that nothing will hurt his brothers again.

I envisioned Madness of Lord Ian not so much as a standard romance as Part 1 of a family saga. The first four books tie together, even though each is a single romance about each of the bothers.

Armed with all these ideas, I set to work.

Never in my wildest dreams did I expect what happened with this book to happen. *The Madness of Lord Ian Mackenzie* was published by Dorchester, the middle book of a three-book contact, and was simply designated in the contract as "a historical romance." I told my editor I wanted to write an hero on the spectrum, and she, fortunately, was interested to see what I'd do.

The book was published with little fanfare, and to my dismay, a large chunk of the orders to a major bookseller was lost. Another of the giant retailers decided to pass on it (which means they carried zero copies). Not only that, but the e-book version took a month and a half to show up on the online sites. By that time, any hope of touching a bestseller list was gone, and I thought *The Madness of Lord Ian* would die in obscurity.

However, word of mouth made Ian a sensation. I watched in astonishment as blog after blog, discussion board after discussion board started talking about this book. The book had almost no support from the publisher, but readers picked it up and made it a hit. I hadn't thought anyone but me would much like Ian's story, but I was very wrong!

The Madness of Lord Ian has made it onto many "best of" lists, including best historical romance, best romance hero, and best romance in general, and the like. I am thrilled that Ian found a place in so many hearts—he certainly has a large part of my own.

The original publisher for Lord Ian went out of business soon after this, and I was never paid the royalties for it. I was fortunately able to rescue Lord Ian and resell the book to Berkley, who also put out the rest of the series.

Madness of Lord Ian continues to be one of my most successful historical romances to this day, in e-, print, and audio, and has been my most translated book.

I am so grateful to the readers who embraced Ian Mackenzie and encouraged me to write the rest of what has become a very long series!

SYNOPSIS

1881, LONDON, PARIS, SCOTLAND

IAN MACKENZIE HAS JUST PURCHASED A MING BOWL FROM A MAN he considers a complete fool—Lyndon Mather—and learns that Mather is engaged. Ian, curious about a woman who would agree to marry this man, discovers that Mather will escort his fiancee to the opera at Covent Garden that evening. Ian vows to go to find out whether she is "genuine" or fake, like many of the Ming bowls in Mather's collection.

When Ian sees Beth Ackerley on Mather's arm, his world changes. He senses that the woman is completely unaware of Mather's darker side, and pens her a note explaining just how dark Mather can be. Beth reads the letter in bewilderment and soon finds herself in a private box in the opera house, alone with Ian Mackenzie—where he proposes to her.

Beth rejects Ian's proposal and decides to set off for Paris, to use her money to see the world. Ian goes right after her.

Ian's sudden interest in Beth is reported Ian's oldest brother, Hart. Hart, the Duke of Kilmorgan, has been severely protective of Ian all Ian's life. It was Hart who went to the asylum and extracted Ian, Hart who makes sure the world leaves mad Ian alone. He fears Beth, who has a murky past, is after Ian's money, and decides to do everything he can to thwart her.

Beth, meanwhile has met Ian's brother's estranged wife—Isabella—who is enchanted with Beth. Isabella, astounded at the change in Ian since he has become interested in Beth, does everything in her power to make sure the two can be together. Isabella is separated from her husband, Mac Mackenzie, an artist, but the two find some common cause in helping Ian and Beth.

Another complication comes in the form of Scotland Yard Inspector Lloyd Fellows. Fellows has been convinced for years that Ian and Hart Mackenzie have something to do with the murder of a young woman in a bawdy house, owned by Hart's longtime mistress. In this house, Hart and others practice darker forms of pleasure, and Fellows is convinced the young woman died in these circumstances. He also nurses a hatred for the Mackenzies, and will do anything to destroy them.

Ian, regardless of the obstacles in his way, pursues Beth with single-minded purpose, intrigued by the way she so openly talks to him and is one of the few people in the world who doesn't fear him. When Beth asks him whether he would mind having an affair with her, because she misses the pleasure she used to find with her husband, Ian is both astonished and happy to comply.

Beth is opening a world to him he never knew existed, one of emotion, light, and happiness, and Ian begins to think that perhaps he could learn about and understand love for the first time in his life.

EXCERPT: THE MADNESS OF LORD IAN MACKENZIE

1881

I find that a Ming bowl is like a woman's breast," Sir Lyndon Mather said to Ian Mackenzie, who held the bowl in question between his fingertips. "The swelling curve, the creamy pallor. Don't you agree?"

Ian couldn't think of a woman who would be flattered to have her breast compared to a bowl, so he didn't bother to nod.

The delicate vessel was from the early Ming period, the porcelain barely flushed with green, the sides so thin Ian could see light through them. Three gray-green dragons chased one another across the outside, and four chrysanthemums seemed to float across the bottom.

The little vessel might just cup a small rounded breast, but that was as far as Ian was willing to go.

"One thousand guineas," he said.

Mather's smile turned sickly. "Now, my lord, I thought we were friends."

Ian wondered where Mather had got that idea. "The bowl is worth one thousand guineas." He fingered the slightly chipped rim, the base worn from centuries of handling.

Mather looked taken aback, blue eyes glittering in his overly handsome face.

"I paid fifteen hundred for it. Explain yourself."

There was nothing to explain. Ian's rapidly calculating mind had taken in every asset and flaw in ten seconds flat. If Mather couldn't tell the value of his pieces, he had no business collecting porcelain. There were at least five fakes in the glass case on the other side of Mather's collection room, and Ian wagered Mather had no idea.

Ian put his nose to the glaze, liking the clean scent that had survived the heavy cigar smoke of Mather's house. The bowl was genuine, it was beautiful, and he wanted it.

"At least give me what I paid for it," Mather said in a panicked voice. "The man told me I had it at a bargain."

"One thousand guineas," Ian repeated.

"Damn it, man, I'm getting married."

Ian recalled the announcement in the *Times*——verbatim, because he recalled everything verbatim: *Sir Lyndon Mather of St. Aubrey's, Suffolk, announces his betrothal to Mrs. Thomas Ackerley, a widow. The wedding to be held on the twenty-seventh of June of this year in St. Aubrey's at ten o'clock in the morning.*

"My felicitations," Ian said.

"I wish to buy my beloved a gift with what I get for the bowl."

Ian kept his gaze on the vessel. "Why not give her the bowl itself?"

Mather's hearty laugh filled the room. "My dear fellow, women don't know the first thing about porcelain. She'll want a carriage and a matched team and a string of servants to carry all the fripperies she buys. I'll give her that. She's a fine-looking woman, daughter of some froggie aristo, for all she's long in the tooth and a widow."

Ian didn't answer. He touched the tip of his tongue to the bowl, reflecting that it was far better than ten carriages with matched teams. Any woman who didn't see the poetry in it was a fool.

Mather wrinkled his nose as Ian tasted the bowl, but Ian had learned to test the genuineness of the glaze that way. Mather wouldn't be able to tell a genuine glaze if someone painted him with it.

"She's got a bloody fortune of her own," Mather went on, "inherited from that Barrington woman, a rich old lady who didn't keep her opinions to herself. Mrs. Ackerley, her quiet companion, copped the lot."

Then why is she marrying you? Ian turned the bowl over in his hands as he speculated, but if Mrs. Ackerley wanted to make her bed with Lyndon Mather, she could lie in it. Of course, she might find the bed a little crowded. Mather kept a secret house for his mistress and several other women to cater to his needs, which he loved to boast about to Ian's brothers. *I'm as decadent as you lot,* he was trying to say. But in Ian's opinion, Mather understood pleasures of the flesh about as well as he understood Ming porcelain.

"Bet you're surprised a dedicated bachelor like myself is for the chop, eh?" Mather went on. "If you're wondering whether I'm giving up my bit of the other, the answer is no. You are welcome to come 'round and join in anytime, you know. I've extended the invitation to you, and your brothers as well."

Ian had met Mather's ladies, vacant-eyed women willing to put up with Mather's proclivities for the money he gave them.

Mather reached for a cigar. "I say, we're at Covent Garden Opera tonight. Come meet my fiancée. I'd like your opinion. Everyone knows you have as exquisite taste in females as you do in porcelain." He chuckled.

Ian didn't answer. He had to rescue the bowl from this philistine. "One thousand guineas."

"You're a hard man, Mackenzie."

"One thousand guineas, and I'll see you at the opera."

"Oh, very well, though you're ruining me."

He'd ruined himself. "Your widow has a fortune. You'll recover."

Mather laughed, his handsome face lighting. Ian had seen women of every age blush or flutter fans when Mather smiled. Mather was the master of the double life.

"True, and she's lovely to boot. I'm a lucky man."

Mather rang for his butler and Ian's valet, Curry. Curry produced a wooden box lined with straw, into which Ian carefully placed the dragon bowl.

Ian hated to cover up such beauty. He touched it one last time, his gaze fixed on it until Curry broke his concentration by placing the lid on the box.

He looked up to find that Mather had ordered the butler to pour brandy. Ian accepted a glass and sat down in front of the bankbook Curry had placed on Mather's desk for him.

Ian set aside the brandy and dipped his pen in the ink. He bent down to write and caught sight of the droplet of black ink hanging on the nib in a perfect, round sphere.

He stared at the droplet, something inside him singing at the perfection of the ball of ink, the glistening viscosity that held it suspended from the nib. The sphere was perfect, shining, a wonder.

He wished he could savor its perfection forever, but he knew that in a second it would fall from the pen and be lost. If his brother Mac could paint something this exquisite, this beautiful, Ian would treasure it.

He had no idea how long he'd sat there studying the droplet of ink until he heard Mather say, "Damnation, he really is mad, isn't he?"

The droplet fell down, down, down to splash on the page, gone to its death in a splatter of black ink.

"I'll write it out for you, then, m'lord?"

Ian looked into the homely face of his manservant, a young

Cockney who'd spent his boyhood pickpocketing his way across London.

Ian nodded and relinquished the pen. Curry turned the bankbook toward him and wrote the draft in careful capitals. He dipped the pen again and handed it back to Ian, holding the nib down so Ian wouldn't see the ink.

Ian signed his name painstakingly, feeling the weight of Mather's stare.

"Does he do that often?" Mather asked as Ian rose, leaving Curry to blot the paper.

Curry's cheekbones stained red. "No 'arm done, sir."

Ian lifted his glass and swiftly drank down the brandy, then took up the box. "I will see you at the opera."

He didn't shake hands on his way out. Mather frowned, but gave Ian a nod. Lord Ian Mackenzie, brother to the Duke of Kilmorgan, socially outranked him, and Mather was acutely aware of social rank.

Once in his carriage, Ian set the box beside him. He could feel the bowl inside, round and perfect, filling a niche in himself.

"I know it ain't me place to say," Curry said from the opposite seat as the carriage jerked forward into the rainy streets. "But the man's a right bastard. Not fit for you to wipe your boots on. Why even have truck with him?"

Ian caressed the box. "I wanted this piece."

"You do have a way of getting what you want, no mistake, m'lord. Are we really meeting him at the opera?"

"I'll sit in Hart's box." Ian flicked his gaze over Curry's baby-innocent face and focused safely on the carriage's velvet wall. "Find out everything you can about a Mrs. Ackerley, a widow now betrothed to Sir Lyndon Mather. Tell me about it tonight."

"Oh, aye? Why are we so interested in the right bastard's fiancée?"

Ian ran his fingertips lightly over the box again. "I want to know if she's exquisite porcelain or a fake."

Curry winked. "Right ye are, guv. I'll see what I can dig up."

———

Lyndon Mather was all that was handsome and charming, and heads turned when Beth Ackerley walked by on his arm at Covent Garden Opera House.

Mather had a pure profile, a slim, athletic body, and a head of golden hair that ladies longed to run their fingers through. His manners were impeccable, and he charmed everyone he met. He had a substantial income, a lavish house on Park Lane, and he was received by the highest of the high. An excellent choice for a lady of unexpected fortune looking for a second husband.

Even a lady of unexpected fortune tires of being alone, Beth thought as she entered Mather's luxurious box behind his elderly aunt and companion. She'd known Mather for several years, his aunt and her employer being fast friends. He wasn't the most exciting of gentlemen, but Beth didn't want exciting. *No drama,* she promised herself. She'd had enough drama to last a lifetime.

Now Beth wanted comfort; she'd learned how to run a houseful of servants, and she'd perhaps have the chance to have the children she'd always longed for. Her first marriage nine years ago had produced none, but then, poor Thomas had died barely a year after they'd taken their vows. He'd been so ill, he hadn't even been able to say good-bye.

The opera had begun by the time they settled into Sir Lyndon's box. The young woman onstage had a beautiful soprano voice and an ample body with which to project it. Beth was soon lost in the rapture of the music.

Mather left the box ten minutes after they'd entered, as he usually did. He liked to spend his nights at the theatre seeing everyone of importance and being seen with them. Beth didn't mind. She'd grown used to sitting with elderly matrons and preferred it to exchanging inanities with glittering society ladies. *Oh, darling did you hear? Lady Marmaduke had three inches of lace on her dress instead of two. Can you imagine anything more vulgar? And her pleats were limp, my darling, absolutely limp.* Such important information.

Beth fanned herself and enjoyed the music while Mather's aunt and her companion tried to make sense of the plot of *La Traviata.* Beth reflected that they thought nothing of an outing to the theatre, but to a girl growing up in the East End, it was anything but ordinary. Beth loved music, and imbibed it any way she could, though she thought herself only a mediocre musician. No matter, she could listen to others play and enjoy it just fine. Mather liked to go to the theatre, to the opera, to musicales, so Beth's new life would have much music in it.

Her enjoyment was interrupted by Mather's noisy return to the box. "My dear," he said in a loud voice, "I've brought you my *very* close friend Lord Ian Mackenzie. Give him your hand, darling. His brother is the Duke of Kilmorgan, you know."

Beth looked past Mather at the tall man who'd entered the box behind him, and her entire world stopped.

Lord Ian was a big man, his body solid muscle, the hand that reached to hers huge in a kid leather glove. His shoulders were wide, his chest broad, and the dim light touched his dark hair with red. His face was as hard as his body, but his eyes set Ian Mackenzie apart from every other person Beth had ever met.

She at first thought his eyes were light brown, but when Mather almost shoved him down into the chair at Beth's side, she saw that they were golden. Not hazel, but amber like brandy, flecked with gold as though the sun danced on them.

"This is my Mrs. Ackerley," Mather was saying. "What do you think, eh? I told you she was the best-looking woman in London."

Lord Ian ran a quick glance over Beth's face, then fixed his gaze at a point somewhere beyond the box. He still held her hand, his grip firm, the pressure of his fingers just shy of painful.

He didn't agree or disagree with Mather, a bit rudely, Beth thought. Even if Lord Ian didn't clutch his breast and declare Beth the most beautiful woman since Elaine of Camelot, he ought to at least give some polite answer.

Instead he sat in stony silence. He still held Beth's hand, and his thumb traced the pattern of stitching on the back of her glove. Over and over the thumb moved, hot, quick patterns, the pressure pulsing heat through her limbs.

"If he told you I was the most beautiful woman in London, I fear you were much deceived," Beth said rapidly. "I apologize if he misled you."

Lord Ian's gaze flicked over her, a small frown on his face, as though he had no idea what she was talking about.

"Don't crush the poor woman, Mackenzie," Mather said jovially. "She's fragile, like one of your Ming bowls."

"Oh, do you have an interest in porcelain, my lord?" Beth grasped at something to say. "Sir Lyndon has shown me his collection."

"Mackenzie is one of the foremost authorities," Mather said with a trace of envy.

"Are you?" Beth asked.

Lord Ian flicked another glance over her. "Yes."

He sat no closer to her than Mather did, but Beth's awareness of him screamed at her. She could feel his hard knee against her skirts, the firm pressure of his thumb on her hand, the weight of his *not*-stare.

A woman wouldn't be comfortable with this man, she thought with a shiver. *There would be drama aplenty.* She sensed that in the restlessness of his body, the large, warm hand that gripped her own, the eyes that wouldn't quite meet hers. Should she pity the woman those eyes finally rested on? Or envy her?

Beth's tongue tripped along. "Sir Lyndon has lovely things. When I touch a piece that an emperor held hundreds of years ago, I feel … I'm not sure. *Close* to him, I think. Quite privileged."

Sparks of gold flashed as Ian looked at her a bare instant. "You must come view my collection." He had a slight Scots accent, his voice low and gravel-rough.

"Love to, old chap," Mather said. "I'll see when we are free."

Mather lifted his opera glasses to study the large-bosomed soprano, and Lord Ian's gaze moved to him. The disgust and intense dislike in Lord Ian's unguarded expression startled Beth. Before she could speak, Lord Ian leaned to her. The heat of his body touched her like a sharp wave, bringing with it the scent of shaving soap and male spice. She'd forgotten how heady was the scent of a man. Mather always covered himself with cologne.

"Read it out of his sight."

Lord Ian's breath grazed Beth's ear, warming things inside her that hadn't been touched in nine long years. His fingers slid beneath the opening of her glove above her elbow, and she felt the folded edge of paper scrape her bare arm. She stared at Lord Ian's golden eyes so near hers, watching his pupils widen before he flicked his gaze away again.

He sat up, his face smooth and expressionless. Mather turned to Ian with a comment about the singer, noticing nothing.

Lord Ian abruptly rose. The warm pressure left Beth's hand, and she realized he'd been holding it the entire time.

"Going already, old chap?" Mather asked in surprise.

"My brother is waiting."

Mather's eyes gleamed. "The duke?"

"My brother Cameron and his son."

"Oh." Mather looked disappointed, but he stood and renewed the promise to bring Beth to see Ian's collection.

Without saying good night, Ian moved past the empty chairs

and out of the box. Beth's gaze wouldn't leave Lord Ian's back until the blank door closed behind him. She was very aware of the folded paper pressing the inside of her arm and the trickle of sweat forming under it.

Mather sat down next to Beth and blew out his breath. "There, my dear, goes an eccentric."

Beth curled her fingers in her gray taffeta skirt, her hand cold without Lord Ian's around it. "An eccentric?"

"Mad as a hatter. Poor chap lived in a private asylum most of his life, and he runs free now only because his brother the duke let him out again. But don't worry." Mather took Beth's hand. "You won't have to see him without me present. The entire family is scandalous. Never speak to any of them without me, my dear, all right?"

Beth murmured something noncommittal. She had at least heard of the Mackenzie family, the hereditary Dukes of Kilmorgan, because old Mrs. Barrington had adored gossip about the aristocracy. The Mackenzies had featured in many of the scandal sheets that Beth read out to Mrs. Barrington on rainy nights.

Lord Ian hadn't seemed entirely mad to her, although he certainly was like no man she'd ever met. Mather's hand in hers felt limp and cool, while the hard pressure of Lord Ian's had heated her in a way she hadn't felt in a long time. Beth missed the intimacy she'd felt with Thomas, the long, warm nights in bed with him. She knew she'd share a bed with Mather, but the thought had never stirred her blood. She reasoned that what she'd had with Thomas was special and magical, and she couldn't expect to feel it with any other man. So why had her breath quickened when Lord Ian's lilting whisper had touched her ear; why had her heart beat faster when he'd moved his thumb over the back of her hand?

No. Lord Ian was drama, Mather, safety. She would choose safety. She had to.

Mather managed to stay still for five minutes, then rose again. "Must pay my respects to Lord and Lady Beresford. You don't mind, do you, m'dear?"

"Of course not," Beth said automatically.

"You are a treasure, my darling. I always told dear Mrs. Barrington how sweet and polite you were." Mather kissed Beth's hand, then left the box.

The soprano began an aria, the notes filling every space of the opera house. Behind her, Mather's aunt and her companion put their heads together behind fans, whispering, whispering.

Beth worked her fingers under the edge of her long glove and pulled out the piece of paper. She put her back squarely to the elderly ladies and quietly unfolded the note.

Mrs. Ackerley, it began in a careful, neat hand.

I make bold to warn you of the true character of Sir Lyndon Mather, with whom my brother the Duke of Kilmorgan is well acquainted. I wish to tell you that Mather keeps a house just off the Strand near Temple Bar, where he has women meet him, several at a time. He calls the women his "sweeties" and begs them to use him as their slave. They are not regular courtesans but women who need the money enough to put up with him. I have listed five of the women he regularly meets, should you wish to have them questioned, or I can arrange for you to speak to the duke.

I remain,
Yours faithfully,
Ian Mackenzie

The soprano flung open her arms, building the last note of the aria to a wild crescendo, until it was lost in a burst of applause.

Beth stared at the letter, the noise in the opera house smothering. The words on the page didn't change, remaining painfully black against stark white.

Her breath poured back into her lungs, sharp and hot. She glanced quickly at Mather's aunt, but the old lady and her companion were applauding and shouting, "Brava! Brava!"

Beth rose, shoving the paper back into her glove. The small box with its cushioned chairs and tea tables seemed to tilt as she groped her way to the door.

Mather's aunt glanced at her in surprise. "Are you all right, my dear?"

"I just need some air. It's close in here."

Mather's aunt began to fumble among her things. "Do you need smelling salts? Alice, do help me."

"No, no." Beth opened the door and hurried out as Mather's aunt began to chastise her companion. "I shall be quite all right."

The gallery outside was deserted, thank heavens. The soprano was a popular one, and most of the attendees were fixed to their chairs, avidly watching her.

Beth hurried along the gallery, hearing the singer start up again. Her vision blurred, and the paper in her glove burned her arm.

What did Lord Ian mean by writing her such a letter? He was an eccentric, Mather had said—was that the explanation? But if the accusations in the letter were the ravings of a madman, why would Lord Ian offer to arrange for Beth to meet with his brother? The Duke of Kilmorgan was one of the wealthiest and most powerful men in Britain—he was the Duke of Kilmorgan in the peerage of Scotland, which went back to 1300-something, and his father had been made Duke of Kilmorgan in the peerage of England by Queen Victoria herself.

Why should such a lofty man care about nobodies like Beth Ackerley and Lyndon Mather? Surely both she and Mather were far beneath a duke's notice.

No, the letter was too bizarre. It had to be a lie, an invention.

And yet … Beth thought of times she'd caught Mather looking at her as though he'd done something clever. Growing up in the East End, having the father she'd had, had given Beth the ability to spot a confidence trickster at ten paces. Had the signs been there with Sir Lyndon Mather, and she'd simply chosen to ignore them?

But, no, it couldn't be true. She'd come to know Mather well when she'd been companion to elderly Mrs. Barrington. She and Mrs. Barrington had ridden with Mather in his carriage, visited him and his aunt at his Park Lane house, had him escort them to musicales. He'd never behaved toward Beth with anything but politeness due a rich old lady's companion, and after Mrs. Barrington's death, he'd proposed to Beth.

After I inherited Mrs. Barrington's fortune, a cynical voice reminded her.

What did Lord Ian mean by *sweeties? He begs them to use him as their slave.*

Beth's whalebone corset was too tight, cutting off the breath she sorely needed. Black spots swam before her eyes, and she put her hand out to steady herself.

A strong grip closed around her elbow. "Careful," a Scottish voice grated in her ear. "Come with me."

LADY ISABELLA'S SCANDALOUS MARRIAGE

CHARACTERS

Main Characters

"Mac" (Roland Ferdinand) Mackenzie

THE WILD YOUNGER BROTHER OF THE MACKENZIE FAMILY, MAC Mackenzie is comfortable in the knowledge that there are several heirs between him and the dukedom. He ran away at sixteen and found refuge in the Paris art scene. He had been an artist from boyhood, but ordered by his father—who went so far as to try to break his fingers—to not pursue such an unmanly profession. Mac is a brilliant painter, creating with zeal and passion, but he doesn't sell his work—he gives it away or donates it, and is patron to promising, penniless young painters.

One night, his disreputable friends leftover from university wager that Mac cannot walk into a society ball to which he has not been invited and not only dance with but kiss the young lady making her first bow.

Mac takes the challenge, thinking to head inside, waltz with the debutant, kiss her to outrage the company, and stroll out. He

"

imagines an insipid chit as he perceives most Englishwomen are and prepares to shock her senseless.

He is stunned when he lays eyes on Lady Isabella Scranton. She is a haughty beauty with flame-red hair and green eyes, who dares look him in the face and demand to know what he is doing there. Mac scrawls his name across her dance card and tows the young woman to the ballroom floor. After whirling her around a few times, he dances her out the door to the terrace, where he proceeds to kiss her.

And is transformed. Both Mac and Isabella are dumbfounded by the kiss and the heat generated between them. Mac asks Isabella to run away with him that night and marry him, and Isabella, to her astonishment, agrees.

Mac is impetuous, rash, arrogant, decadent. He is so into his own pleasure that he sometimes doesn't see who he's running over to get it—or that they're unhappy, even though he tells himself he's trying for their pleasure as well.

On the good side, Mac is a talented artist and quick to appreciate beauty. He's generous, kind, and likes to help people. He's very loving and giving, close with his brothers, and quick to befriend people of all classes and walks of life.

Lady Isabella is in for a wild, reckless, scandalous marriage.

Lady Isabella Scranton

ELDEST DAUGHTER OF AN EARL, Isabella let herself be dazzled and swept away by Mac on the night of her debut ball. She'd never seen anything like him, and felt a connection to him that never waned.

Her parents never forgave her, because though Mac is a rich aristocrat, he's scandalous, Scots, and an *artist*. Isabella discovers the heights of Mac's wildness when she joins him in Paris for his decadent life with other artists (male and female), artist's models, and tolerant wives. She gets a very fast education on the ways of the world, but Mac proves he can't settle down.

Isabella has been raised to be the perfect hostess and wife. To the relief of Mac's servants, she takes over his household and runs it with calm efficiency. The staff become devoted to her.

The Mackenzie brothers love her from the beginning as well. They are happy to have someone take care of their ne'er-do-well younger brother, and Daniel, Cameron's son, is happy to let her mother him. Isabella also makes a connection with Ian, who lets everyone know, in his own way, that he prefers her company to his brothers'.

Her marriage to Mac lasts three turbulent years before they separate.

Thus begins a tale …

———

IMPORTANT SECONDARY CHARACTERS
  Ian and Beth Mackenzie
  Cameron Mackenzie
  Hart Mackenzie
  Daniel Mackenzie
  Bellamy (Mac's valet)
  Inspector Lloyd Fellows
  Aimee (adopted by Mac)
  Louisa Scranton (Isabella's younger sister)
  Mac's assorted odd friends

AUTHOR'S NOTES

Author's Notes

WRITING THE FOLLOW-UP TO *THE MADNESS OF LORD IAN Mackenzie* was an intimidating task, to say the least. When I started *Lord Ian*, I had no idea the book would take off the way it did, or that it would connect with so many people.

I had already planned Isabella and Mac's story—as I say, the entire family took root in my head and wouldn't let me go. I was curious as to why the two were separated, what that meant in the Victorian age, and how they would get back together.

I did enjoy spending more time with the Mackenzies as I wrote the story, and learning more about the family. I got to bring back Daniel, Cameron's son, and deepen his relationship with his father. I also hinted at Cameron's tragic past life, and showed a glimpse of a young lady he had a connection with.

The book let me explore what really happens after the rake-hell sweeps the innocent young woman off her feet. I researched the legal aspects of separation and divorce at the time, and thought about the ways a couple who might seem perfect for each other could fall apart.

I made rules for myself—no cheating, no jealousy, no "other woman." The couple's problems had to come from within themselves, not an outside person trying to break them up.

Another thing I explored was alcoholism—its effect on a relationship and Mac's courageous fight against it. However, I didn't want this to be a "recovery" book, so Mac has already kicked his drinking by the time the story opens, and is ready to take the next step—winning back Isabella.

The book was published in a transition period for me. The publisher that had brought out *Madness of Lord Ian* (Dorchester / Leisure) was out of business, and *Lord Ian* was out of print and off the shelves.

Therefore *Lady Isabella* was Book 2 of a series that launched into bookstores without Book 1 anywhere to be found (including in e-book). Because almost 15 months had passed since publication of the first book, readers had either forgotten about the series or hadn't realized I was continuing it.

Because of this *Lady Isabella* kind of hung in limbo for a while, before I could write and publish Book 3. Happily, since then it has sold quite well, one of my top selling historicals ever.

SYNOPSIS

LONDON 1881

LADY ISABELLA'S SCANDALOUS MARRIAGE BEGINS WHEN ISABELLA pays a visit to Mac Mackenzie to inform him she's discovered someone is forging his paintings.

Mac is stunned to see her—three years before, Isabella had left Mac and requested a separation. He grieved but was not surprised. Mac's up-and-down life, fueled by drink, drove her to distraction. They would quarrel and make up in the most dramatic fashion, and after a time, Isabella simply grew exhausted.

Mac has not taken a drink of alcohol for years, going sober when he realized he'd chased her away.

Mac is not much interested in another artist forging his paintings—let them. He paints for the love of it, not fame or monetary gain.

Isabella's visit does fuel a determination, however, to have her back, at any cost. He wants it all—Isabella in his life, his house, and his bed.

Isabella has no intention of letting Mac flare her love for him, and avoids him at all costs. But events push them together, the forger turns dangerous, and Isabella can no longer avoid the consequences of her impetuous marriage to the wildest Mackenzie.

EXCERPT: LADY ISABELLA'S SCANDALOUS MARRIAGE

All of London was amazed to learn of the sudden marriage of Lady I — S— and Lord M— M—, brother of the Duke of K— last evening. The lady in question had her Come-Out and her Wedding the same night, leading debutantes to plead with fathers to make their coming-out balls just as eventful.

—From a London society newspaper, February 1875

SEPTEMBER, *1881*

Isabella's footman rang the bell at the house of Lord Mac Mackenzie on Mount Street, while Isabella waited in the landau, wondering for the dozenth time since she'd set off whether this were wise.

Perhaps Mac would be out. Maybe the unpredictable man had gone off to Paris, or to Italy, where summer would linger for a time. She could investigate the matter she'd discovered by herself. Yes, that would be best.

As she opened her mouth to call back her footman, the large black door swung open, and Mac's valet, a former pugilist, peered out. Isabella's heart sank. Bellamy being here meant Mac was here, because Bellamy never strayed far from Mac's side.

Bellamy peered into the landau, and a look of undisguised astonishment crossed his scarred face. Isabella hadn't approached this house since the day she'd left it three and a half years ago. "M'lady?"

Isabella took Bellamy's beefy hand to steady herself as she descended. The best way to do this, she decided, was simply to do it.

"How is your knee, Bellamy?" she asked. "Are you still using the liniment? Is it too much to hope that my husband is at home?"

As she talked, she breezed into the house, pretending not to notice the parlor maid and a footman popping out to stare.

"The knee's much better, m'lady. Thank you. His lordship is . . ." Bellamy hesitated. "He's painting, m'lady."

"So early? There's a wonder." Isabella started up the stairs at a quick pace, not letting herself think about what she was doing. If she thought about it, she'd run far and fast, perhaps lock herself into her house and not come out. "Is he in his studio? No need to announce me. I'll go up myself."

"But m'lady." Bellamy followed her, but his damaged knee wouldn't let him move quickly, and Isabella reached the landing, three floors up, before Bellamy had mounted the second flight.

"M'lady, he said not to be disturbed," Bellamy called upward.

"I won't be long. I need only ask him a question."

"But, m'lady, he's . . ."

Isabella paused, hand on the white doorknob of the right-hand attic room. "I shall take full blame for invading his lordship's privacy, Bellamy."

She lifted her skirts as she swung open the door and walked into the room. Mac was there, all right, standing in front of a long easel, painting with fervor.

Isabella's skirts slid from her nerveless fingers, the beauty of her estranged husband striking her like a blow. Mac wore a kilt, threadbare and paint-flecked, and he was naked from the waist up. Though it was cool in the studio, Mac's torso gleamed with sweat, his skin tanned from spending the summer on the warmer continent. He wore a red kerchief on his head, gypsy style, to keep paint out of his hair. He'd always done that, she remembered with a pang. It made his cheekbones more prominent, emphasized the handsomeness of his face. Even the rough boots, much worn and paint-splotched, were familiar and dear.

Mac laid paint on his canvas with energy, obviously not hearing Isabella open the door. He held the palette in his left hand, arm muscles tight, while his right moved the brush in swift, jerking strokes. Mac was a stunning man, made still more attractive when absorbed in doing something he loved.

Isabella had used to sit in this very studio on an old sofa strewn with cushions, simply watching him paint. Mac might not say one word to her while he worked, but she had adored watching the play of muscles on his back, the way he'd smear paint on his cheek when he'd absently rub it. After a particularly good session, he'd turn to her with a wide smile and pull her into his arms, never minding that paint now smeared all over *her* skin.

So absorbed was she in Mac that Isabella didn't notice what he painted with such intensity until she forced herself to look away from him and across the room. She barely stifled her dismay.

A young woman lay on a raised platform draped with yellow and red coverings. She was nude, which came as no surprise—Mac generally painted women who wore nothing or very little. But Isabella had never seen him paint anything so blatantly erotic. The model lay on her back with her knees bent, her legs wide apart. Her hand rested on her private place, and she was spreading herself open without shame. Mac scowled at the offering and painted with rapid brushstrokes.

Behind Isabella, Bellamy reached the top landing, puffing from exertion and distress. Mac heard him and growled but didn't look 'round.

"Damn it, Bellamy, I told you I didn't want to be disturbed this morning."

"I'm sorry, sir. I couldn't stop her."

The model raised her head, spied Isabella, and grinned. "Oh, hello, yer ladyship."

Mac glanced behind him once, twice, then his copper gaze riveted to Isabella. Paint dripped, unheeded, from his brush to the floor.

Isabella strove to keep her voice from shaking. "Hello, Molly. How is your little boy? It's all right, Bellamy, you can leave us. This won't take long, Mac. I only came to ask you a question."

Damnation.

What the hell was Bellamy playing at, letting her up here?

Isabella hadn't set foot in the Mount Street house in three and a half years, not since the day she'd left him with nothing but a short letter for explanation. Now she stood in the doorway, in hat and gloves donned for calling. Today of all days, while Mac painted Molly Bates in her spread glory. This wasn't part of his plan, the one that had made him leap onto a train to London after his brother's wedding and follow her down here from Scotland. He'd call this a grievous miscalculation.

Isabella's dark blue jacket hugged her torso and cupped her full bosom, and a gray skirt of complicated ruffles spread over a small bustle. Her hat was a concoction of flowers and ribbons, her gloves a dark gray that wouldn't show London grime. The gloves outlined slender fingers he wanted to kiss, hands he longed to have slide up his back as they lay together in bed.

Isabella had always known how to dress, how to present herself in colors dear to his artist's eye. Mac had loved to help her dress in the mornings, lacing her gowns against her soft, sweet-smelling skin. He'd dismiss her maid and perform the tasks himself, though those mornings it took them a long time to descend for breakfast.

Now Mac drank in every inch of her, and *damn it,* grew hard. Would she see, and would she laugh?

Isabella crossed to the dressing gown Molly had left in a heap on the floor. "You'd better wrap up in this, dear," she said to the model. "It's chilly up here. You know Mac never believes in feeding the fire. Why don't you warm up downstairs with a nice cup of tea while I have a chat with my husband?"

Molly leapt to her feet, her grin wide. Molly was a beautiful female in the way many men liked—large-bosomed, round-hipped, doe-eyed. She had a mass of black hair and a perfect face, an artist's dream. But next to the glory of Isabella, Molly faded to nothing.

"Don't mind if I do," Molly said. "It's stiff work posing for naughty pictures. My fingers are that cramped."

"Some teacakes ought to loosen you again," Isabella said as Molly slid on the dressing gown. "Mac's cook always used to keep currant ones in large supply, in case of emergencies. Ask her if she still does."

Molly's dimples showed. "I've missed you, no lie, your ladyship. 'Is lordship forgets we 'ave to eat."

"It's his lordship's way," Isabella said. Molly strolled from the studio without worry, and Mac watched as though from far away as Bellamy followed Molly out and closed the door.

Isabella turned her lush green eyes to him. "You're dripping."

"What?" Mac stared at her then heard a glob of paint hit his board floor. He let out a growl, slammed the palette onto the table, and thrust the brush into a jar of oil of turpentine.

"You've begun early today," Isabella said.

Why did she keep on in that friendly, neutral voice, as though they were acquaintances at a tea party?

"The light was good." His own voice sounded stiff, harsh.

"Yes, it's a sunny morning for a change. Don't worry, I'll let you get back to it soon. I only want your opinion."

Blast her, had she come here to throw him off guard on purpose? When had she gotten so good at the game?

"My opinion on what?" he asked. "Your new hat?"

"Not my hat, although thank you for noticing. No, I want your opinion on this."

Mac found the hat in question right under his nose. Gray and blue ribbons trailed into glossy curls that beckoned to be lifted, smoothed.

The hat tilted back until he was looking into Isabella's eyes, eyes that had snared him across a ballroom so long ago. She hadn't been aware of her power then, the sweet debutante, and she didn't know it now. Her simple look of inquiry, of interest, could pin a man and give him the most erotic dreams imaginable.

"On this, Mac," she said impatiently.

She was lifting a handkerchief toward him. In the middle of its snowy whiteness lay a piece of yellow-covered canvas about an inch long and a quarter inch wide.

"What color would you say this was?" she asked.

"Yellow." Mac quirked a brow. "You drove all the way here from North Audley Street to ask me whether something is yellow?"

"Of course I know it's yellow. What kind of yellow, specifically?"

Mac peered at it. The color was vibrant, almost pulsing. "Cadmium yellow."

"More specific than that?" She wiggled the handkerchief as though the motion would reveal the mystery. "Don't you understand? It's *Mackenzie* yellow. That astonishing yellow you mix for your paintings, the secret formula known only to you."

"Yes, so it is." With Isabella standing so close to him, her heady scent in his nostrils, he didn't give a damn if the paint was

Mackenzie yellow or graveyard black. "Have you been amusing yourself slicing up my pictures?"

"Don't be silly. I took this from a painting hanging in Mrs. Leigh-Waters's drawing room in Richmond."

Curiosity trickled through Mac's impatience. "I've never given a painting to Mrs. Leigh-Waters of Richmond."

"I didn't think you had. When I asked her about it, she told me she bought the picture from an art dealer in the Strand. Mr. Crane."

"The devil she did. I don't sell my paintings, especially not through Crane."

"Exactly." Isabella smiled in triumph, the red curve of her lips doing nothing to ease his arousal. "The painting is signed *Mac Mackenzie,* but you didn't paint it."

Mac looked again at the strip of brilliant yellow on the handkerchief. "How do you know I didn't paint it? Maybe some ungrateful blackguard I gave a picture to sold it to raise money to pay a debt."

"It's a scene from a hill, overlooking Rome."

"I've done many scenes overlooking Rome."

"I know that, but this wasn't one of yours. It's your style, your brushwork, your colors, but you didn't paint it."

Mac pushed the handkerchief back at her. "How do you know? Are you intimately acquainted with all my works? I've painted quite a few Rome pictures since you . . ." He couldn't bring himself to say "since you left me." He'd gone to Rome to soothe his broken heart, painting the bloody vista day after day. He'd done too damn many pictures of Rome, until he'd grown sick of the place. Then he'd moved to Venice and painted it until he never wanted to see another gondola as long as he lived.

That was when he'd still been a debauched, drunken sot. Once he'd sobered up, replacing his obsession for single-malt with one of tea, he'd retreated to Scotland and stayed put. The Mackenzies didn't view whiskey as strong drink—they viewed it as essential to life—but Mac's drink of choice had changed to oolong, which Bellamy had learned to brew like a master.

At his words, Isabella flushed, and Mac felt a flash of sudden glee. "Ah, so you *are* intimately acquainted with everything I've painted. Kind of you to take an interest."

Her blush deepened. "I see notices in art journals, is all, and people tell me."

"And you've become so familiar with each of my pictures that you know when I didn't paint one?" Mac gave her a slow smile. "This from a woman who changed her hotel when she knew I was staying in it?"

Mac hadn't thought Isabella could grow any more red. He felt the dynamics in the room change, from Isabella in a bold frontal attack to Isabella in hasty retreat.

"Don't flatter yourself. I happen to notice things, is all."

And yet she'd known straightaway that he hadn't painted what she'd seen in Mrs. Leigh-Waters's drawing room. He grinned, liking her confusion.

"What I'm trying to tell you is that someone out there is forging Mac Mackenzies," Isabella said impatiently.

"Why would anybody be fool enough to forge something by me?"

"For the money, of course. You are very popular."

"I'm popular because I'm scandalous," Mac countered. "When I die, the paintings will be worthless, except as souvenirs." He set the slice of paint and handkerchief on the table. "May I keep this? Or do you plan to restore it to Mrs. Leigh-Waters?"

"Don't be silly. I didn't tell her I was taking it."

"You left the painting on her wall with a bit sliced out, did you? Won't she notice that?"

"The picture is high up, and I did it carefully so it doesn't show." Isabella's gaze moved to the painting on his easel. "That is quite repulsive, you know. She looks like a spider."

Mac didn't give a damn about the painting, but when he glanced at it he wanted to groan. Isabella was right: It was terrible. All of his paintings were terrible these days. He hadn't been able to paint a decent stroke since he'd gone sober, and he had no idea why he'd thought this one would be any better.

He let out a frustrated roar, picked up a paint-soaked rag, and hurled it at the canvas. The rag landed with a splat on Molly's painted abdomen, and brown-black rivulets ran down the rosy skin.

Mac turned from the picture in time to see Isabella swiftly exiting the room. He sprinted after her and caught up to her halfway down the first flight of stairs. Mac stepped around her, slamming one hand to the banister, the other to the wall. Paint smeared on the wallpaper Isabella had picked out when she'd redecorated his house six years ago.

Isabella gave him a cold look. "Do move, Mac. I have half a dozen errands to attend before luncheon, and I'm already late starting."

Mac took long breaths, trying to still his rage. "Wait. *Please.*" He made himself say the word. "Let us go down to the drawing room. I'll have Bellamy bring tea. We can talk about the paintings you think are forged." Anything to keep her here. He knew in his heart that if she walked away from this house again, she'd never return.

"There is nothing more to say about the forged paintings. I only thought you'd want to know."

Mac was aware that his entire household lurked below, listening. They wouldn't do anything so gauche as peer up the staircase, but they'd be in doorways and in the shadows, waiting to see what happened. They adored Isabella and had mourned the day she'd left them.

"Isabella," he said, pitching his voice low. "Stay."

The tightness around her eyes softened the slightest bit. Mac had hurt her, he knew it. He'd hurt her over and over again. The first step in winning her back was to stop the hurting.

Her lips parted, red and lush. Because he was two steps below her, Isabella's face was on level with his. He could close the few inches between them and kiss her if he chose, feel her mouth on his, taste her warm moisture on his tongue.

"Please," he whispered. *I need you so much.*

Molly chose that moment to climb toward them up the stairs. "Are you ready for me again, yer lordship? You still want me sticking me fingers in me Mary Jane?"

Isabella closed her eyes, her lips thinning into a long, immobile line. Mac's temper splintered.

"Bellamy!" he shouted over the banisters. "What the devil is she doing out of the kitchen?"

Molly came closer, her smile good-natured. "Oh, her ladyship don't mind me. Do you, yer ladyship?" Molly sidled around first Mac, then Isabella, her dressing gown rustling as she headed back up to the studio.

"No, Molly," Isabella said in a cool voice. "I don't mind *you.*"

Isabella lifted her skirt in her gloved hand and prepared to start around Mac. Mac reached for her.

Isabella shrank away. Not in loathing, he realized after the first frozen heartbeat, but because the hand he stretched toward her was covered in brown and black paint.

Mac slammed himself back against the stair railing. He wouldn't trap her. At least not now, with all his servants watching and listening, and Isabella looking at him in that way.

Isabella moved down the stairs around him, very carefully not touching him.

Mac strode after her. "I'll send Molly home. Stay and have luncheon. My staff can run your errands for you."

"I very much doubt that. Some of my errands are quite personal." Isabella reached the ground floor and took up the parasol she'd left on the hall tree.

Bellamy, don't you dare open that door.

Bellamy swung the door wide, letting in a wash of London's fetid air. Isabella's landau stood outside, her footman ready with the door open.

"Thank you, Bellamy," she said in a serene voice. "Good morning."

She walked out.

Mac wanted to rush after her, grab her around the waist, drag her back into the house. He could have Bellamy lock and bolt the doors so she couldn't leave again. She'd hate him at first, but she'd gradually understand that she still belonged with him. Here.

Mac made himself let Bellamy close the door. Tactics that worked for his barbaric Highland ancestors would be useless on Isabella. She'd give him that cool look from her beautiful eyes and have him on his knees. He had prostrated himself for her often enough in the past. The feeling of carpet on his knees had been worth her sudden laughter, the cool tinge leaving her voice as she said, "Oh, Mac, don't be so absurd." He'd pull her down to the carpet with him, and the forgiveness would take an interesting turn.

Mac sat down heavily on the bottom stair and put his head in his paint-stained hands. Today had been a misstep. Isabella had caught him off guard, and he'd ruined the beautiful opportunity she'd handed him.

"Oh, the painting's all spoiled." Molly hurried from the floors above in a flurry of silk. "Mind you, I think I look a bit funny in it."

"Go on home, Molly," Mac said, his voice hollow. "I'll pay you for the full day."

He expected Molly to squeal in pleasure and hurry off, but instead she sank down next to him. "Oh, poor lamb. Want me to make you feel better?"

Mac's arousal had died, and he didn't want it to rise again for anyone but Isabella. "No," he said. "Thank you."

"Suit yourself." Molly stroked slender fingers through his hair. "It's the absolute worst when they don't love you back, ain't it, me lord?"

"Yes." Mac closed his eyes, his rage and need swirling around him until he was sick with it. "You're right, it is the absolute worst."

THE MANY SINS OF LORD CAMERON

CHARACTERS

Lord Cameron Mackenzie

Cameron was the second-oldest son of the Duke of Kilmorgan, and the next in line for the dukedom if something were to befall his currently childless older brother, Hart—a circumstance Cameron dreads.

Cameron is the most reckless and scandalous of the brothers, openly taking mistresses right and left, married and unmarried. He is the father of Daniel, sixteen at the opening of Cameron's book, who is as uncontrollable as his father.

Cameron married young and against his father's wishes, eloping with Lady Elizabeth Cavendish, who was beautiful, scandalous, and unpredictable. Cameron quickly learned that she was a bit mad, made more so after the birth of their son, Daniel. Lady Elizabeth, after trying to kill both Cameron and Daniel, ends her life. The only two people who witnessed her suicide were Cameron and infant Daniel, which caused rampant speculation that Cameron murdered her himself.

Cameron spent the next years burying his tragedy with affairs, travel, and looking after his impetuous son. One night, he returns to his room at Kilmorgan Castle to find a young Ainsley Douglas searching for something in his night table. Outrage turns to intrigue when he sees how beautiful and mysterious Ainsley is ...

———

Ainsley Douglas nee McBride

AINSLEY, born Ainsley McBride, is the only daughter in a family of men. Her parents died when she was a child, and she and her brothers were raised by their oldest brother, Patrick, who was eighteen at the time. Her other three brothers—Elliot, Sinclair, and Steven—helped raise Ainsley, who learned to be robust enough to keep up with them.

Ainsley attended Miss Pringle's Academy for young women, and there met Lady Isabella. Ainsley was good at picking locks and sneaking about the school to procure midnight snacks, thus earning much admiration from Isabella and the rest of her friends.

She married at eighteen to the much older John Douglas, for reasons only her brother Patrick was privy to. She also became a lady in waiting to Queen Victoria, as her mother had been one of Victoria's confidants.

It is while she is married to John Douglas that she steals into Cameron's chamber, convinced Cameron has stolen something from a woman to use against her—Ainsley in indignation agrees to get it back.

She doesn't expect to be caught by Cameron, and then to nearly succumb to his seduction. She vows to be true to her husband, and Cameron, touched by her devotion, sends her off.

And then, a few years later, Ainsley, now a widow, sneaks into Cameron's chamber once again, this time to find compromising letters written by the Queen to John Brown—she believes Cameron and his current mistress have stolen them for nefarious purposes.

When Cameron catches her again, and this time, all bets are off.

———

Important secondary characters

Angelo: Cameron's valet and horse-training partner

Ian and Beth Mackenzie

Mac and Isabella Mackenzie

Hart Mackenzie

Daniel Mackenzie, Cameron's son

Jamie Mackenzie (Beth and Ian's son)

Lloyd Fellows (Inspector of Scotland Yard)

Lady Eleanor Ramsay (Hart's former fiancée)

The McBrides (Ainsley's brothers): Patrick, Elliot, Sinclair, Steven

Phyllida Chase (an unwitting matchmaker)

AUTHOR'S NOTES

Author's Notes

CAMERON'S BOOK IS ONE OF MY FAVORITES OF THIS SERIES. CAM IS a complicated man—large, loud-voiced, dangerous, and yet so careful and gentle with his horses and unashamed in his love for his son. He's also the single father of a teenaged boy, with all the challenges that brings.

I loved writing the flashback scene where Cameron first tries to seduce Ainsley, then is moved by her devotion to her husband. He realizes she's a truly kind and loyal person and doesn't wish to hurt her.

Ainsley has a past she keeps secret, which intrigues Cameron mightily. Why on earth did she marry the older John Douglas, and why is she loyal to a queen who treats her like a servant?

Writing Queen Victoria, elderly by this time and set in her ways, living in dark and freezing Balmoral, was a lot of fun. I've read quite a lot about Victoria's life, her connection with John Brown, details of her many homes, and the lives of her ladies-in-waiting. I was happy to have a chance to put that research to use.

I also love horses, so the horse racing aspect of Cameron's book was satisfying as well, as was continuing his relationship with his valet and trainer, the Angelo.

In this book, we meet Lady Eleanor Ramsay, the woman who had been engaged to Hart and then jilted him. She's an unusual woman—smart, courageous, and a non-stop talker!

But mostly I loved this book because of Cameron and Ainsley. The "buttons" scenes are some of my favorites, as is the "honey" scene. Daniel also has a large part in this story, and we witness him growing up.

Cameron's past is a little different from many romance heroes'. He was married to a woman who went through post-partum depression, and she was also physically abusive to him. Cameron had his reasons for not banishing her, but he also learned how to keep himself safe from her.

Watching Ainsley uncover Cameron layer by layer, and also watching Cameron bring Ainsley out from hiding, was a delight. These are two people who needed each other. Three, actually—Daniel needs Ainsley and Cameron, and they need him.

It was a relief when *Many Sins of Lord Cameron* was finally published. *The Madness of Lord Ian* had just been re-released after being unavailable for a year and a half. I had answered email after email about Lord Ian's book for those eighteen months, and it was grueling! I was as frustrated as the readers who couldn't find it, but there was nothing I could do. (This was *right* before self-publishing was a viable option—if I could have self-published *Madness*, I would have!)

At last, the first three books in the series were available together. Needless to say, sales of the entire series went up, readers again connected to the stories, and I breathed a heartfelt sigh of relief.

SYNOPSIS

SEPTEMBER 1882

Lord Cameron Mackenzie is intrigued when he finds the pretty widow, Ainsley Douglas, hiding in the window seat of his bedchamber. Cam remembers Ainsley Douglas all right—six years ago, he'd caught her in this very bedchamber, during a house party in the Mackenzies' Scottish manor. Enchanted by her ingenuous excuses, he decided to seduce her, but stopped shy when she'd made a rather touching appeal about her "good husband who didn't deserve to be heartbroken."

Later, Cameron learned that her visit to his bedchamber was part of some female intrigue against him, the kind his late wife used to practice. Ainsley protested her innocence, but Cameron's anger made him never want to see her again. Now she's back, at another house party—and Cameron finds the gray-eyed minx in his bedchamber, again. Her excuses are just as ingenuous, but this time Cameron is determined to teach her a lesson.

They have unfinished business, Cameron tells her. He asks her how many of her many buttons she'll let him unclasp, promising that before the house party is over, she'll be asking him to undo them all.

Ainsley's dismay is real. She's on a mission to prevent embarrassment to Queen Victoria, and time is running out. Though the needs he'd stirred long ago during her unhappy marriage rise again, she knows it would be foolish to fall for love-them-and-leave-them Cameron Mackenzie.

But he asks her a question that challenges her beliefs about love and happiness, and she finds herself risking all to be with the black sheep of the Mackenzie family.

EXCERPT: THE MANY SINS OF LORD CAMERON

SCOTLAND, SEPTEMBER 1882

I saw Mrs. Chase slide that letter into Lord Cameron's pocket. She did it almost under my nose. Bloody woman.

Ainsley Douglas sank to her knees in her ball dress and thrust her arms deep into Lord Cameron Mackenzie's armoire.

Why did it have to be Cameron Mackenzie, of all people? Did Mrs. Chase know? Ainsley's heart thrummed before she calmed it down. No, Phyllida Chase could not know. No one did. Cameron must not have told her, because the tale would have come 'round to Ainsley again with breathtaking speed, society gossip being what it was. Therefore, it stood to reason that Cameron had kept the story to himself.

Ainsley felt only marginally better. The queen's letter hadn't been in the pockets of any of the coats in the dressing room. In the armoire, Ainsley found shirts neatly folded, collars stacked in collar boxes, cravats carefully separated with tissue paper. Rich cambric and silk and softest lawn, costly fabrics for a rich man.

She pawed hastily through the garments, but nowhere did she find the letter tucked carelessly into a pocket or fallen between the shirts on the shelf. The valet had likely gone through his master's pockets and taken away any stray paper to return it to Lord Cameron or put it somewhere for safekeeping. Or Cameron had already found it, thought it female silliness, and burned it. Ainsley prayed fast and hard that he'd simply burned it.

Not that such a thing would completely solve Ainsley's dilemma. Phyllida, blast the woman, had more of the queen's letters stashed away somewhere. Ainsley's assignment: Retrieve them at all costs.

The immediate cost was to Ainsley's dove gray ball dress, the first new gown she'd had in years that wasn't mourning black. Not to mention the cost to her knees, her back, and her sanity.

Sanity was further disturbed by the sound of the door opening behind her.

Ainsley backed swiftly out of the wardrobe and turned around, fully expecting Cameron's rather frightening Romany valet to be glaring down at her. Instead, the door blocked whoever had pushed it open, giving Ainsley a few more seconds to panic.

Hide. Where? The door to the dressing room lay across the length of the chamber, the armoire behind her too full for a young woman in a ball dress. Under the bed? No, she'd never dash across the carpet and wriggle beneath it in time.

The window with its full seat was two steps away. Ainsley dove for it, stuffed her skirts beneath her and jerked the curtains closed.

Just in time. Through the crack in the drapes, she saw Lord Cameron himself back into the room with Phyllida Chase, former maid of honor to the queen, hanging around his neck.

The sudden burn in Ainsley's heart took her by surprise. She'd known weeks ago that Phyllida had stuck her claws into Cameron Mackenzie. Why should Ainsley mind? Phyllida was the sort of woman Lord Cameron preferred: lovely, experienced, uninterested in her husband. Likewise Cameron was the sort Phyllida liked: rich, handsome, not looking for a deep attachment. They suited each other well. What business was it of Ainsley's?

Even so, a lump formed in her throat as Lord Cameron shut the door with one hand and slid the other to the small of Phyllida's back. He leaned down and took her mouth in a leisurely kiss.

There was desire in that kiss, unashamed, unmistakable desire. Once, long ago, Ainsley had felt Cameron Mackenzie's desire. She remembered rippling heat softening her body, the point of fire of his kiss. Years had passed, but she still remembered the imprint of his mouth on her lips, on her skin—his hands so skilled.

Phyllida melted to Cameron with a hungry noise, and Ainsley rolled her eyes. She knew full well that *Mr.* Chase was still in the gardens, following the house party on a ramble, the paths lit by paper lanterns under the midnight sky. Ainsley knew this because she'd slipped away from the party as they moved from ballroom to gardens, so that she could search Lord Cameron's chamber.

They couldn't have let her search in peace, could they? No, the bothersome Phyllida could not stay away from her Mackenzie male and had dragged him up here for a liaison. Selfish cow.

Cameron's coat slid to the floor. The waistcoat and shirt beneath outlined muscles hardened by years of riding and training horses. Lord Cameron moved with ease for such a big man, comfortable with his height and strength. He rode with the same grace, the horses under him responding to his slightest touch. Ladies responded to the same touch, she had reason to know.

The deep scar on his cheekbone made some say that his handsomeness was ruined, but Ainsley disagreed. The scar had never unnerved her, but his tallness had taken Ainsley's breath away when Isabella had introduced her to him six years ago, as had the way his gloved hand swallowed her smaller one. Cameron hadn't looked much interested in an old school friend of his sister-in-law's, but later . . . *Oh, that later.*

At *this* moment, Cameron's gaze was reserved for the slim, dark-haired beauty of Phyllida Chase. Ainsley happened to know that Phyllida kept her hair black with the help of a little dye, but Ainsley would never say so. She wouldn't be that petty. If she and Isabella had a good giggle over it, what harm was there in that?

Cameron's waistcoat came off, then his cravat and collar, giving Ainsley a fine view of his bare, damp throat.

She looked away, an ache in her chest. She wondered how long she would have to wait before attempting to slip away—surely once the couple was on the bed they'd be too engrossed in each other to notice her crawling for the door. Ainsley drew a long breath, becoming more unhappy by the minute.

When she summoned the nerve to peek back through the drape, Phyllida's bodice was open, revealing a pretty corset over plump curves. Lord Cameron bent to kiss the bosom that welled over the corset cover, and Phyllida groaned in pleasure.

The vision came to her of Lord Cameron pressing his lips to *Ainsley's* bosom. She remembered his breath burning her skin, his hands on her back. And his kiss. A deep, warm kiss that had awakened every single desire Ainsley had ever had. She remembered the exact pressure of the kiss, the shape and taste of his mouth, the rough of his fingertips on her skin.

She also remembered the icicle in her heart when he'd looked at her and through her the next day. Her own fault. Ainsley had been young and allowed herself to be duped, and she'd compounded the problem by insulting him.

Phyllida's hand was under Cameron's kilt now. He moved to let her play, and the plaid inched upward. Cameron's strong thighs came into view, and Ainsley saw with shock that scars marked him from the back of his knees to the curve of his buttocks.

They were deep, knotted gashes, old wounds that had long since closed. Good heavens, Ainsley hadn't seen *that*. She couldn't stop the gasp that escaped her lips.

Phyllida raised her head. "Darling, did you hear something?"

"No." Cameron had a deep voice, the one word gravelly.

"I'm certain I heard a noise. Would you be a love and check that window?"

Ainsley froze.

"Damn the window. It's probably one of the dogs."

"Darling, *please*." Her pouting tone was done to perfection. Cameron growled something, and then Ainsley heard his heavy tread.

Her heart pounded. There were two windows in the bedchamber, one on either side of his bed. The odds were two-to-one that Lord Cameron would go to the other window. Even bet, Ainsley's youngest brother, Steven, would say. Either Cameron would jerk back the curtain and reveal Ainsley sitting there, or he would not.

Steven didn't like even bets. Not enough variables to be interesting, he insisted. That was because Steven wasn't the one huddled on a window seat waiting to be revealed to Lord Cameron and the woman who was blackmailing the Queen of England.

Lord Cameron's broad brown hands grasped the edges of the drapes in front of Ainsley and parted them a few inches.

Ainsley gazed up at Cameron, meeting his topaz gaze for the first time in six years. He looked at her fully, like a lion on a veldt eyeing a gazelle, and the gazelle in her wanted to run, run, run. The defiant tomboy from Miss Pringle's Academy, however, now a lofty lady-in-waiting, stared boldly back at him.

Silence stretched. Cameron's large body blocked her from the room behind him, but he could so easily turn and reveal her.

Cameron owed her nothing. He must know good and well that she was hiding in his bedchamber because of another intrigue. He could betray Ainsley, hand her to Phyllida, and think it served her right.

Behind Cameron, Phyllida said, "What is it, darling? I saw you jump."

"Nothing," Cameron said. "A mouse."

"I can't bear mice. Do kill it, Cam."

Cameron let his gaze tangle with Ainsley's while she struggled to breathe in her too-tight lacings.

"I'll let it live," he said. "For now." Cameron jerked the curtains closed, shutting Ainsley back into her glass and velvet tent. "We should go down."

"Why? We've just arrived."

"I saw too many people coming back into the house, including your husband. We'll go down separately. I don't want to embarrass Beth and Isabella."

"Oh, very well."

Phyllida didn't seem much put out, but then, she likely assumed she could hole up with her Mackenzie lord anytime she pleased to enjoy his touch.

For one moment, Ainsley experienced deep, bone-wrenching envy.

The two fell silent, no doubt restoring clothing, and then Phyllida said, "I'll speak with you later, darling."

Ainsley heard the door open, more muffled conversation, and then the door closed, and all was silent. She waited a few more heart-pounding minutes to make certain they'd gone, before she flung back the draperies and scrambled down from the window seat.

She was across the room and reaching for the door handle when she heard a throat clear behind her.

Slowly, Ainsley turned around. Lord Cameron Mackenzie stood in the middle of the room in shirtsleeves and kilt, his golden gaze once more pinning her in place. He held up a key in his broad fingers.

"So tell me, Mrs. Douglas," he said, his gravelly voice flowing over her. "What the devil are you doing in my bedchamber—this time?"

THE DUKE'S PERFECT WIFE

CHARACTERS

Hart Mackenzie, Duke of Kilmorgan

HART MACKENZIE: HE'S MAD, BAD, AND DANGEROUS TO KNOW. He has dark secrets, and people speak of his "proclivities." He rules Kilmorgan Castle with an iron hand, and lives for the day Scotland is independent again. He's decadent but practical, isolated but in control of all around him.

Who really is Hart Mackenzie? I immersed myself in his background, his mistakes, his loves, his losses, his grief, his triumphs.

Hart comes across as a hard man, controlling of his brothers (or at least he tries to). I wanted in Hart's book to show that if he was controlling, it was because he'd do anything, absolutely anything, to protect his younger brothers and keep them from harm. Hart took beatings for them when they were younger, and he did even more to keep them safe when they were all older (though the brothers don't know what).

As for his proclivities, Hart was more or less a dom in his younger years. He owned the house of his mistress (Mrs. Parker) who would do anything for him. Later, when he became more interested in politics, he sold the house to her and eased back on his activities.

Hart had chosen Lady Eleanor Ramsay to be his wife. She was the right age, class, spirits, and Scottish. Unfortunately for Hart, Eleanor was not the type to meekly agree that she should hitch herself to him for his own glory.

She also learned much about him—his controlling mania, his hard attitude, and decided she didn't want a marriage like that. She loved Hart but not enough to let him walk on her and everyone else in his life.

So, she broke it off.

Hart made things worse for himself by trying to force her to marry him, though he recognized this was a bad idea the instant he did it.

He decided Eleanor was right, turned away, and married a woman who *would* become the meek duchess and do whatever he said. Unfortunately, she passed away giving birth to their son (who also died), and Hart learned what true grief was.

To recover, he threw himself into his political career, with an eye to becoming Prime Minister and prying Scotland free of England's dominion.

In the middle of this, Eleanor Ramsay comes into his life again ...

———

Lady Eleanor Ramsay

I LOVE ELEANOR! When I met Hart Mackenzie, I knew I'd need a woman who could stand up to him and give him hell. Hart would run roughshod over any woman who didn't—and Eleanor never let him.

Eleanor is the daughter of a Scottish earl (Lord Alec Ramsay), her mother deceased. She and her father live in a rambling, tumble-down manor house on an impoverished estate, their meager income made from the sales of Lord Ramsay's complicated books on botany that Eleanor helps him write.

She's astonished when Hart Mackenzie begins to court her, but she doesn't mind at first. She sees something behind the arrogant, wild youth who will be duke one day, a caring heart he hides behind a protective shell. She allows him to seduce her—she's perfectly happy to let him, he's a master at it—and she allows herself to fall in love.

When she learns more about Hart and realizes that reaching him might be beyond even her powers—and she envisions a long, hard marriage ahead of her—she calls things off. It breaks her heart, but Hart's rage is much like his abusive father's, and she knows it.

Eleanor doesn't abandon Hart completely, however. She watches him from afar, keeping up with his career, trying to feel happy for him when he marries, and weeping for him when his wife and son die.

She and Hart begin to write to each other, easing back on passion to simply communicate with each other, getting to know each other.

When someone appears to try to blackmail Hart over nude photos he allowed his mistress to take, Eleanor decides she must act to save him.

She springs back into his life and tells him she'll help him ferret out the blackmailer. Hart agrees, though he has reasons of his own to want her back in his life …

———

IMPORTANT SECONDARY CHARACTERS
    Ian and Beth Mackenzie
    Mac and Isabella Mackenzie

Cameron and Ainsley Mackenzie

Daniel Mackenzie, Cameron's son

Jamie and Belle Mackenzie (Beth and Ian's son and daughter)

The McBides (Ainsley's brothers): Patrick, Elliot, Sinclair, Steven

David Fleming (Hart's righthand man and descendent of one of the Mackenzie's cousins. He's even more decadent than Hart, and had been in love with Eleanor.)

Aimee, Eileen, and Robert Mackenzie (Mac and Isabella's children)

Gavina Mackenzie (Ainsley and Cam's daughter)

Lord Alec Ramsay (Eleanor's father)

Louisa Scranton (Isabella's younger sister)

Wilfred (Hart's secretary)

Mrs. Whitaker (an unlikely ally)

AUTHOR'S NOTES

Author's Notes

Now we come to Hart.

Writing Hart Mackenzie's story was a challenge, to say the least. I love Hart and especially Eleanor, and I wanted to get these two people together.

One of the challenges I faced was the fact of Hart's past. He'd more or less lived in a brothel with his mistress and was into BDSM.

I know some readers wanted a book all about Hart the Dom. They wanted the historical version of Christian Grey (just my luck *50 Shades* came out a few months before this book did. I also got accused of copying it, though I'd turned in the final book to my publisher a year or so before that. So goes the whacky world of publishing).

However, this book wasn't meant to be erotic romance. My point in writing Hart's book was to write about *Hart*, not his journey from Dom to not-Dom. His interest in BDSM was only a part of him, an outlet for his need for control (and his lack of it under his father's thumb). He'd given all this up well before Ian's book, and definitely before he let Eleanor back into his life.

If anything, Eleanor made Hart see that this part of himself wasn't shameful, and she didn't mind (in fact, our Eleanor is intrigued, and wishes Hart wouldn't hold himself back).

I explored Hart and Eleanor's journey together, from their turbulent but mostly happy courtship, to their falling out, to the older Hart and Eleanor learning about each other again.

What they uncovered was heartbreaking and loving. I don't regret one word I wrote in Hart and Eleanor's tale.

We also learn a lot more about Hart's role in freeing his brothers from their father, and the terrible things he went through in order to protect the rest of the family. Only Eleanor knows, which gives them another bond.

I introduced David Fleming, Hart's oldest friend, who is distantly related to the Mackenzies. He too had once hoped Eleanor would be his wife, but knew that Eleanor wanted only Hart. David is decadent and interesting, and he finds his HEA in *A Rogue Meets a Scandalous Lady*.

We also get a glimpse of all the new Mackenzie children, and see Ian's love for his son and daughter, and his new life.

The Duke's Perfect Wife was my first historical romance to hit the *New York Times*.

Eleanor and Hart's tale wrap up the stories of the original four brothers. But more, of course, was to come!

SYNOPSIS

Lady Eleanor Ramsay is the only one who knows the truth about Hart Mackenzie. Once his fiancee, she is the sole woman to whom he could ever pour out his heart.

Hart has it all—a dukedom, wealth, power, influence, whatever he desires. Every woman wants him—his seductive skills are legendary. But Hart has sacrificed much to keep his brothers safe, first from their brutal father, and then from the world. He's also suffered loss—his wife, his infant son, and the woman he loved with all his heart though he realized it too late.

Now, Eleanor has reappeared on Hart's doorstep, with scandalous nude photographs of Hart taken long ago. Intrigued by the challenge in her blue eyes—and aroused by her charming, no-nonsense determination—Hart wonders if his young love has come to ruin him . . . or save him.

EXCERPT: THE DUKE'S PERFECT WIFE

LONDON 1884

HART MACKENZIE.

It was said that he knew every pleasure a woman desired and exactly how to give it to her. Hart wouldn't ask what the lady wanted, and she might not even know herself, but she would understand once he'd finished. And she'd want it again.

He had power, wealth, skill, and intelligence, and the ability to play upon his fellow man—or woman—to make them do anything he wanted and believe it to be their own idea.

Eleanor Ramsay knew firsthand that all of this was true.

She lurked among a flock of journalists in St. James's Street on an unexpectedly mild February afternoon, waiting for the great Hart Mackenzie, Duke of Kilmorgan, to emerge from his club. In her unfashionable gown and old hat, Lady Eleanor Ramsay looked like any other lady scribbler, as hungry for a story as the rest of them. But while they craved an exclusive story about the famous Scottish duke, Eleanor had come to change his life.

The journalists snapped alert when they spied the tall duke on the threshold, his broad shoulders stretching out a black coat, Mackenzie plaid swathing his hips. He always wore a kilt to remind everyone who set eyes on him that he was, and always would be, Scottish first.

"Your Grace!" the journalists shouted. "Your Grace!"

The sea of male backs surged past Eleanor, shutting her out. She jostled her way forward, using her folded parasol without mercy to open her way to the front of the pack. "Oh, I do beg your pardon," she said, when her bustle shoved aside a man who tried to elbow her in the ribs.

Hart looked neither left nor right as he pulled on his hat and walked the three steps between the club and the door of his open landau. He was master of not acknowledging what he did not wish to.

"Your Grace!" Eleanor shouted. She cupped her hands around her mouth. "Hart!"

Hart stopped, turned. His gaze met hers, his golden stare skewering her across the twenty feet of space between them.

Eleanor's knees went weak. She'd last seen Hart on a train, almost a year ago, when he'd followed her into her compartment, his hand warm on her arm, and made her take a gift of money from him. He'd felt sorry for her, which had rankled. He'd also tucked one of his cards into the collar of her bodice. She remembered the heat of his fingers and the scrape of the card, with his name, against her skin.

Hart said something to one of the pugilist-looking bodyguards who waited next to his carriage. The man gave Hart a nod then turned and shouldered his way to Eleanor, breaking a path through the frantic journalists.

"This way, your ladyship."

Eleanor clutched her closed parasol, aware of the angry glares around her, and followed. Hart watched her come, his gaze never moving. It had been heady, once upon a time, to be the center of that very studied attention.

When she reached the landau, Hart caught her by the elbows and boosted her up and inside.

Eleanor's breath went out of her at his touch. She landed on the seat, trying to slow her pounding heart, as Hart followed her in, taking the seat opposite, thank heavens. She'd never be able to get through her proposition if he sat too close to her, distracting her with the heat of his very solid body.

The footman slammed the door, and Eleanor grabbed at her hat as the landau jerked forward. The gentlemen of the press shouted and swore as their prey got away, the landau heading up St. James's Street toward Mayfair.

Eleanor looked back over the seat at them. "Goodness, you've made Fleet Street unhappy today," she said.

"Damn Fleet Street," Hart growled.

Eleanor turned around again to find Hart's gaze hard on her. "What, all of it?"

This close to him, she could see the gold flecks in his hazel eyes that gave him the eagle look, and the red highlights in his dark hair from his Scottish ancestry. He'd cropped his hair shorter since she'd seen him last, which made his face sharper and more forbidding than ever. Eleanor was the only one among the crowd of journalists to have seen that face soften in sleep.

Hart stretched one big arm across the seat, his large legs under the kilt crowding the carriage. The kilt shifted upward a little, letting her glimpse thighs tanned from all the riding, fishing, and tramping about he did on his Scottish estate.

Eleanor opened her parasol, pretending that she was relaxed and happy to be in the same carriage as the man to whom she'd once been engaged. "I apologize for accosting you on the street," she said. "I did go to your house, but you've changed your majordomo. He did not know me, nor was he by any means impressed by the card you gave me. Apparently ladies make a habit of trying to gain your house by false pretenses, and he assumed me one of those. I really cannot blame him. I could have stolen the card, for all he knew, and you have always been quite popular with the ladies."

Hart's gaze didn't soften under her barrage of words as it used to do. "I will speak to him."

"No, no, don't shout at the poor man *too* much. He wasn't to know. I expect you tell him very little, in your maddening way. No, I came all this way from Aberdeen to talk to you. It's really quite important. I called in at Isabella's, but she was not at home, and I knew that this could not wait. I managed to get it out of your footman—dear Franklin, how he's grown—that you'd be at your club, but he was too terrified of the majordomo to let me wait in the house. So I decided to lurk and catch you when you emerged. It was such fun, pretending to be a scribbler. And here I am."

She threw out her hands in that helpless gesture Hart remembered, but woe to any man who thought this woman helpless.

Lady Eleanor Ramsay.

The woman I am going to marry.

Her dark blue serge dress was years out of date, her parasol had one broken spoke, and her hat with faded flowers and short veil perched lopsidedly on her head. The veil did nothing to hide the delphinium blue of her eyes or the spread of sweet freckles that ran together when she wrinkled her nose, all the while smiling her little smile. She was tall for a woman, but filled out with generous curves. She'd been breathtakingly beautiful at age twenty, when he'd first seen her flitting about a ballroom, her voice and laughter like music, and she was beautiful now. Even more so. Hart's hungry gaze feasted on her, he imbibing her like a man who'd gone without sustenance for a very long time.

He forced his voice to remain steady, casual even. "What is this important thing you need to speak to me about?" With

Eleanor it could be anything from a lost button to a threat to the British Empire.

She leaned forward a little, the hook at the top of her collar coming loose from the frayed fabric. "Well, I cannot tell you, here, in an open carriage plodding through Mayfair. Wait until we are indoors."

The thought of Eleanor following him into his house, breathing the same air he did, made his chest constrict. He wanted it, he craved it. "Eleanor . . ."

"Goodness, you can spare me a *few* minutes, can't you? Consider it my reward for distracting those rabid journalists. What I have discovered could border on the disastrous. I decided it best I rush down and tell you in person instead of write."

It must be serious to make Eleanor leave her ramshackle house outside Aberdeen, where she lived with her father in genteel poverty. She went few places these days. Then again, she could have some covert motive in that head of hers. Eleanor could do nothing simply.

"If it is that important, El, for God's sake, tell me."

"Goodness, your face looks like granite when you scowl. No wonder everyone in the House of Lords is terrified of you." She tilted back the parasol and smiled at him.

Soft flesh beneath his, her blue eyes half closed in sultry pleasure, Scottish sunshine on her bare skin. The feeling of moving inside her, her smile as she said, "I love you, Hart."

Old emotions rose swiftly. He remembered their last encounter, when he hadn't been able to stop himself touching her face, saying, "Eleanor, whatever am I going to do with you?"

She popping up here before he was ready would force him to alter the timing of his plans, but Hart had the ability to rearrange his schemes with lightning speed. That's what made him so dangerous.

"I will tell you in due time," Eleanor went on. "And give you my business proposition."

"Business proposition?" With Eleanor Ramsay. God help him. "What business proposition?"

Eleanor, in her maddening way, ignored him to look around at the tall houses that lined Grosvenor Street. "It has been so long since I've been to London, and for the Season, no less. I am looking forward to seeing everyone again. Good heavens, is that Lady Mountgrove? It is, indeed. Hello, Margaret!" Eleanor waved heartily to a plump woman who was alighting from a carriage in front of one of the painted doors.

Lady Mountgrove, one of the most gossipy women in England, fixed her mouth in a round O. Her stare took in every detail of Lady Eleanor Ramsay waving at her from the Duke of Kilmorgan's carriage, the duke himself planted opposite her. She gaped a long time before lifting her hand in acknowledgment.

"Goodness, I haven't seen her in donkey's years," Eleanor said, sitting back as they rolled on. "Her daughters must be, oh, quite young ladies now. Have they made their come-outs yet?"

Her mouth was still kissable, closing in a little pucker while she awaited his answer.

"I haven't the faintest bloody idea," Hart said.

"Really, Hart, you must at least *glance* at the society pages. You are the most eligible bachelor in all of Britain. Probably in the entire British Empire. Mamas in India are grooming their girls to sail back to you, telling them, *You never know. He's not married yet.*"

"I'm a widower." Hart never said the word without a pang. "Not a bachelor."

"You're a duke, unmarried, and poised to become the most powerful man in the country. In the world, really. You should give a thought to marrying again."

Her tongue, her lips, moved in such a sultry way. The man

who'd walked away from her had to be insane. Hart remembered the day he'd done so, still felt the tiny *smack* of the ring on his chest when she'd thrown it at him, rage and heartbreak in her eyes.

He should have refused to let her go, should have run off with her that very afternoon, bound her to him forever. He'd made mistake after mistake with her. But he'd been young, angry, proud, and . . . embarrassed. The lofty Hart Mackenzie, certain he could do whatever he pleased, had learned differently with Eleanor.

He let his voice soften. "Tell me how you are, El."

"Oh, about the same. You know. Father is always writing his books, which are brilliant, but he couldn't tell you how much a farthing is worth. I left him to amuse himself at the British Museum, where he is pouring over the Egyptian collection. I do hope he doesn't start pulling apart the mummies."

He might. Alec Ramsay had an inquisitive mind, and neither God nor all the museum authorities in the land could stop him.

"Ah, here we are." Eleanor craned to look up at Hart's Grosvenor Square mansion as the landau pulled to a halt. "I see your majordomo peering out the window. He looks a bit dismayed. Do not be too angry with the poor man, will you?" She put her fingers lightly on the hand of the footman who'd hurried from Hart's front door to help her down. "Hello again, Franklin. I have found him, as you see. I was remarking upon how tall you've become. And married, I hear. With a son?"

Franklin, who prided himself on his forbidding countenance while guarding the door of the most famous duke in London, melted into a smile. "Yes, your ladyship. He's three now, and the trouble he gets into." He shook his head.

"Means he's robust and healthy." Eleanor patted his arm. "Congratulations to you." She folded her parasol and waltzed into the house while Hart climbed down from the landau behind her. "Mrs. Mayhew, how delightful to see you," he heard her say. He entered his house to see her holding out her hands to Hart's housekeeper.

The two exchanged greetings, and were talking about, of all things, recipes. Eleanor's housekeeper, now retired, apparently had instructed her to obtain Mrs. Mayhew's recipe for lemon cakes.

Eleanor started up the stairs, and Hart nearly threw his hat and coat at Franklin as he followed. He was about to order Eleanor into the front drawing room when a large Scotsman in a threadbare kilt, loose shirt, and paint-spattered boots came barreling down from the top floor.

"Hope you don't mind, Hart," Mac Mackenzie said. "I brought the hellions and fixed myself a place to paint in one of your spare bedrooms. Isabella's got the decorators in, and you wouldn't believe the racket—" Mac broke off, a look of joy spreading across his face. "Eleanor Ramsay, by all that's holy! What the devil are you doing here?" He raced down the last of the stairs to the landing and swept Eleanor off her feet into a bear hug.

Eleanor kissed Mac, second youngest in the Mackenzie family, soundly on the cheek. "Hello, Mac. I've come to irritate your older brother."

"Good. He needs a bit of irritating." Mac set Eleanor down again, eyes glinting with his grin. "Come up and see the babies when you're done, El. I'm not painting them, because they won't hold still; I'm putting finishing touches on a horse picture for Cam. Night-Blooming Jasmine, his new champion."

"Yes, I heard she'd done well." Eleanor rose on her tiptoes and gave Mac another kiss on the cheek. "That's for Isabella. And Aimee, Eileen, and Robert." *Kiss, kiss, kiss.* Mac absorbed it all with an idiotic smile.

Hart leaned on the railing. "Will we get to this proposition sometime today?"

"Proposition?" Mac asked, eyes lighting. "Now, that sounds interesting."

"Shut it, Mac," Hart said.

Screaming erupted from on high—shrill, desperate, Armageddon-has-come screaming. Mac grinned and jogged back up the stairs.

"Papa's coming, hellions," he called. "If you're good, you can have Auntie Eleanor for tea."

The shrieking continued, unabated, until Mac reached the top floor, dodged into the room from whence it issued, and slammed the door. The noise instantly died, though they could still hear Mac's rumbling voice.

Eleanor sighed. "I always knew Mac would make a good father. Shall we?"

She turned and headed up to the next floor and the study without waiting for Hart. At one time, she'd become well acquainted with all the rooms in his house, and she apparently hadn't forgotten her way around.

The study hadn't changed at all, Eleanor noted when she entered. The same dark paneling covered the walls, and bookcases filled with what looked like the same books climbed to the high ceiling. The huge desk that had belonged to Hart's father still reposed in the middle of the room.

The same carpet covered the floor, though a different hound dozed by the fire. This was Ben, if she remembered correctly, a son of Hart's old dog, Beatrix, who'd passed on a few months after her engagement to Hart had ended. The news of Beatrix's death had nearly broken her heart.

Ben didn't open his eyes as they entered, and his gentle snore blended with the crackle of the fire on the hearth.

Hart touched Eleanor's elbow to guide her across the room. She wished he wouldn't, because the steel strength of his fingers made her want to melt, and she needed to maintain her resolve.

If all went well today, she'd not have to be close to him again, but she had to make the first approach in private. A letter could have gone too easily into the wrong hands, or be lost by a careless secretary, or burned unopened by Hart.

Hart dragged an armchair to his desk, moving it as though it weighed nothing. Eleanor knew better, though, as she sat on it. The heavily carved chair was as solid as a boulder.

Hart took the desk chair, his kilt moving as he sat, showing sinewy strength above his knees. Anyone believing a kilt unmanly had never seen Hart Mackenzie in one.

Eleanor touched the desk's smooth top. "You know, Hart, if you plan to be the first minister of the nation, you might give a thought to changing the furniture. It's a bit out of date."

"Bugger the furniture. What is this problem that made you drag yourself and your father down from the wilds of Scotland?"

"I am worried about you. You've worked so hard for this, and I can't bear to think of what it would do to you if you lost everything. I've lay awake and pondered what to do for a week. I know we parted acrimoniously, but that was a long time ago, and many things have changed, especially for you. I still care about you, Hart, whatever you may believe, and I was distressed to think that you might have to go into hiding if this came out."

"Into hiding?" He stared at her. "What are you talking about? My past is no secret to anyone. I'm a blackguard and a sinner, and everyone knows it. These days, that's almost an asset to being a politician."

"Possibly, but this might humiliate you. You'd be a laughing-stock, and that would certainly be a setback."

His gaze became sharp. Gracious, he looked like his father when he did that. The old duke had been handsome, but a monster, with nasty, cold eyes that made you know you were a toad beneath his heel. Hart, in spite of it all, had a warmth that his father had lacked.

"Eleanor, cease babbling and tell me what this is all about."

"Ah, yes. It's time you saw, I think." Eleanor dug into a pocket inside her coat and withdrew a folded piece of pasteboard. She laid this on the desk in front of Hart, and opened it.

Hart went still.

The object inside the folded card was a photograph. It was a full-length picture of a younger Hart, shot in profile. Hart's body had been a little slimmer then but still well muscled. In the photograph, he rested his buttocks against the edge of a desk, his sinewy hand bracing on the desk's top beside his hip. His head was bent as he studied something at his feet, out of the frame.

The pose, though perhaps a bit unusual for a portrait, was not the unique thing about the picture. The most interesting aspect of this photograph was that, in it, Hart Mackenzie was quite, quite naked.

A MACKENZIE FAMILY CHRISTMAS: THE PERFECT GIFT

CHARACTERS

A MACKENZIE FAMILY CHRISTMAS WAS A CHANCE TO BRING BACK all the characters of the first four books and to take a look at those in upcoming books. The story switches from couple to couple as they celebrate the first Christmas with all the married brothers together, giving us a peek at their happily ever after. We also get a look at the Mackenzie children gathered in one place while the family awaits the birth of Hart and Eleanor's first child.

Main Characters

Ian and Beth Mackenzie
Mac and Isabella Mackenzie
Cameron and Ainsley Mackenzie
Hart and Eleanor (Duke and Duchess of Kilmorgan)
Daniel Mackenzie (Cam's oldest son)
Lloyd Fellows
Lady Louisa Scranton
Elliot and Julian McBride (Note: I did not spend much time

on these two, or their children, because at the time, their book, *The Seduction of Elliot McBride,* had not yet been published.)
Sinclair McBride
Steven McBride
David Fleming
Curry, Bellamy, and Angelo (valets to Ian, Mac, and Cam)

Mackenzie / McBride children

Jamie, Belle, and Megan (Ian and Beth)
Aimee, Eileen, and Robert (Mac and Isabella)
Gavina (Cameron and Ainsley)
Hart Alec Graham Mackenzie (Hart and Eleanor)
Andrew and Caitriona (Sinclair McBride)

AUTHOR'S NOTES

Author's Notes

I HAD THE IDEA FOR WRITING A "WHAT HAPPENS AFTER THE HEA" story, because I know so many readers like seeing the couples happy down the road.

I am a firm believer that marriage is only the beginning, and that love grows stronger and deeper as time passes (though I realize, in the real world, it doesn't always work out). I wanted to show the brothers and their ladies living life but being happy at the same time, no matter what obstacles came their way.

With that in mind, I gathered the brothers and their new families at Kilmorgan Castle for Christmas and Hogmanay. Eleanor is expecting her and Hart's first child, Daniel is coming home for the holidays, and Ainsley's brothers are also invited.

I came up with threads for each couple—Ian and Beth and the Ming bowl, a worrying adventure for Ainsley and Cam, romantic secrets between Isabella and Mac, and the birth of Eleanor's baby. I threw in a few more things for Daniel and let some secondary characters have a role. David Fleming arrives, as does Sinclair McBride and his two terrifying children. Lloyd Fellows also appears, and we have a glimpse of Lloyd as he starts to lose his heart to Isabella's sister, Louisa.

This novel is light in tone, meant to be a true happy ever after. I hope to write more of these Mackenzie gatherings.

SYNOPSIS

The Mackenzies have gathered for Christmas, the first since all four brothers have begun their married lives. With wives and children, the Mackenzie brothers descend on Kilmorgan Castle for feasting and merrymaking.

Ian has ordered a new Ming bowl, which he shows Beth, and then ... disaster. Beth drops the bowl and smashes it.

Beth fears the loss of Ian's precious Ming bowl will send him into one of what he calls his "muddles," thought those have been few and far between since they married. When Ian disappears for hours at a time in an upstairs room, letting in only Daniel, Beth's worry escalates, as do the fears of the rest of the family.

Ian, on the other hand, has turned his attention to other matters ...

Elsewhere in the story, Eleanor is awaiting the birth of her first child, and is confined to bed, which does not suit her exuberant nature. Hart fears to lose her, but he keeps up his tough exterior.

Daniel is in his element, taking wagers on the sex and exact hour of the birth of Eleanor and Hart's baby. He also sets up a boxing match between Bellamy, Mac's valet and former fighter, and Cameron, organizing the betting again.

Christmas Day brings surprises, as does New Year's.

Join the Mackenzie family for revelry and Scottish fun!

EXCERPT: A MACKENZIE FAMILY CHRISTMAS

DECEMBER 1884

"By the way," Curry said, coming to Ian with the decanter. "While you were out, it came."

Ian waited while Curry filled his glass, Ian taking in the flow of the amber liquid, the exact way the droplets splashed into the glass and spread in perfect ripples.

When Curry finished and took a step back, his words, along with Beth's excited smile, connected in Ian's brain.

"It's here?" Ian asked.

"Aye, m'lord. Waiting for you in the Ming room. With the Russian gentleman's compliments, his man who delivered it said."

Ian didn't hear the last. He left his seat, his brothers, their wives, and Curry a blur as he strode out of the room and down the enormous corridor, not realizing until halfway that he still clutched a full glass of whiskey, the liquid sloshing out over his hand.

Beth walked out after Ian, her skirts rustling, but she didn't hurry. She knew where her husband was going and why.

This summer, Ian had found an illustration of a Ming bowl in a book he'd read with his usual speed, and nothing would do but that he acquired said bowl, no matter what the cost.

He'd scoured antiques stores in London, Edinburgh, Paris, and down into Italy. He'd visited dealers, written letters, sent telegrams, and waited anxiously for the answers. Because Ian was one of the foremost collectors of Ming bowls in Great Britain and Europe, many came forward to say they had a bowl exactly like it, but Ian had always known that none of them were right. *It isn't the same,* he'd tell the disappointed merchant or collector.

At long last, he'd pinned down the current owner of the bowl in the book—an aristocrat in Russia. The Russian gentleman had agreed to the price and said he'd send the bowl by courier. Impatient Ian had thought of little else from that day to this.

Beth found him at a table in the middle of the Ming room, his broad hands tearing back the paper and straw in a wooden box. She paused to observe him, her tall husband with a blue and green Mackenzie kilt hugging his hips, his dark formal coat stretched across his shoulders. He'd mussed his close-cropped hair, lamplight burnishing auburn streaks in it.

He worked quickly, gaze intent on the box. The room around him was filled floor to ceiling with glassed-in shelves and glass cases on the floor, each bearing a Ming bowl on a little stand, each precisely labeled.

Bowls only. Ian had no interest in vases or in porcelain from any other period. His early Ming collection, however, was priceless, the envy of all other Ming aficionados.

Ian lifted the bowl from the wrappings and swiftly examined it, holding it up to the light and studying every side. Beth held her breath, fearing the Russian had cheated him, and wondering what Ian's reaction would be if he had.

Then Ian relaxed into his devastating smile, his golden gaze seeking hers. "My Beth, come and see."

He held the bowl with steady fingers as he waited for her. Beth marveled that his hands, so large and strong, could be so gentle—with his Ming bowls, on her skin, while holding his son and daughter.

The bowl was certainly beautiful. Its thin porcelain sides were covered with interwoven flowers and tiny dragons in blue, one object flowing into another in delicate strokes. The inside of the bowl held more flowers dancing around the rim, and on the bottom was a single lotus flower. The underside held a dragon, four claws curled around the bowl's bottom lip. The blue, the only color, was incredible—dark and intense across the centuries.

"Lovely," Beth breathed. "I understand now why you hunted for it so hard."

Ian kept his gaze on the bowl, his face betraying joy he didn't know how to convey. He said nothing, but his look, his happiness, was enough.

"The perfect Christmas gift," Beth said. "How on earth will I find something for you to compete with it?"

"Today isn't Christmas," Ian said in his matter-of-fact voice, still looking at the bowl. "It's the twelfth. And we give our gifts at Hogmanay."

"No, I meant . . . Never mind." Ian could be so very literal, and though he did try to understand Beth's little jokes, he didn't always catch when she meant to be funny. *Poor Beth,* she imagined him thinking, *She doesn't understand a word she's saying.*

Ian set the bowl into her cupped palms. "Hold it up to the light. The pattern is deep. You can see the layers when th' light is behind them."

He kept hold of her wrists as he guided her to raise her

hands, holding the bowl toward the warm yellow wall sconce, which dripped with long, clear crystals.

The light unfolded more flowers from between the dragons and vines, small and light blue. "Oh, Ian, it's exquisite."

Ian released her wrists to let her turn the bowl this way and that, but he remained behind her, his warmth on her back. Her bustle crushed against her legs, Ian's arm coming around her waist. He leaned to kiss her neck, the love in the kiss rippling heat through her.

Beth held the bowl up again, her fingers trembling. She needed to tell Ian of the outcome of their nights in bed this autumn, but she'd not had the chance yet. But now . . .

Beth started to turn, to lower the bowl, to hand it back to him.

Her shoe caught on the edge of the Aubusson carpet, its fringe snagging the high heel of her boot. She rocked, and Ian caught her by the elbow, but the bowl slipped from her fingers.

She lunged for it, and so did Ian, but the porcelain evaded their outstretched hands.

Beth watched in horror as the blue and white bowl fell down, down, down to the wooden floor beyond the rug, and smashed into shower of beautiful, polished bits.

THE UNTAMED MACKENZIE

CHARACTERS

Lloyd Fellows

Lloyd Fellows grew up the son of a charwoman barmaid, knowing he is illegitimate. He learns that he is indeed the bastard son of the Duke of Kilmorgan, a Scottish duke of vast wealth. Hearing that the duke is due to drive through a part of London, the boy Lloyd tries to accost him and tell the duke he is his long, lost son.

Unfortunately, the duke only swats Lloyd aside, thinking him a street boy, while his oldest son, Hart, rides in luxury in the carriage.

Thus, Lloyd grew up vowing hatred of the Mackenzie family and doing all he can to bring them down.

This changes when he actually meets the Mackenzie brothers and gets drawn into their world. They accept him—greet him with open arms, even—and he realizes he has to revise his opinion.

While Lloyd believes he'll never be one of the Mackenzies in truth, he works at his own life with the same obsession they work at theirs. He becomes a policeman and rises through the ranks to Chief Inspector, one of the best detectives in the new Criminal Investigation Division of Scotland Yard.

It is this expertise, as well as his connections to the Mackenzies, that causes him to be sent to the murder of a prominent man on a wealthy estate. To his dismay he finds that one of the primary suspects is Lady Louisa Scranton, the sister of Isabella Mackenzie (Mac's wife), and the woman he's falling in love with …

———

Lady Louisa Scranton

Louisa, the youngest daughter of Earl Scranton, has lived in her sister's shadow all her life, but at the same time loved Isabella with all her heart.

Her life changed dramatically when first Isabella elopes with Lord Mac Mackenzie and then leaves him, causing a great scandal which hurts Louisa's chances on the marriage mart. Not long later, her father goes bankrupt and dies, leaving Louisa in an even worse situation.

Isabella makes sure Louisa and their mother are taken care of financially, but Louisa wants more than that. She tells Isabella she wants help in finding a suitable husband—she doesn't need anyone exciting, but she believes any husband is better than being left on the shelf.

Until, that is, she meets Lloyd Fellows at Eleanor and Hart's wedding, and they share a spontaneous kiss.

They meet again in A Mackenzie Family Christmas, spying each other in the staircase hall:

"Louisa's face flooded with heat, but she would not let herself look away. Yes, she had kissed him. She'd been filled with the joy of the wedding, even with its complications, and a sadness that she'd likely never have such a wedding herself. She'd found this handsome man, as sad and alone as she was, and she'd wanted his warmth."

They share another kiss at the Christmas ball, but both are convinced that nothing will come of it.

The next time Louisa sees Lloyd Fellows, she is about to be arrested for murder.

IMPORTANT SECONDARY CHARACTERS
Ian and Beth Mackenzie
Mac Mackenzie
Isabella Mackenzie (nee) Scranton (wife to Mac)
Cameron and Ainsley Mackenzie
Hart and Eleanor Mackenzie
Daniel Mackenzie
Mrs. Fellows (Lloyd's mother)
Sergeant Pierce
Sir Richard Cavanaugh (doctor)
Constable Dobbs

AUTHOR'S NOTES

Because of the success of *A Mackenzie Family Christmas* and my self-published shorter novels in my Shifters Unbound series, my publisher convinced me to pen three shorter novels for the Mackenzie series, which would be published by their e-first imprint, InterMix.

I was persuaded, but in retrospect I'm not sure it was the best idea. Choosing which books should be short and which long was difficult, plus there was no promise of a print edition for any of them.

Also, I did not know whether I'd be given a contract for any more full-length books. I wanted to make sure Lloyd Fellows' story was told, so I agreed to make him the first Intermix short novel.

But on to Lloyd—when he came on the scene in *Madness of Lord Ian Mackenzie*, I was intrigued. Who was this man, and why was he so adamant about persecuting the Mackenzies? When I realized, I was even more intrigued.

I enjoy writing villains, sometimes even more than writing heroes, because I see them as real people who don't know they're villains. They think they are perfectly justified in whatever cruel thing they're doing.

My favorite villains of all have become heroes (Alexander in *The Mad, Bad Duke*—villain in *Penelope and Prince Charming*; James Ardmore in *The Pirate Hunter*—villain in *The Pirate Next Door;* and James Denis in the Captain Lacey Regency mysteries —although he's still a villain!). These men are interesting to me because they're already complex, and I like to get into their point of view and also give them a satisfying ending.

I paired Lloyd with Lady Isabella's younger sister, liking the contrast between the world-weary Lloyd, and the young, spirited Louisa. She's lost at life a bit herself (dead father gone bankrupt, and she's left on the shelf), but she's kind and sunny natured. What better way for she and Lloyd to be thrown together than to have her be accused of a murder Lloyd then must investigate?

I am a mystery author in my other life (see my books writing as Ashley Gardner plus the Below Stairs Mystery series), and I enjoy exploring the history of policing, especially before technology took over. Detectives had to rely on witnesses, their own eyes at a crime scene, reasoning, intuition, and dogged persistence. Because Lloyd is falling in love, he has to solve this case quickly and rescue the woman who makes him happy. Now can he, a lowly police detective, make *her* happy?

SYNOPSIS

JUNE 1885, LONDON

To redeem her family's disgraced name, Lady Louisa Scranton has decided to acquire a proper husband. He needs to be a man of fortune and highly respectable in order to restore both her family's lost wealth and reputation. She enters the Marriage Mart with all flags flying, determined to find the right bachelor.

But Louisa's hopes are dashed when the Bishop of Hargate drops dead at her feet–and she is shockingly accused of murder! Soon, Louisa's so-called friends begin shunning her, because the company of a suspected killer is never desirable in polite society.

The problem comes to the ears of Detective Inspector Lloyd Fellows, by-blow of the decadent Scottish Mackenzie family and an inspector for Scotland Yard. He has shared two passionate kisses with Lady Louisa-and vows to clear her name. For not only does he know she's innocent, he recognizes he's falling for the lovely lady.

Fellows is Louisa's only hope of restoring her family's honor–and it is he alone who intrigues Louisa in a way that may be even more scandalous than murder...

EXCERPT: THE UNTAMED MACKENZIE

APRIL 1885

He's dead, all right," Sergeant Pierce said.

He and Fellows knelt next to the body while a doctor called Sir Richard Cavanaugh stood nearby and gave them his medical opinion in the most condescending way possible.

"Histotoxic hypoxia," Sir Richard said. "See his blue coloring? Prussic acid, most likely. In the tea, I would think, a fatal dose. Would have been quick. Only a few moments from ingestion to death."

Fellows disliked arrogant doctors who presumed ahead of the facts, but in this case, the man was probably right. Fellows had seen death by prussic-acid poisoning before. Still, he preferred to hear conclusions from the coroner after a thorough postmortem, not to mention a testing of food and drink the victim had taken, than speculations by a doctor to the elite.

Fellows ordered Pierce to gather up what was left of the broken teacup with the liquid inside, and also the full teacup that stood next to the pot on the table. He had Pierce pour off the tea still in the pot into a vial for more testing. Fellows scraped up cream from a pastry that had been smashed on the ground, and the remains of the plate that had held it, handing all to Pierce.

He left Pierce sealing up the vials with wax and had a look around the tea tent. Unfortunately too many people had trampled in here; the place was a mess. The grass was filled with footprints—ladies' high heels, gentlemen's boots, servants' sturdy shoes—all overlapping one another.

The local police sergeant stood well outside the tent as though washing his hands of the affair. Fellows approached him anyway. The fact that the local police had sent no one higher than a sergeant meant the chief constable wanted to keep well out of the way. He wondered why.

"Your thoughts, Sergeant?" Fellows asked the local man.

The sergeant shrugged, but the man had a keen eye and didn't look in the least bit stupid. "The doc says poison in the tea, and I don't disagree. The young lady they think did it is in the house—my constable's on the lookout up there. She's an aristo's daughter, though, so the lady of the house didn't want the likes of us questioning her. Says we had to wait for you." The sergeant gave Fellows a dark nod. "Better you than me, if you don't mind me saying so, guv."

He meant better *Fellows* lost his job for arresting a rich man's spoiled daughter, which was exactly what could happen. Fellows' Mackenzie connections might be able to save him from a lawsuit by the girl's father, but his career could be over.

Not that Fellows wanted to go begging, hat in hand, to his half brothers for their charity. An invitation to the races was one thing. Owing a monumental obligation to Hart Mackenzie was another.

"Go help Sergeant Pierce," Fellows growled at the man. "I'll need statements from everyone. Who was where and what they saw—in minute detail. Understand?"

The sergeant did not look happy, but he saluted and said, "Yes, sir."

Fellows left him behind and made for the house and the aristocrat's daughter. He reflected as he approached the large house that running down a killer six feet three and weighing eighteen stone was much more satisfying than having to face a silly girl who probably didn't understand what exactly she'd done. She likely felt herself perfectly justified in poisoning a man who'd annoyed her. She'd be highly strung and more than a little mad, or else too stupid to realize the consequences of her actions.

Fellows looked up at the giant brick house trimmed in white, strategically positioned for a view to the river at the bottom of a meadow. The very rich lived here, the sort who existed in their own world, with their own rules; no outsiders need enter.

He climbed the marble steps at the rear of the house and stepped into the dim coolness of its interior. Mrs. Leigh-Waters, the lady of the house, hurried toward him from the front hall. She was a large-bosomed woman with hair pressed into tight, unnatural curls, and was garbed in a gray bustle gown that made her look a bit like a pigeon.

"I'm so glad you've come, Chief Inspector," she gushed. "They've always spoken highly of you, which is why I told the chief constable to telegraph you. The local constables can be a bit . . . hasty . . . and she needs a bit of sympathy, doesn't she?"

"Of course," Fellows said, forcing his tone to be polite. "I will keep the interview brief."

"Thank you." Mrs. Leigh-Waters sounded relieved. "I'm certain she will thank you too."

She led Fellows through the cool, high-ceilinged hall whose draped window at the end cut out most of the light. Mrs. Leigh-Waters tapped on a door halfway along and opened it to a sitting room with back windows overlooking the garden and the view.

Two women rose from the sofa to face him. Fellows halted three steps inside the room, unable to move.

The features of the two red-haired women were heartbreakingly similar, the younger a little taller than the older. The older wore a gown of bottle green with black buttons up its bodice. The younger woman's gown had a blue and brown striped underskirt, the blue overskirt folded back to reveal a lining of blue and brown checks. Her bodice was buttoned to her chin with brown cloth-covered buttons. Fellows noted every detail even as his gaze fixed to her face.

The older sister, Lady Isabella, was married to Lord Mac Mackenzie, one of Fellows' half brothers. The younger sister, Lady Louisa Scranton, had petal-soft skin, lips that could kiss with heat, and a smile that had been haunting Fellows' dreams since the day he'd met her.

Louisa stared back at him, as frozen as he, her lips slightly parted.

Isabella unlinked herself from Louisa and came forward. "Thank heavens you're here," Isabella said to Fellows, both relief and worry in her voice. "They're claiming *Louisa* did this, can you imagine? You'll clear this up and tell them she didn't, won't you?"

Isabella spoke, but Fellows could only see Louisa. Louisa looked back at him, fixed in place, her face as white as the plaster ornamentation on the cornice above her.

The other two ladies in the room faded, as did the sound of voices outside the windows, the sunshine, the fine afternoon. Fellows could be alone in a whirling fog, where nothing existed but himself and Louisa.

At Christmas this year, Fellows had found himself alone in a hallway with her, in the Duke of Kilmorgan's obscenely large house. Louisa had tried to talk to Fellows, bantering as she did with the other young men at the celebration. Fellows had heard only her voice, sweet and clear, and then he'd had her up against the doorframe, his mouth on hers, her body pliant beneath him. Fellows could still taste the kiss, hot and beautiful, and remember his need for her rising high.

She was the aristo's daughter the doctor and local sergeant were convinced had poisoned the bishop. Lady Louisa Scranton, earl's daughter, sister-in-law to the scandalous Mackenzies, the woman Fellows dreamed about on nights he couldn't banish the thoughts of her any longer.

He'd have to pull himself from the investigation. He'd never be able to get through it, because anything Fellows found against Louisa he'd toss aside or try to pin to someone else. He knew he'd do anything to keep from seeing this woman led away in manacles, put into a cell, charged and tried, convicted and hanged until dead.

The proper thing would be to excuse himself, summon Pierce to take her statement, and tell the Yard they needed to assign another detective to the case.

Another detective who might find evidence that Louisa had committed murder. Fellows's heart beat sickeningly fast. If he backed away, Louisa might be convicted for the crime by people too impatient to prove she could be nothing but innocent.

Now was the time to speak. To say good day to Mrs. Leigh-Waters and explain that Sergeant Pierce would take over the questioning of Isabella and Louisa.

Fellows opened his stiff lips. "It shouldn't be too much to clear up, ma'am," he found himself saying to Mrs. Leigh-Waters. "I'll need to speak to Lady Louisa alone."

THE SEDUCTION OF ELLIOT MCBRIDE

CHARACTERS

Elliot McBride

Elliot fell in love with Juliana when he was very young, and nursed his love for her all his life.

He joins the army to make a living, is shipped to India, and there is captured and held for a long time by hostile tribesmen in the mountains between the Punjab and what is now Pakistan. Thoughts of Juliana are all that keep him sane.

Elliot emerges from the ordeal with what we now call PTSD, but he is convinced he's mad. He comes home for good from India, ready to buy a house from his uncle, who has run out of money, and settle down and forget.

When he learns that the woman he's always loved, Juliana, is getting married, he makes himself go to the wedding. The crowds and stress are too much for him, so he ends up alone in a side chapel, nursing his hurts with whiskey.

When Juliana, left at the altar, accidentally sits down on top of him and then asks him to marry her, he seizes on the hope and agrees.

Elliot was a complicated character to write—he has to deal

with the horrible things that have happened to him, but he's also courageous and resourceful, and has experience of the world, its brutality but also its beauty. He is also very quiet—unlike the three older Mackenzie brothers who have no problem with words, Elliot keeps his thoughts to himself.

His love for Juliana is strong, though, and his determination to make it work with her and keep her safe is as strong.

Elliot is one of the characters who has stuck with me and one of my top favorite heroes.

Juliana St. John

JULIANA WAS RAISED to be the perfect Victorian young lady—quiet, competent, organized, and to keep her opinions to herself. The fact that her mother had been a fluttery creature who escaped her dull life by shopping and taking laudanum encourages Juliana to be even more competent and organized (she loves her lists).

Juliana took care of her father and ran the house since childhood, taking even more responsibility at age fourteen after her mother dies.

Juliana has loved Elliot, her friend Ainsley's brother, ever since they were children, but she thought she had no hope of his noticing her.

Elliot was always clever and breathtakingly male, and when he joined the army and became a dashing soldier she figured he would stay in India and make a long career of it.

Juliana worried until she was ill when Elliot was captured—the day she heard he'd escaped and returning to Scotland the happiest of her life. She still doesn't believe Elliot has any interest in her and so she decides, reluctantly, to marry the "correct" husband. Also, her father has remarried, and Juliana feels that she is in the way.

She's not the only one surprised when Elliot accepts her spontaneous proposal, after the man who was supposed to be a safe husband left her at the altar.

Juliana, however, has a backbone of steel and a determination that matches Elliot's. She vows to take care of him, and defends him against all comers.

Juliana and Elliot need each other, they understand that about each other, and their love deepens as the story goes on. I very much love this couple!

IMPORTANT SECONDARY CHARACTERS
Cameron Mackenzie
Ainsley Mackenzie
Uncle McGregor
Hamish
Mahindar
Channan (Mahindar's wife)
Nandita (Channan's sister)
Komal (Mahindar's mother)
Priti
Archibald Stacy
Mrs. Rossmoran

AUTHOR'S NOTES

I BECAME INTRIGUED WITH THE CHARACTER OF ELLIOT MCBRIDE when Ainsley told Cameron about her family in *The Many Sins of Lord Cameron*. I was especially interested in Elliot who had suffered such an ordeal and was working through what sounded like PTSD.

I decided to add the McBride brothers into the mix and wanted to write about Elliot first. I thought about the opening scene—a bride dumped at the altar (poor Juliana!) and pictured her and Elliot finding each other again, when she seeks a quiet place to compose herself.

Research for this book took me to India, more specifically, the Punjab, in the very north of India where it borders what was then Afghanistan. The troubles in the 1880s were very similar to what they are now, with border clashes and raids. Elliot, who went to India to get over Juliana, is captured by such a band of raiders and held prisoner for a long time before he manages to escape.

He's found and taken in by a Punjabi family, who nurses him back to health, and he returns to Scotland for a time. He quickly grows tired of being the invalid everyone tiptoes around, so he heads back to India to the family who helped him, and also to find something precious he left behind.

The Punjabi family interested me, so I had them accompany Elliot back to Scotland (they wanted to make sure he was all right). As someone who has lived outside my native country several times, I know what it's like to leave behind all you know and be dropped into a culture completely different to yours. At the time of the story, many immigrants from India, Africa, and the West Indies were making their way to Britain. I wanted to explore what it was like for people to leave India and end up on the far side of the world, in the cold, damp north.

The family of Mahindar, his wife and sister-in-law, and especially his mother, Komal, who has a tumultuous and humorous relationship with Elliot's Uncle McGregor, have become the favorites of many readers.

I enjoyed writing this book and watching Juliana's gentle heart and steely determination help pull Elliot back from the worst place of darkness.

SYNOPSIS

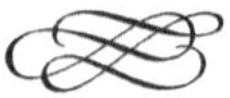

JUNE 1885, LONDON

Juliana St. John was raised to be very proper. After a long engagement, her wedding day dawns—only for Juliana to find herself jilted at the altar.

Fleeing the mocking crowd, she stumbles upon Elliot McBride, the tall, passionate Scot who was her first love. His teasing manner gives her an idea, and she asks Elliot to save her from an uncertain future—by marrying her...

After escaping brutal imprisonment, Elliot has returned to Scotland a vastly wealthy yet tormented man. Now Juliana has her hands full restoring his half-ruined manor in the Scottish Highlands and trying to repair the broken heart of the man some call irredeemably mad. Though beautiful and spirited, Juliana wonders if that will be enough to win a second chance at love.

EXCERPT: THE SEDUCTION OF ELLIOT MCBRIDE

SCOTLAND 1884

ELLIOT SAT FROZEN, HIS HAND GRIPPING THE BACK OF THE PEW SO hard he was surprised the wood didn't splinter. He watched as Juliana laughed, as her glorious hair fell to her bared shoulders. She smiled though her blue eyes were wet, and the hands that plucked the flower from her lap were long fingered and trembling.

Elliot wanted to put his arms around her and cradle her close. *There now,* he'd say. *You're better off without the idiot.* An even stronger instinct made him want to go find Grant Barclay and shoot him for hurting her.

But Elliot knew that if he made the mistake of touching Juliana, he wouldn't stop at comfort. He'd tilt her head back and kiss her lips, as he'd done at her debut ball, the night she'd permitted the one kiss.

They'd both been eighteen. Before Elliot had gone to hell and back, that chaste kiss would have been enough for him. This time, it would not be enough, not by a long way.

He'd kiss down her pretty throat to her bosom, nuzzle her gown's neckline with its points of lace, and feather kisses to her shoulders. Then he'd lick his way back up to her ripe lips, seam them with his tongue, coax her to let him inside.

He'd kiss her with long, careful kisses, tasting the goodness of her mouth while he held her and did not let her go.

Elliot would want to take everything, because Lord only knew when he'd have the chance again. A broken man learned to savor what he could when he had the opportunity.

"It will stay with me forever," Juliana was saying. *"Poor Juliana St. John. Don't you remember? She'd already put on her wedding clothes and gone to the church, poor darling."*

What did a man say to a woman in this state? Elliot wished for the eloquence of his barrister brother, who stood up in court and made elegant speeches for a living. Elliot could only ever speak the truth.

"Let them say it, and to the devil with them."

Juliana gave him a sad smile. "The world is very much about what *they* say, my dear Elliot. Perhaps it's different in India."

Dear God, how could anyone think that? "The rules there are damn strict. You can die—or get someone else killed—by not knowing them."

Juliana blinked. "Oh. Very well, I concede that such a thing sounds worse than people expecting me to hide in shame and knit socks for the rest of my life."

"Why the devil should you knit socks? Do what you like."

"Very optimistic of you. Not fair to me, but I'm afraid I will be talked about for a long while now. *And* I am now on the shelf. Thirty years old, and no longer an ingénue. I know that women do all sorts of things these days besides marry, but I am too old to attend university, and even if I did, my father would die of shame that I was such a bluestocking. I was raised to pour tea, organize fêtes, and say correct things to the vicar's wife."

Her words slid over Elliot without him registering them, her musical voice soothing. He lay back and let her talk, realizing he'd not felt so at ease in a long while.

If I could listen to her forever, if I could drift into the night hearing her voice, I might get well again.

No, nothing would be well, never again, not after the things he'd seen and done, and what had been done to him. He'd thought that once he took refuge in Scotland again, it would stop. The dreams, the waking terrors, the utter darkness when time passed and he knew nothing of it. But it hadn't, and he'd known he had to put the next part in his plan to work.

Juliana was studying him, her blue eyes clear like a summer lake. The beauty of her, the memory of those eyes, had sustained him for a long time in the dark.

Sometimes he'd dreamed she was with him, trying to wake him, her dulcet voice filling his ears. *Come on, now, Elliot. You must wake up. My kite's tangled in tree, and you're the only one tall enough to get it down.*

He remembered the day when he'd first realized what he felt for her—they must have both been about sixteen. She'd been flying a kite for children of her father's friends, and Elliot had come to watch. He'd retrieved the kite from a tree for her and earned a red-lipped smile, a soft kiss on his cheek. From that day forward, he'd been lost.

"Elliot, are you awake?"

His eyes had drifted closed on memories, and now Juliana's voice blended with the remembered dream. He pried his eyes open. "I think so."

"You did not hear me, did you?" Her face was pink in the dim light.

"Sorry, lass. I'm a bit drunk."

"Good. Not that you're drunk, but that you didn't hear me. Never mind. It was a foolish idea."

He opened his eyes wider, his brain coming alert. What the hell had he missed?

The darkness did that to him sometimes. Elliot could slide past large portions of conversation without noticing he had done so. He'd come back to himself realizing people were waiting for his response and wondering what was the matter with him. Elliot had decided that avoiding people and conversation was the best solution.

With Juliana, he wanted to know. "Tell me again."

"I don't think I ought. If it were a cracking-good idea, you'd have leapt on it at once. As it is . . ."

"Juliana, I swear to you . . . I drift in and out. I want to hear your cracking-good idea."

"No, you don't."

Females. Even ones he'd been secretly in love with for years could drive him insane.

Elliot sat up and moved closer to her, his feet on the floor. He stretched his arm along the back of the pew, not touching her but close enough to feel her warmth. "Juliana, tell me, or I'll tickle you."

"I'm not eight years old anymore, Elliot McBride."

He wanted to laugh at her haughty tone. "Neither am I. When I say *tickle*, I no longer mean what I did then." He touched her bare shoulder with one finger.

A mistake. The contact shot heat up his arm and straight into his heart.

Her lips were close to his, lush and ripe. She had faint freckles across her nose, ten of them. She'd always had them, had always tried to rid herself of them, but to Elliot, every one was kissable.

Her eyes went still, and her voice was a whisper of breath. "What I asked, Elliot, was whether *you* would marry me."

THE WICKED DEEDS OF DANIEL MACKENZIE

CHARACTERS

Daniel Mackenzie

DANIEL WAS A READER FAVORITE FROM HIS FIRST APPEARANCE IN *The Madness of Lord Ian Mackenzie*. The only son of Cameron Mackenzie, he's been raised in the chaos of his uncle's homes, moving from one to the other. It's clear his father loves him and wants to take care of him, but also that Cameron doesn't much know what to do with him.

Daniel took it all in his stride, and in *Wicked Deeds of Daniel Mackenzie,* we see him grown up and ready to take on the world.

Daniel's restless nature and his quick mind draw him to the latest technology and devices of the time, from learning about or adapting the inventions of others to inventing his own gadgets. He is especially interested in automobiles and combustion engines, determined to make his own cars and make them the best and fastest in the world.

Young women easily fall for his charm, but Daniel is in no hurry. He has a loving family, now full of aunts who dote on him. He hasn't quite found his place—hovering between the his father and uncles and now his baby cousins—but he cheerfully assumes all will be well.

When Daniel meets Violet, a lady who is beautiful, resourceful, inventive, and also a damsel in distress, he falls headlong in love, and then pursues her with the thorough determination of all the Mackenzie men.

Violet Devereaux

I LOVE UNUSUAL HEROINES, and Violet is certainly unusual. She is a fraudulent medium and very skilled at deception, but she does it for survival. She's had a rough past, and she doesn't believe she'll ever be valued for herself … until she meets Daniel.

She's also clever at gadgets and technology, fascinated by Daniel's engines, his cars, and Daniel himself.

Violet it probably one of the most complex heroines I've written. She isn't the usual, sunny-natured "good" girl waiting for her Prince Charming. She's been kicked around by the world, and must take care of a mother who is convinced she's psychic, that is, when she can gain the energy to leave her bed. Violet's cleverness and her sacrifices are why she and her mother survive and stay out of jail.

Violet has never had the chance at a normal life, and she knows she's nothing like the young women a man like Daniel Mackenzie should marry. Violet tries not to let herself be dazzled by Daniel, but Daniel Mackenzie is hard to ignore.

IMPORTANT SECONDARY CHARACTERS
  Cameron and Ainsley Mackenzie
  Ian and Beth Mackenzie

Mac and Isabella Mackenzie
Hart and Eleanor, Duke and Duchess of Kilmorgan
Celine Devereaux (Violet's mother)
Mary (Violet's faithful maid)
Simon (Daniel's valet and bodyguard)

AUTHOR'S NOTES

I KNOW SOME READERS WERE A LITTLE PUZZLED WHEN I LEAPT forward in time to 1890 to tell Daniel's story, then back again for the next books (*Scandal and the Duchess* and *Rules for a Proper Governess*).

The answer has nothing to do with storytelling and everything to do with the publishing industry. I had a contract for Elliot's book and one more Mackenzie, but authors, no matter how successful, can't count on landing a contract for further books in a series. The publisher might drop the author altogether after a contract is up or ask the author to write something different, or an author's editor can leave and the next editor might not be interested in continuing the series.

With all that in mind, I had no way of knowing, after I wrote Elliot's book, whether I'd have any more contracts for the Mackenzies. I wanted to make sure Daniel's book got written, so I went ahead and wrote it and turned it in.

Of course, after that, I *did* get another Mackenzie contract, and I wanted to pick up the rest of the McBrides, so I had to go back to the 1880s for those.

Such is the life of an author.

Daniel was such a joy to write about. He's spontaneous, fun-loving, and reaches out and grabs as much out of life as he can. He wasn't the usual dark, brooding, alpha romance hero—he's plenty alpha, but he's like a comet.

I chose Violet as his heroine, because she was the dark, brooding, broken one in need of rescue, and she was also resilient enough to take Daniel's energy. They worked off each other—Daniel bringing Violet out of herself and showing her what joy was, Violet calming Daniel a little and making him stop and think.

They connect over their inventions—Violet with her wind machine and Daniel with his automobile engines. Once they shed their issues, they make a perfect couple.

To write this story I had to do a ton of research on the early automobile. Amazing stuff! Daniel is a little bit advanced for his time, because much of what he came up with for his car design wasn't in use until later in the 1890s, but Daniel is a prodigy! Learning about early combustion engines and drive trains and what an intricate process goes into running a car was eye-opening. Plus I got to look at all kinds of very cool vintage cars. Like Violet, I would have insisted on driving them.

One interesting fact I learned was that the very first long-distance automobile trip was done by a woman—Bertha Benz. She wanted to visit her mother, and because it was a bit of a journey to her house from Mannheim, Bertha decided to take this automobile her husband had invented. She didn't tell him—she just put her bag in the back, took her sons, and left. She stopped at pharmacies to buy the petrol to run the engine (the only places that carried it), and puttered along the back roads until she safely reached her mother's house about sixty miles away. And then she drove back home after her visit. Go, Frau Benz!

And that balloon ride! One of my favorite scenes in all my books is Daniel's and Violet's balloon ride over the French countryside, which entailed a large amount of research on ballooning.

Daniel again was ahead of his time. Most ballooning in the 1890s was with hydrogen balloons, the balloons being a closed bubble. These balloons were a little easier to navigate than hot air ones, but not by much.

Hot air balloons are open at the bottom, and the mechanism used nowadays to keep feeding the balloon hot air during travels hadn't yet been invented. Once the hot air was gone, the balloon came down. Daniel is trying to come up with the engine that keeps the balloon aloft and allows it to be steered. But of course, this was an early attempt, and things do not go smoothly …

Daniel's book was one of those that I loved every second of writing.

SYNOPSIS

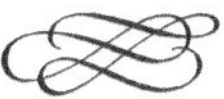

JUNE 1885, LONDON

DANIEL MACKENZIE LIVES UP TO THE REPUTATION OF THE scandalous Mackenzie family—he has wealth, looks, and talent, and women love him. When he meets Violet Bastien—one of the most famous spiritual mediums in England—he immediately knows two things: that Miss Bastien is a fraud, and that he's wildly attracted to her.

Violet knows she can't really contact the other side, but she's excellent at reading people. She discerns quickly that Daniel is intelligent and dangerous to her reputation, but she also finds him generous, handsome, and outrageously wicked. But spectres from Violet's past threaten to destroy her, and she flees England, adopting yet another identity.

Daniel is determined to find the elusive Violet and pursue the passion he feels for her. And though Violet knows that her scandalous past will keep her from proper marriage, her attraction to Daniel is irresistible. It's not until Daniel is the only one she can turn to that he proves he believes in something more than cold facts. He believes in love.

EXCERPT: THE WICKED DEEDS OF DANIEL MACKENZIE

They were in a balloon, a hundred and more feet above the earth, winter wind knifing past them, and Violet realized Daniel wanted her. He had to be mad.

And yet . . . if it could be only Daniel and herself, floating forever, the troubles of the world left on the rocky slopes below them, Violet could find happiness. The basket pushed at her feet as the balloon lifted her away from the petty worries of her life.

Up here, she could enter a world of true sweetness, if only for a little while. This was her magical barge, and Daniel was the magician who could banish all the monsters.

For answer, Violet rose on her tiptoes and kissed his lips.

The spanner fell with a clatter to the bottom of the basket, Daniel's strong hand splaying across her buttocks to lift her to him. His kiss turned harder, masterful. His mouth opened hers, tongue sweeping in to take. Violet met him halfway, her heart beating wildly.

His arms were hard, his shirt a thin layer over solid muscle. Violet let her hands play over him as he kissed her, running her touch up his arms and down the firm length of his back.

Daniel's strength took her breath away, and yet at the same

time, he poured strength into *her*. Her magician was working his magic, taking away all pain, all sorrows.

When Daniel pulled back from the kiss, cold slapped at her. "Oh, you tempt me, Vi," Daniel said, a warm glow in his eyes. "You tempt me much. I'm sorry I told Dupuis and Simon to chase us."

Violet glanced down, the ground so far away it was heart-stopping. A man on a large horse—the draft horse she'd seen in the barn—trotted along a road that cut through the valley below them. Much farther behind was a man driving a cart. The horseman looked up and waved, and Daniel waved back.

"It is only a kiss," Violet said. Her voice still didn't work right. She who could master five languages and various accents in each one now could barely pronounce scratchy words in English.

"*Only* a kiss?" Daniel's arms tightened around her. "Grind me to powder beneath your heel, why don't you?" His hand on her buttocks lifted her again, the touch intimate and yet freeing. "Let me—"

He broke off and looked up. *Let me . . . Let me what? Have my wicked way with you?* Violet leaned closer to him, caring for nothing but the words on his lips, his lips themselves, the radiant heat of his body. *I need you, Daniel. And I'm scared.*

Daniel released her suddenly as the balloon swayed hard. The basket shoved upward, a strong gust sending it rocking. Violet shouted, her yell carried away on the wind, as Daniel grabbed ropes, pulling hard until the basket stopped its sickening spin.

He thrust the ropes at her. "Hang on to these. Now we see if my hot-air personal dirigible is truly dirigible."

"*Now we see?*" Violet stared at him as she grasped the lines. "You said you'd done this before."

"Flown a balloon before, yes. Never tried to steer one with

this system. Now, when I tell you *right*, you pull the rope in your right hand, *left*, the one in your left. Can you do that?"

"I think I can remember right from left," Violet answered shakily and started to wrap the ropes around her hands.

Daniel grabbed her. "No. You *hold* them. If one jerks wild, I don't need it pulling you out of the basket at worst, tearing off your fingers at best."

Violet's eyes widened, and she unwrapped the ropes. Daniel retrieved the crankshaft, stuck it into his engine, and wound it again. A larger flame jumped from the top of the open box, the basket tipped, and Violet let out another yelp.

Daniel laughed. "I like that you like to scream. Left, now. *Left!*"

Violet yanked the rope as Daniel continued to crank, the flame spurting. The basket righted from its horrible listing, and the balloon rose higher still.

Wind buffeted them. Violet watched Daniel's body move as he worked, and wondered why he wanted to go so high. It was freezing now, the wind dry but icy.

Violet glanced ahead of them, and suddenly understood why he wanted the height. Rocks and cliffs rushed at them, the trees on them looking so close she might be able to reach out and touch them. She sucked in a breath.

"Higher!" she shouted. "We need to go higher!"

"What the bloody hell do ye think I'm doing? Pull the right rope! *Right!*"

"I'm pulling it!" Violet yanked on it with all her strength.

Daniel kept pumping the fire. The rocks rushed at them. At any moment they'd hit, the basket would splinter, and she and Daniel would tumble down. Would they land on rocks, arms around each other, hurting but surviving? Or be plunged to their deaths?

Violet didn't want to plunge to her death just yet. She

wanted to be pulled back into Daniel's embrace, to feel his desire for her and taste it on his lips.

At one time in her life, Violet would have welcomed death. But not today. Not when she'd finally found this *aliveness*.

Daniel kept cranking. Violet's wind machine blew the hot air up into the balloon's silken envelope. The basket soared upward, over the cliffs. The crags at the top of the little peak seemed to reach up to grab for them, but then the balloon was clear. After a minute of soaring inches above trees on the other side of the ridge, the land fell away to the next valley, and the balloon floated gently above it.

Daniel stopped the crankshaft and straightened up, stretching his arms high. He whooped. "Well done, lass!"

Laughing, he caught Violet in his arms, lifting her from her feet and kissing her. His face was cold now, cheeks ruddy, hair mussed by the wind. Violet, still holding the ropes, kissed him back.

Daniel's gaze was all for her as he lowered her to her feet and gently took the ropes from her. "Thank ye, love. We make a good team."

"Yes." The word came out a croak, Violet unable to think of anything else to say.

Daniel turned around to look at the world, and spread his arms, the ropes moving with him. "Never been this high before." He whooped again, and Violet laughed.

The land opened out before them, a long river valley dotted with farms and small villages. Patches of snow clung to the shadows of trees and rocks on the slopes of the ridge they'd just crossed. Far below, smoke rose from the scattered farmhouses, and one or two people moved about on the remote roads.

No one in the wide world knew where Violet was at this moment. Though she'd told Mary she was accompanying Mr. Mackenzie to a village outside Marseille, Violet had not known Daniel would take her aboard this wonderful machine and off into spaces unknown. No one but Daniel knew where she was now—they'd even left Monsieur Dupuis and Simon behind in the last valley.

Violet was truly alone, floating on air, with only a man who was nearly a stranger to keep her aloft. Daniel had isolated her from everyone she knew, taken her far from the help of anyone. Violet should be terrified, brought to her knees in one of her attacks of panicked hysteria.

But she could feel no fear. She watched Daniel as he dropped the ropes, held the side of the basket, and looked around, enraptured. The world was beautiful, Violet was alone with the man who'd shown her its beauty, and her heart was light. This must be what happiness felt like.

When Daniel turned and looked at her, Violet wished the moment could be suspended in time. She never wanted to forget *how* he was looking at her. Not in lechery, not demanding anything from her. He studied her as though he liked looking at Violet, for herself, as though nothing in the world mattered to him but her and this moment.

I could love you, Daniel Mackenzie.

In this place of contentedness and freedom, the warmth of the words took form, and wouldn't leave her.

Daniel turned away, scanning the horizon again. "We should find a place to set down."

"I don't want to." Violet spoke before she could stop herself.

Daniel glanced at her again, his smile returning. "I don't either. But those clouds are thickening, and a balloon is not a good place to be in a rainstorm. Or possibly a snowstorm, this far from the coast."

True, now that the Mediterranean's breezes had been left behind, the wind had a wintry bite.

"Over there, I'm thinking." Daniel pointed to a flat space of land covered with bare black fields, plowed furrows making dark crisscrosses in the ground.

"How do we land?" Violet looked up at the balloon, which was stretched full. "Do you know where we are?"

Daniel shrugged. "Somewhere in France. When we bring this thing down, I plan to ask."

How wonderful to go where the wind blew, to not worry about where you were or where you were going. Daniel moved through life expecting it to get out of his way, while Violet frantically scrambled to survive.

Daniel started working with ropes again, and turned knobs on his engine. The fire in the machine died down, and the balloon slowly, regretfully began to descend.

"Hmm," Daniel said.

"What?" Violet was at his side again. "What do you mean, *hmm?*"

Daniel gave her a dark look. "Better hold on to something."

Violet clutched the side of the basket, her heart hammering. "Why?"

A gust of wind caught them. The balloon rocketed sideways, at the same time the basket rapidly slid toward the earth.

Daniel pulled down hard on a rope, and high above them, a hole opened in the silk to let out the air. He yanked on the steering ropes some more, then finally let go of everything and slammed his arms around Violet from behind, grabbing the basket on either side of her. He shielded her with his body as the plowed field rushed at them, the balloon deflating.

SCANDAL AND THE DUCHESS

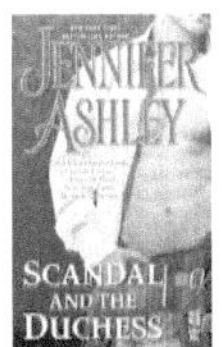

CHARACTERS

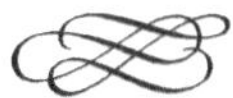

Steven McBride

THE YOUNGEST OF THE MCBRIDE BROTHERS, STEVEN IS A CAREER soldier. Unlike Elliot, he was sent to Africa, where he lived and worked for years. He loves Africa—the huge skies, open lands, the heat, and he people. Like me, Steven loves to be warm, and he finds England and Scotland far too chilly and damp for his taste.

He almost marries a woman who threw herself at him, but gives her up so she can marry his best friend, and returns to Africa.

He is back in England for one errand, but he plans to return to his regiment and the African sunshine as soon as he can. He doesn't think he'll ever find a woman who would be willing to live an adventurous life with him, until he meets Rose …

———

Rose Barclay, Duchess of Southdown

ROSE HAS HAD AN UNLUCKY LIFE. She married the elderly Duke of Southdown because she liked him, and they had a happy marriage before his death, but of course because she was much younger than he was, tongues wagged. She was accused of causing the duke's death with her youthful exuberance in bed on their honeymoon.

Because of the journalists who like to write scurrilous stories about her, Rose mostly stays at home, venturing out only to visit good friends and always protected by her servants. She's alone in the world now, and her stepson (who is older than she is), is trying to keep her from her widow's portion.

As Rose tells Steven:

"I'm a duchess, because I married a duke. I was plain Miss Barclay before that, but my family is all gone now." The sorrow of that tore at her, and it always would. "I'm stopping with my coachman, because I'm skint. I had been staying with a friend, but she asked me to leave last night—or, rather, hinted strongly that I should go. Can't blame her, really. Journalists follow me about, waiting for me to do something scandalous, which happens all the time, unfortunately. I'm telling you this to warn you, because I'm certain the story of you coming home with me is all over London this morning. If you keep your head down, I think you'll be all right."

Rose doesn't think she'll ever find happiness or any of the money her husband promised her, but Steven will prove her wrong on both counts.

IMPORTANT SECONDARY CHARACTERS
Miles (Rose's coachman and bodyguard)

Mrs. Miles (Miles's wife who dotes on Rose)
Sinclair McBride
Ian and Beth Mackenzie
Cameron and Ainsley Mackenzie
Albert Francis, Duke of Southdown (Rose's stepson)

141

Mrs. Miles (Miles's wife who dotes on Rose)
Sinclair McBride
Ian and Beth Mackenzie
Cameron and Ainsley Mackenzie
Albert Francis, Duke of Southdown (Rose's stepson)

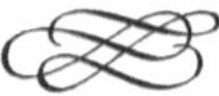

THIS SHORTER BOOK WAS A BIT UNLIKE MY USUAL FARE. STEVEN was a bachelor and thought he'd always be so, and Rose, though she'd married a duke, was down on her luck.

This was another case of two people needing each other, and each making the other stronger. Rose's realistic outlook on life and her ability to make fun of it endeared her to Steven, and Steven's ability to think on his feet complimented Rose's situation well.

I like pretend engagement stories, and used that trope in this one. Steven comes up with the ruse both to protect Rose and to keep him from a bad situation of his own, but of course, sparks begin to fly...

I have an interest in furniture and its history (witness my dollhouses full of period furniture), and I had fun researching the furnishings that play a major role in the plot.

The furniture Rose's husband left her came from the Regency period: a cabinet made by George Bullock and a settee in what was called "Egyptian style."

Regency furniture could be over-the-top garish. Egypt was the rage after Napoleon's expedition, and the British army brought back artifacts and writing from the Nile. Exhibits fired imaginations, and furniture makers began to create furniture and interior design accessories in ebony with much gilding, carving, cameos, marble, plaster, marquetry, and any other decorative item that could fit onto a surface. The result could be hideously gaudy or quite elegant.

Bullock designed beautiful cabinets and grew famous for it until his untimely death in 1817. I imagine my character, Grenville, from the Captain Lacey Regency mysteries, owning the elegant sort of Regency furnishings Bullock made.

I also enjoy a good puzzle and a treasure hunt, and of course I had to bring back Ian Mackenzie to help them solve it. Ian's unique way of looking at the world was key to finding the answer.

I have to say, though, that this book nearly broke me. I finished it not long after I'd finished *Rules for a Proper Governess*, and I was exhausted. I thought at the time that I would never write again—I was done.

I am happy to be wrong. Since the day I recovered from the burnout this book pushed me into, I have written nearly 5 million words and published many, many more books.

I hope that encourages anyone else suffering from burnout. If you let yourself cool down and return to doing things for the love of it, the creativity returns.

SYNOPSIS

JUNE 1885, LONDON

SCANDAL FOLLOWS ROSE BARCLAY, YOUNG WIDOW OF THE DUKE of Southdown, wherever she goes. It's never her fault, but newspapers love to write about the young woman from Scotland, and the much older duke she married, who died on their honeymoon. The duke left her with a large widow's portion, now contested by his son, who kicks Rose out of the estate's dower house and uses it to kennel his dogs.

Rose does not need to be found with a large, handsome Scot passed out at her feet, fueling gossips and giving her son-in-law more ammunition. The Scot is Steven McBride–a decorated soldier who is notorious for heavy gambling and womanizing during his leave time. Steven is happy to open his eyes and find the beautiful woman standing over him, and happy to help spirit her away. He comes up with a ruse to foil the journalists, but Rose will have to go along with his very scandalous proposal

EXCERPT: SCANDAL AND THE DUCHESS

NOVEMBER 1885

WHEN HE WAS THIS DRUNK, THERE WAS ONLY ONE THING TO DO. Steven McBride laid the rest of his money on the table and got unsteadily to his feet.

"Divide it," he said to the assembled men, his Scots accent slurring. "I cannae see my cards anymore, and you'll have it off me anyway. Good night."

His friends and acquaintances, some as drunk as himself, either laughed or grunted and went back to their cards. Bloody Scottish upstart, he knew many of them thought.

Some thought much worse than that—those who knew the story—by their dark looks. Army should have slung him out.

Steven knew exactly why he was imbibing to his eyeballs on his leave, and why he'd come home earlier this year. Knowing why did not make it any easier to leave the card room, navigate his way down the stairs—who the devil had put the card room upstairs?—and stagger into the street.

He looked up and down for his carriage, then remembered he'd hired a carriage to bring him to the soiree tonight. Steven vaguely remembered dismissing it, blast it all, telling the coachman he'd make his own way home.

The November cold was bitter, a wind sweeping down the street to cut straight through Steven's uniform coat. Steven's regiment was currently in West Africa, a land of warmth. Bloody great heat, actually, but Africa was an amazing world full of amazing people. Nothing there like this frozen London passage, wind howling down it, stinging him even in his drunken state.

Which way were his lodgings? Steven didn't have a permanent house in London, so he usually hired rooms whenever he came to town—flats that catered to single gentlemen. He stayed in the same area each time, but rarely in the same house or even the same street. Sometimes he didn't bother with rooms at all and stayed in a hotel like the Langham.

The Langham—had a familiar ring to it. Was Steven living there now? Or had that been last year?

Steven realized he was standing befuddled in the street, buffeted by the wind. Passersby, what there were of them on this bone-cold night, were looking at him askance.

The pungent, grassy smell of horse dung caught his attention. A carriage clopped slowly by, the horses doing what horses did even when walking about. Wildcats in Africa were cagey about where they relieved themselves, hiding it from all but the most canny hunters. London horses simply let it fall to the street, and humans came along behind and swept it up for them. Which animal was the more clever?

Steven half jogged, half stumbled toward the carriage. A hansom, that's what he needed. He could tell the cabby to take him to the Langham, where they'd find him a room, whether he'd booked in already or not.

The shape was wrong for a hansom, but Steven was past caring. He had to get somewhere, or he'd fall down in the street and spend the rest of the night unconscious on the cobbles. Even in this part of London, even in this weather, he doubted he'd have much left on him when he woke up.

The carriage stopped. Wind cut Steven, making his eyes water. He folded his arms against the cold, and ran toward the carriage, head down.

A woman bundled in a thick cloak and hood came out of the lighted house the carriage had halted before. As soon as she crossed the threshold, four or five other persons appeared out of nowhere to block her way.

"There she is!"

"Duchess . . . Your Grace . . ."

"Your Grace, my readers would love a description of your gown tonight . . . Are you still in mourning?"

"Your Grace, how did it feel to have ensnared a duke, only to have him perish in the wedding bed?"

"Your Grace, there are rumors of you carrying on a flirtation with the Earl of Posenby. Or his son. Some speculate both. Would you tell us which it is?"

Bloody journalists, Steven thought in disgust. They were after some aristo, more dirt for the scandal sheets. Steven had no idea who the cloaked woman was and had no interest. He only wanted to climb into the carriage—private or not, he'd pay the coachman handsomely to take him anywhere.

Of course, he'd just thunked a large wad of money to the game table. Steven wondered vaguely if he had any left as he made a lunge for the coach.

The cloaked woman broke from the vultures—"Your Grace, is it true you're wintering in Nice with a comte?"

She put on a burst of speed. Steven stumbled on his drunken feet, and he and the woman met in a crash of flesh and breathlessness.

Steven found himself landing face-first on a bosom of exceptional quality. The woman's cloak had pulled away, revealing a gown fairly modestly cut but giving Steven enough bosom to enjoy. His cheek rested on warm flesh, his lips pressed onyx beads, and he inhaled a heady, womanly perfume.

He heard a heart beating rapidly under his ear, and a voice vibrating through a body of fine plumpness.

"Oh dear."

Steven tried to raise his head—not that he wanted to—but he couldn't. He could only lever himself up by grasping the woman by the hips and pulling himself upright.

The hips were a warm handful, the thighs beneath her skirts and stiff bustle even better. Steven climbed the poor woman, unbending himself as he went.

Unfortunately, his legs had stopped working. They gave way again, throwing his weight onto her. She retreated to compensate, but her back met the carriage door. Steven kept falling, his body landing full-length against hers, plastering her to the coach.

The woman's hood slipped down. Steven saw eyes of clearest green, a round face haloed by golden hair, flushed cheeks, and a wide mouth that begged for kisses. It would be rude to kiss her without asking first, but Steven didn't have the words to inquire.

His face and hers were very close together, the kissable lips an inch away.

"My dear fellow," the woman said breathlessly. "Are you all right?"

"No," Steven tried to say. "Damn, woman, but you're beautiful." The words came out a jumbled mess, in broad Highland Scots, but the journalists heard them.

"Your Grace, who is he?" "A regimental affair, is it? Or a Highland fling?" "What about the comte? And the earl?"

"Good Lord," came the impatient voice of Steven's angel. "Leave the poor man alone. Can't you see he's ill?"

"Falling down drunk is more like it," one of the journalists said, and laughed. "Who is he? Give us a name."

"You lot, clear off!"

The coachman had come down off the box, and flapped his

hands at the journalists like a woman shooing chickens out of her garden. Steven wanted to burst out laughing. At the same time, a footman exited the house from which the woman had emerged and laid hands on Steven. Steven heard the cry of a constable coming up the street, along with the man's heavy footsteps.

"Off with you," the footman growled at Steven. The constable came faster, his tall helmet bobbing out of the gloom and making Steven laugh harder.

Laughter and the footman's heavy hands made Steven slide down the woman's body. He found the hard street beneath his knees, his face buried in her abdomen, the black bombazine of her gown smooth against his nose.

She smelled wonderful. The perfume didn't come from a bottle. It was her—soap and the scent of fabric, warmth and woman. Steven pressed his face to her belly, wanting to take his ease with her.

"Sir." Her hands were on his hair. Steven snuggled in closer. If they'd been alone and without so many clothes, this would be the perfect way to finish the night.

She leaned to him, his angel, and whispered, "What on earth are you doing?"

"Loving you," Steven said. "You deserve every bit of loving a man can give you."

"Oh," she said. "You are very drunk, I believe. Perhaps the nice constable will see you home."

"No home." His home was a tent in Africa, under huge sky, in blessed warmth. "I have no home."

"Dear me, that's sad. Do you need money? Perhaps a meal?"

Steven's laughter returned. She thought him a homeless, helpless sot, and maybe he was.

The journalists surged forward. More people seemed to be on the street, and someone threw a stone. "Tart!" a woman yelled. "Be off with ye."

The coachman growled. He flung open the door of the coach and more or less hoisted the woman inside. Steven grabbed the door as it swung shut, hanging on to it to keep him upright. The coachman started to wrench him away, but the journalists pushed in, as did the sudden crowd. London loved a riot—best way to keep warm in the winter, Steven mused—any excuse to begin one.

"Miles, let him in. He'll get trampled."

Steven heard her voice, felt himself be hauled up under the arms by a man of amazing strength, and then he met the floor of the carriage. The door slammed, bumping Steven's booted foot. After a moment, the carriage jerked forward, and things splattered against it—the denizens making good use of the handy horse apples in the street.

The angel seemed to be speaking to him. Steven heard her clear voice but no words. He laid his head on her skirt, blissfully warm, and drifted off to sleep.

WHEN STEVEN CRACKED open his eyes, it was daylight; at least as much daylight that could filter through the narrow, dirty window on a London winter day.

The narrow window went with the narrow room, wide enough only for a single bed and a corner washstand. That was all. No curtain or blind, no bureau, no cheerful fire, only a brick chimney that went up through the room and gave off a modicum of heat.

Where the hell was he? The last thing Steven remembered was a card game . . .

No, a cold London street, someone throwing things . . .

Green eyes, red lips curving into a little smile, and a scent like roses. Deep red roses, heady and intense.

Had Steven dreamed her? If so, he wanted to go back to sleep.

But the cold, Steven's pounding head, and details of the night were knocking for attention. He should climb out of bed, dress, and face his problems like a Scotsman and a soldier.

The bed was warm, and raising his head hurt like hell. Steven laid it back down.

He must have slept again, because when he next opened his eyes, the room was brighter. The door swung open, and in came his angel with a wooden tray heaped with crockery.

"Good morning," she said brightly. "Would you like some tea?"

RULES FOR A PROPER GOVERNESS

CHARACTERS

Sinclair McBride

Sinclair McBride is a widower with two children. He lost his wife several years before, and is left to raise the children he loves but doesn't know what to do with.

Andrew, the younger at eight years old, is wild and uncontrollable, but also exuberant and cheerful. Caitriona, about eleven, is much quieter, withdrawn into herself since her mother passed.

Sinclair, of the Scottish McBride family, was once a soldier, like his brothers Elliot and Steven, but instead of remaining in the army, he returned to Edinburgh and studied law.

Now he is a barrister, which means he puts on a white wig and gown, and stands up in court to argue cases in front of judges. He's by now what's called a "silk," which means he's a senior barrister, who has impressed enough people in the profession to rise through the ranks.

Sinclair began his career in Scotland, but found a place in a chambers in London, where he rose to fame by ruthlessly prosecuting criminals and not backing down until he won. His performance in court won him the name of the "Scots Machine" to the other barristers and "Basher McBride," to the criminals.

However, Sinclair is a man of compassion and conscience, and when he realizes an accused man or woman is innocent, he does his best to turn the tables and make sure they go home free.

He's as withdrawn from the rest of the world, though, as is his daughter, moving through his life half asleep.

And then he meets Bertie.

Sinclair's other troubles are his children. He loves them but he knows they are out of control. It's a running joke in the family that the nannies or governesses stay only one day, some only hours. Sinclair has no idea how to raise children and he's desperate for help, but none of the governesses he finds can handle the children any better than he can.

And then, as I say, he meets Bertie ...

Roberta "Bertie" Frasier

BERTIE FRASIER IS from a different world than Sinclair. She's a pickpocket from London's East End, but neither that life nor taking care of her father have made her hard. She's optimistic and caring, dreaming of a happier life, but she's also realistic enough to believe she'll probably be stuck where she is the rest of her days.

When she sees Sinclair in court, prosecuting one of her friends, whom Bertie knows is innocent, she immediately falls under the spell of his voice. She's determined to know more about him, especially after her father demands Bertie get back at him for getting one of his friends arrested, and Bertie picks his pocket.

Bertie discovers who Sinclair is and where he lives,

wondering at her own infatuation, because nothing will ever come of it. She's fascinated by him, though, seeing a man of deep sadness who also can be amazingly eloquent and intelligent.

She knows their worlds are far apart, but they are both able bridge the gap through the children.

Bertie recognizes the restlessness and need for affection in Andrew and Catriona, because she has the same feeling inside herself. The two children connect to Bertie because she's unusual, and also not afraid of them. They respond to her natural affection, and it is they who ask her to stay and look after them.

Bertie is only too delighted.

Important Secondary Characters
    Caitriona ("Cat") McBride
    Andrew McBride
    Hart and Eleanor, Duke and Duchess of Kilmorgan
    Cameron and Ainsley Mackenzie
    Macauley (Sinclair's valet)
    Mac and Isabella Mackenzie
    Ian and Beth Mackenzie
    Elliot and Juliana McBride
    Franklin (Sinclair's coachman)
    Jeffrey (Bertie's supposed boyfriend)
    Edward Davies (brother to Sinclair's deceased wife)

AUTHOR'S NOTES

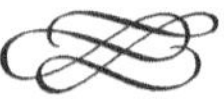

I'D HAD BERTIE IN MY HEAD FOR A LONG, LONG TIME—ONE OF the first heroines who came to me when I began writing romance, in fact. But she never had a story to go with her! Until, that is, I met Sinclair McBride and his out-of-control children who needed a governess. What better governess than an unconventional young woman from the wrong side of town?

I have been criticized for pairing a working-class young woman from the East End with a barrister of Mayfair, but my response is: 1) This is romance! We can have fun and enjoy the ride; and 2) Sinclair is not a titled aristocrat, nor is he an English gentleman. He's a Scotsman who worked his way up through his profession from scratch after a short career in the army.

While marrying a working-class woman might shock his fellow English barristers and the judges who want to control him, it is not a scandal to Sinclair's family and friends in Scotland.

Working for a living was not anathema to the Victorian Scots, which is why the Mackenzies are not simply landed gentlemen who while away their time. They work at professions—Ian runs the distillery, Hart was an MP, Cameron runs a racing stables, Mac teaches painting, and Daniel is training to be an engineer. Likewise Sinclair is a barrister, and Steven and Elliot have successful military careers.

Writing Bertie's character was a lot of fun, and I was glad to see Sinclair, who was far too sad, get his happy ending. The kids too!

SYNOPSIS

JUNE 1885, LONDON

Scottish barrister Sinclair McBride can face the most sinister criminals in London–but the widower's two unruly children are a different matter. Little Caitlin and Andrew go through a governess a week, sending the ladies fleeing in tears. There is, however, one woman in town who can hold her own.

Roberta "Bertie" Frasier enters Sinclair's life by stealing his watch–and then stealing a kiss. Intrigued by the handsome highlander, Bertie winds up saving his children from a dangerous situation and returning them to their father. Impressed with how they listen to her, Sinclair asks the lively beauty to be their governess, never guessing that the unconventional lady will teach him a lesson or two in love.

EXCERPT: RULES FOR A PROPER GOVERNESS

WINTER, 1885

His voice drew her, and Bertie wanted to hear more of it. She leaned forward in the balcony to watch the man standing upright and arrogant, one hand touching an open book on a table in front of him, the other gesturing as he made his argument.

The villains Bertie knew called the barrister Basher McBride, because Mr. McBride always got a conviction. He wore one of the silly wigs, but his face was square and handsome, and far younger than that of the judge who sat above him. A wilted nosegay reposed in a vase in front of the judge, both judge and flowers looking weary in the extreme.

The case had caught the attention of journalists up and down the country—the sensational murder of a lady by one of her downstairs maids. The young woman in the dock, Ruthie, had been accused of stabbing her employer and making off with a hundred pounds' worth of silver.

Bertie knew Ruthie hadn't done it. The deed had been done by Jacko Small and his mistress, only they'd set up Ruthie to take the blame for it. Bertie had known, had heard Jacko's plans, but did the police listen to the likes of Roberta Frasier? No.

Not that Bertie was in the habit of talking to constables most days. She stayed as far away from them as possible, and her dad and Jeffrey, Bertie's self-styled beau, made sure she did. But she'd tried for Ruthie's sake.

Hadn't mattered. They'd arrested Ruthie anyway, and now Ruthie would get hanged for something she didn't do.

The handsome Basher McBride, with his mesmerizing voice, was busy making the case that Ruthie *had* done it. Ruthie couldn't afford a defense, so she was here on her own in the dock, thin and small for her age, a maid who'd been in the wrong place at the wrong time. Bertie could only clench her fists and pray for a miracle.

Mr. McBride, despite his dire statements, had a delicious Scots accent. His voice was deep and rich, rolling over the crowd like an intoxicating wave. Even the bored judge couldn't take his eyes off him.

Mr. McBride had broad shoulders and a firm back, obvious even in the black robes. He was tall, dominating all in the room, the strength in his big, bare hands apparent. He looked as though he'd be more at home out on a Highland hillside, sword in hand as he fended off attackers. One glare from those gray eyes, and his attackers would be running for their lives.

His accent wasn't so thick Bertie couldn't understand it, but his *R*s rolled pleasantly, and his vowels were long, especially the *U*s.

"If your lordship pleases," Mr. McBride said, his voice warming Bertie again, "I would like to call Jacko Small back to the witness box."

Bertie swallowed, nervous. Jacko had already given evidence that he'd found the body in the sitting room of the London house, then seen Ruthie down in the kitchen, crying, with blood on her apron. The silver had been gone, and no one had found it, so Ruthie must have hidden it somewhere, hadn't she? The police had tried to get its location out of her, but of course

Ruthie hadn't known, as she hadn't stolen the silver in the first place.

The judge sighed. "Is it *relevant*, Mr. McBride? This witness has already told us his version of events."

"One or two more questions, your lordship," Mr. McBride said without hurry. "You will understand my reasons in due time."

In duuui time. The vowel came out of his mouth with a round, full sound.

Jacko came back in, was reminded he was under oath, and faced Mr. McBride with all innocence on his face.

"Now, then Mr. Small." Mr. McBride smiled pleasantly, but Bertie saw a gleam in his eyes that was a cross between anger and glee.

Now what was he up to?

"Mr. Small," Mr. McBride said smoothly. "You say you opened the door of the sitting room to find the lady of the house on the floor, her dress covered in blood. You'd been asked to refill the coal bin on your return from your day out and had gone up there to do so." Mr. McBride glanced down at the notes on his bench. "That day was the seventh of July. The middle of the afternoon, in the middle of summer. Quite the warmest day anyone could remember, the newspapers reported. A bit too warm for a fire, wouldn't you say?"

Jacko blinked. "Well . . . I . . . the nights were still nippy. I remember that."

"Yes, of course. Bloody English weather. Begging your pardon, your lordship."

People tittered. The judge scowled. "Please get on with it, Mr. McBride."

"You say in your statement that you saw quite a lot of blood," Mr. McBride said, not missing a beat. "On the sofa, on the floor, smeared on the door panels and on the doorknob."

"'Sright." Jacko put his hand to his heart. "Gave me a turn, it did."

"So you fled the room and went down to the kitchen, where you saw the accused wearing an apron stained with blood. *She* says she got the blood on her because she thought she'd help out the cook by stuffing the chickens for dinner. The chickens were still a bit bloody, and she wiped her hands on her apron. Correct?"

"It's what she said, yeah."

"Now, I need your help, Mr. Small. I must ask you a very important question, so think hard. Was there any blood smeared on the doorknob of the door to the back stairs?"

Jacko blinked again. He obviously hadn't rehearsed this question. "Um. I don't think so. I can't be sure. Don't remember. I was, you know, in a state."

"But you remember distinctly the blood on the doorknob in the sitting room. You were quite poetic about it."

More titters. Jacko looked flustered.

What the devil was Mr. McBride doing? Bertie's gloved hand tightened on the railing. He was supposed to be proving Ruthie did it, not that Jacko lied. Which Jacko had, of course, but how did Mr. McBride know that?

Besides, it wasn't his job to expose Jacko. Bertie knew from experience that courtrooms had procedures everyone followed to the letter. It was as if Mr. McBride had stepped onstage and started playing the wrong part.

"Was there blood on the doorknob to the back-stairs door?" Mr. McBride repeated, his deep voice growing stern.

"Um. Yeah," Jacko said. "Yeah, now that I recall it, there was. Another big smudge, like in the sitting room. I had to touch it to open it. It were awful." A few of the jury shifted in their seats in sympathy.

"Except there wasn't," Mr. McBride said.

"Eh?" Jacko started. "Whatcha mean?"

"The door to the back stairs, or the green baize door as it is also known, had a broken panel. It had been taken away, since it was a quiet day, to be mended. There was no door that day, not for you to open, nor for the maid to smear blood on."

"Oh." Jacko opened and closed his mouth. "Well, I don't really remember, do I? I was, watcha call it . . . agitated."

"Though you remember in exact detail the placement of every item and every bloodstain in the sitting room. The accused says she didn't see you at all that day, and never knew about her employer's death until the police arrived. I'm going to suggest you went nowhere near the kitchen and never saw the accused. I suggest you left the sitting room and the house entirely, returned later, found the police there, saw them taking away the accused and her bloody apron, and came up with the story about seeing her."

Jacko looked worried now. "Yeah? And why'd I come back, if I'd killed the old bitch?"

The judge looked pained. Mr. McBride's eyes took on a hard light. "You knew that if you'd disappeared entirely, you'd be screaming your guilt. I suggest you left to dispose of the silver and returned as though you'd been gone all day. And never did I suggest, Mr. Small, that you committed the murder."

Rustling and muttering filled the courtroom. The judge looked annoyed. "Mr. McBride, do I have to remind you that the witness is not on trial?"

"No, he's not," Mr. McBride agreed. "Not yet."

Another round of laughter. Jacko's face was shiny with sweat, although it was nippy in here on this winter day.

"I am finished with the witness, your lordship. In my summing up, I will be putting the case that what we have here is not a conniving young woman who killed her employer, smeared blood all over the room, and then remained quietly in the kitchen with an apron covered with the same blood—and, I might add, no time to dispose of the missing silver. I am instead going to put forth my belief that another person must have had much better opportunity, and strength, to commit the crime, and that we are coming dangerously close to a miscarriage of justice. Perhaps your lordship would like to retire briefly and prepare for my outrageous statements."

The judge growled as laughter began again. "Mr. McBride, I have warned you about your behavior in my courtroom before. This is not the theatre."

Oh, but it was, Bertie thought. Only the play was real, and the curtain, final. Mr. McBride knew that too, she sensed, despite his jokes.

"You are, however, correct that I would like to recess briefly to gather my thoughts," the judge said. "Bailiff, please see that Mr. Small does not leave."

The judge rose, and everyone scrambled to their feet. The judge disappeared through the door into his inner sanctum, the journalists rushed away, and the rest of the watchers filed out, talking excitedly.

Bertie looked over the railing at Mr. McBride, who'd sat down, pushing his wig askew as he rubbed the sunshine-colored hair beneath it. The animation went out of his body as the courtroom emptied, as though he were a marionette whose strings had been cut.

He glanced around and up, but not at Bertie. Mr. McBride looked at no one and nothing.

Bertie was struck by how empty his face was. His eyes were a strange shade of gray, clear like a stormy morning. As Bertie watched, those eyes filled with a vast sadness, the likes of which Bertie had never seen before. His mouth moved a little, as though he whispered something, but Bertie couldn't hear what he said.

Bertie remained fixed in place instead of nipping off for some ale, her hand on the gallery's wooden railing. She couldn't take her eyes off the man below, who'd changed so incredibly the moment his performance had finished.

Mr. McBride didn't leave his bench until the judge returned, and the courtroom started up again. Then he got to his feet, life flowing back into his body, becoming the eloquent, arrogant man with the beautiful voice once more.

The judge signaled for him to begin. Mr. McBride summed up his case so charmingly that all hung on his words. The jury went out and returned very quickly with their verdict about Ruthie, *Not guilty.*

Ruthie was free. Bertie had hoped for a miracle, and Mr. McBride had provided one.

***

AFTER MUCH HUGGING, Ruthie left Bertie and went home with her mum. Bertie found her dad and Jeffrey waiting for her outside the pub across the street. They were furious. Jacko was Jeffrey's best mate, and Jacko had just been arrested for murder and taken away by the police.

"'E's to blame," Jeffery said darkly, jerking his chin at Mr. McBride, who was walking out of the Old Bailey, dressed now in a normal suit and coat. Once again, Bertie noted how Mr. McBride had changed from a man who commanded a room to a man who looked tired of life.

The afternoon was cold, darkening with the coming winter night. Bertie rubbed her hands together in her too-thin gloves and suggested that her dad and Jeffrey take her into the pub and buy her a half.

"Not yet," Bertie's dad said. "Just teach 'im a lesson, Bertie. Go on now, girl."

Girl, when she was twenty-six years old. "Leave him alone," she said. "He saved Ruthie."

"But got Jacko arrested," Jeffrey growled. "Whose side are you on?"

"Jacko *killed* the woman," Bertie said. "He's a villain; he always was. I say good on Ruthie."

Jeffrey grabbed Bertie by the shoulder and pushed her into the shadows of the passage beside the pub. He wouldn't hit her in public—he'd take her somewhere unseen to do that—but his hand clamped down hard. "Jacko is my best friend," Jeffery said, his breath already heavy with gin. "You get over to that fiend of a Scottish barrister and fetch us a souvenir. We deserve it. The traitorous bastard was supposed to take Jacko's part."

Jeffrey's grip hurt. Bertie knew if she protested too much, both Jeffrey and her dad would let her have it. But she couldn't do this.

"That fiend of a Scottish barrister is very smart," she argued. "He'll catch me, then *I'll* be in the cell with Jacko, waiting to go before the magistrate."

Bertie's dad leaned in, his breath already reeking as well. "You just do it, Roberta. You're like a ghost—he'll never know. And if he *does* see you, you know what to do. Now get out there, before I take my hand to you."

They weren't going to leave it. In their minds, Mr. McBride was the villain of the piece and deserved to be punished. If Bertie refused, her dad would drag her away and thrash her until she gave in. If Mr. McBride went home while Bertie was taking her beating, her dad would make her wait here every afternoon until Mr. McBride returned for another case.

Either way, Bertie was doing this. One way would simply be less painful than the other.

Bertie jerked free of Jeffrey's hold. "All right," she snapped. "I'll do it. But you'd better be ready. He's no fool."

"Like I said, he'll never see ya," her dad said. "You've got the touch. Go on with you."

Bertie stumbled when her dad pushed her between the

shoulder blades, but she righted herself and squared her shoulders. Taking a deep breath, she walked steadily toward where Mr. McBride stood waiting, his sad face and empty eyes focused on something far, far from the crowded streets of the City of London.

Sinclair McBride pulled his coat close against the icy wind and drew his hat down over his eyes.

Remember Sir Percival Montague, Daisy? he asked the gray sky. *Well, I potted him good today. Old Monty was nearly rubbing his hands, wanting to pronounce sentence of death on that poor girl. Bloody imbecile. She was no more guilty than a newborn kitten.*

The sky grew darker, rain coming with the night. So damnably cold here, not like the blistering heat of North Africa, where Sinclair had done his army time. His younger brother, Steven, was always trying to talk Sinclair into traveling with him—Spain, Egypt, back to Rome at least, where winters were balmy.

But there was the question of Andrew and Caitriona, Sinclair's very interesting children. Sinclair couldn't bring himself to foist them on Elliot and Juliana while he traveled the world. His brother and sister-in-law were starting their own family, their own life, and needed time alone. *Take them with me?* Sinclair had to smile. *Wouldn't that be an adventure?*

Sinclair imagined his two terrifying bairns on trains, carriages, carts, all the way to Italy. No, not the best answer.

Thinking about Andrew and Cat helped him avoid the one thought Sinclair had been trying to banish all day. Now as he stood in the cold, waiting for his coachman to bring the landau, the thought came unbidden.

Seven years to this day you left me, Daisy.

Margaret McBride, Maggie or Daisy to those closest to her, had died of a fever that threatened to take Sinclair's children as well. Seven years ago today.

My friends and family expect me to move on, can you believe it?

But they've not had the loves of their lives ripped away from them, have they? They wouldn't say such bloody daft things if they had.

"Moving on" sounded like forgetting all about Maggie, his wife, his lover, his helpmeet, his best friend. *And I'll never do that.*

Maggie didn't answer. She never did. But it didn't matter. The comfort Sinclair drew from talking to her, out loud or inside his head, was some days the only thing that kept him sane.

When you're ready for me to move on, I know you'll tell me. Another gust of wind had Sinclair grabbing for his hat and clenching his teeth. Where the devil was Richards with the coach? *I trust you, Daisy . . .*

The crowd was thick, everyone in London going home for the night. Sinclair held on to his hat as he was buffeted. Richards was taking a damn long time. Sinclair wasn't usually in a rush, but tonight was bloody cold, and the rain was starting to come down in earnest.

A shove and a thump sent Sinclair a swift step forward. A young woman had stumbled into him, her shoes skidding on the wet pavement. She struggled to keep her feet, and Sinclair put a steadying hand under her arm.

"Easy now, lass," Sinclair said.

She looked up at him . . . and everything stopped. Sinclair saw a dark hat covered with bright blue violets, then eyes of the same blue—clear and warm in this swirl of gray. The young woman's face was round, her nose slightly tip-tilted, her red lips curving into a charming smile.

He'd never seen her before, and at the same time, Sinclair felt a jolt rock him, as though he'd been waiting for years for this encounter. The two of them stood together in a warm stillness, removed from the rest of the world as it rushed around them.

"I'm *that* sorry, mister," the young woman was saying. "Some bloke put his elbow right in me back, and me feet went clean out from under me. You all right?"

"I'm whole." Sinclair forced himself back to the cold of the real world, and studied her with his professional assessment, honed by a long career of watching criminals. She wasn't a street girl. Game girls had a desperate look, and were too eager to be seductive. *Want me to make ya feel better, lamb?* was the cleanest of the offers Sinclair had gotten as he strode through London's streets.

This young woman was working-class, probably on her way home after a long day's drudgery. She wasn't dirty, but the sleeves of her velvet jacket were frayed at the cuffs, her gloves threadbare and much mended. Poor, but making the best of it.

Still, she didn't have the downtrodden appearance many factory women had. Her smile was sunny, as though telling the world things could be better if given a chance.

"Well, that's good," she said. "Night, mister. Sweet dreams."

Another smile, and in the sudden flare of an approaching light, all Sinclair could see were her eyes.

Deep and blue, like the depths of the ocean. The Mediterranean could be that color. Sinclair remembered southern Italy and its shores from his leave time, when he'd been in the army and traveling the world. He'd known peace there.

This young woman with her blue eyes was beautiful, with a beauty that went beyond her shabby clothes and working-class grin. She was a vision of light in the darkness, in a place where darkness had lasted too long.

Someone else shoved him, and Sinclair turned to step out of the way. When he looked back for the young woman, she was gone. He blinked at the empty space where she'd been, then lifted his gaze and spied her slipping through the crowd, the violets on her hat bobbing.

The detail of her ridiculous hat kept Sinclair from believing he'd dreamed her. But of course he hadn't. Visions of beautiful women were of golden-haired sirens with perfect bodies, strumming on lyres perhaps, luring men to their dooms. Sirens didn't have lopsided smiles and plump faces, and blue eyes that pulled Sinclair out of his despair, if only for a moment.

But she was gone now, vision or no, and Sinclair needed to go home. Andrew and Cat would have locked their new governess into the cellar by now, or accidentally burned down the house. Or both.

They didn't *mean* to be bad, his little ones . . . Well, mostly they didn't. One of the governesses had claimed that Andrew was possessed by the devil. She'd even offered to contact a priest she knew who could have him exorcised. That governess hadn't lasted more than an hour.

A clock struck. Sinclair, out of habit, reached for his watch to compare the time. His watch always ran a few minutes fast and having it repaired made no difference. Buying a new watch was out of the question, because Daisy had given him this one . . .

Which was no longer in his pocket.

Reality rushed back at Sinclair with an icy slap. His gaze went to the violet-covered hat as it disappeared around a corner.

Good God, how stupid had he been? He hadn't pegged the young woman as a pickpocket, because pickpockets usually didn't stop for a chat. They stole and slipped away before the victim was aware.

Her bad luck someone had tripped her. Or had it been luck?

All this went through his head as Sinclair whirled around and strode after the woman, his feet moving faster and faster as he went. Gone was any thought of finding his coach and going home. Nothing mattered but getting that watch back. Sinclair would find the young woman and take it away from her, even if he had to chase her to the ends of the earth.

———

BASHER MCBRIDE WAS COMING after her. Bertie had twigged he was much too smart not to notice if she lifted his timepiece, but she'd told herself not to be a coward. Now she knew her folly, because he was chasing her, and he'd have her nicked in a heartbeat. She should have stuck with taking his handkerchief and been done.

But she'd wanted Mr. McBride to look at her. To see those eyes, gray like the sky before dawn, to hear his rumbling voice. She'd warmed all over when the syllables had poured onto her —*Easy now, lass.*

She'd lingered too long to admire him, and now he was coming. Bertie picked up her pace and dashed around another corner. She knew London better than most, and she could lead him on a merry chase. And if Bertie couldn't shake him . . . well, she'd know where to run.

She scooted into the backstreets behind the grim walls of Newgate, ducking into the warrens and winding streets, lanes so narrow they blotted out the last streaks of light in the sky.

These passages were filled with trash, rats, and layabouts. A few of the men lolling in their gin-soaked stupor tried to grab Bertie's skirts as she went by, but Bertie expertly twitched away from them and kept on running.

Bertie risked a dash across Aldersgate Street and back into the narrower lanes beyond. She jumped over a vagrant who looked to be far gone on opium, her boot heels clicking on the hard-packed street.

And wasn't it just her luck? The Scottish bloke was keeping up with her. A swift glance behind her as she rounded a corner showed McBride running after her, his body moving with athletic competence as he ducked and swerved around carts, dung, and vermin, both human and rodent.

Bertie's breath was coming fast, her corset too tight to keep this up for long. Blast the man. He should be giving up by now, toddling off to his comfortable home in Mayfair or Belgrave Square or wherever he laid his pristine head to rest.

She remembered how he'd stood straight and tall in front of the judge, taunting the old misery, turning the verdict around to surprise them all. Basher McBride's arrogance had rolled off him, with even the judge grudgingly conceding to him.

But then, as soon as his performance was over, all that arrogance drained out of him, leaving Mr. McBride an empty shell. Until now, of course. His energy was back, focused on chasing Bertie and dragging her off to a constable.

Not that, never that. Bertie didn't particularly want to finish her life at the end of a noose. The jury might be sympathetic that Bertie was forced to pickpocket by her father—if they believed her—but that would only mean she'd be transported across the ocean to someplace she knew nothing about or locked up in a grim and terrifying prison.

She should have been able to slip away from him by now, but Mr. McBride was keeping her in sight, whichever passage she took. Bertie knew she'd have to lure him to The Trap, whether she liked it or not, or she'd never get away from him.

That's how she thought of it—*The Trap*—with capital *T*s outlining the jaws of it. No one escaped it, not easily anyway. Mr. McBride was smart—he'd run the other way as soon as he saw what was what, and leave Bertie alone.

"Oi!" she shouted when she was within three feet of the place. "It's Bertie! I'm coming in!"

A door in a squalid wall in a dark alley swung open, and Bertie leapt over the doorsill. She swept up her skirts as she landed, careful not to turn her ankles in the rubble.

Beyond the door was an empty space where a house had stood, pulled down or fallen down long ago. The lot was surrounded on four sides by other buildings that soared five and six stories to the sky. No windows faced the place, nothing to reveal the secrets of the inner emptiness. The space was lit right now with a fire built in the remains of an old stove, and with lanterns of the men and boys who liked to gather here.

The Trap was to be used in dire emergency, when a pursuer became too keen or bullies from another neighborhood strayed too close. The men and boys who made The Trap their haven were usually armed, usually drunk, and always ready to have a go at whoever was mad enough to come through the door.

Bertie fled through the lot, which was strewn with stones and broken bottles, skirting the pile of old rubbish in the middle. A smaller door led out the other side to another passage, where Bertie could slip away and go home.

She turned around to take one last look at her handsome Mr. McBride, to glimpse him again before he sensibly fled.

Except, he wasn't sensibly fleeing. Mr. McBride came on inside, firelight shining on his light-colored hair, his hat gone who knew where. He showed no fear about the toughs who were converging on him, and when he spotted Bertie on the other side of the lot, he roared, with a voice that rang like a warrior's, "Stop her!"

The toughs blinked, not used to victims who didn't scramble away from them in terror. Mr. McBride started around them, straight for Bertie. The lads came out of their shocked state by the time McBride was halfway past the mound of junk, then they struck.

"Aw, bloody *hell!*" McBride's rich Scots rang out, and he grabbed a rusted iron bar from the pile. Before Bertie's stunned eyes, Mr. McBride turned to face the onslaught and started fighting back.

The youths and men charging him had knives, clubs, or coshes. Mr. McBride parried their blows, thrusting and beating at them as they beat on him. Iron rang against steel, and one of the youths cursed as his knife went flying. Mr. McBride had the advantage against the knives, having chosen a bar long enough to keep them back. When they figured out how to get under Mr. McBride's reach, however . . .

They were going to kill him.

These toughs were thieves, murderers, or the sons of such. They'd killed before, wrapping up a body and tipping it into the Thames, with the police none the wiser. Never mind that Mr. McBride was obviously a toff in his fine clothes—they'd kill him, strip him, divide up the spoils, and go for a gin.

Why the devil didn't he just *run*?

Bertie came pounding back to him. She dove around the flailing bars, earning her curses from the youths yelling at her to get out of the way, and closed her hands around Mr. McBride's arm. She found beneath the expensive cloth strength that matched the iron bar he wielded. Mr. McBride started to shake her off, but Bertie dug deeper.

"This way," she shouted. "Run!"

"Get out of it, girl!" one of the toughs yelled. "Fair game."

"No, you leave him be! Come *on*."

She jerked at Mr. McBride, who finally saw wisdom and came with her. The lads, enraged she was depriving them of their fun, poured after them. Bertie ran out the narrow door on the far side, jumping over the sill to the street. Mr. McBride had to turn and fight at the last moment, buffeting back two lads who'd grabbed his coat. The coat tore, but stayed on, and McBride swung away and followed Bertie.

Bertie slammed the door. She grabbed the iron bar from Mr. McBride's hands and wedged the door shut, though she knew it wouldn't hold for long, and the lads could always go around the other side.

She seized him by the sleeve and started running. McBride ran with her, his strides strong.

It wasn't long before Bertie heard the youths coming. A few would give up, losing interest, but some would be determined.

Jeffrey's mates loved a good fight, and they'd want to divide up the spoils they found on Mr. McBride.

"This way," Bertie urged as she dove around a corner.

There was one place in all of London Bertie could go. No one else knew about it but her—not her dad, not Jeffrey, not her own mates. Taking Mr. McBride there was a risk—he could have the constables raid it when she let him go—but maybe it would be worth the sacrifice. This courageous, handsome Scotsman didn't deserve to be beaten to death by East End thugs.

Bertie ran for the end of an alleyway that looked as though it went no farther. Mr. McBride started to argue, but Bertie put her finger to her lips and pulled him around a hidden corner, then down a slippery set of stairs and through a noisome passage. Finally, Bertie squeezed into a space that led between the backs of buildings, corners poking out and seeming to block the way. Bertie had discovered long ago that a lithe young woman *could* push through here and find a refuge.

Mr. McBride grunted a bit as he struggled through the narrower parts, then popped out like a cork behind Bertie as she opened a half-size door and ducked through. This door had led to an old scullery and kitchen for a house that had once been large and fine. But the room had been walled off long ago as the houses had been changed, pulled down, or rebuilt, and this corner of the cellar was lost and forgotten.

"Mind your head," Bertie said.

At the same time she heard a thump and Mr. McBride growled, "Thank you, lass. Very timely."

They went down a set of stairs in the pitch dark, Mr. McBride with a heavy hand on Bertie's shoulder. "Seventeen of 'em," she said, and started counting off.

Mr. McBride's hand was firm, spreading heat beneath her worn velvet coat and wool bodice. Strong too, his fingers blunt and gripping hard.

At the bottom, they went through another door, then Bertie told him to stay put while she groped for the matches she kept on a shelf and started lighting lamps. She had three lamps down here now, which threw a rosy glow over the crumbling bricks and fallen beams that littered the triangular room.

A pile of cushions, carefully formed into the approximation of a sofa, stood against the most solid wall. Bertie had covered it with shawls and blankets, and set up a small folding table near it, strewn now with newspapers and magazines she'd managed to smuggle down here. The passage above was too narrow for her to bring in much furniture, but she'd made the place as cozy as she could. She'd carried down small rugs over the years, overlapping them to keep her feet off the cold, damp floor.

Mr. McBride remained in place by the door until Bertie's lights strengthened. She'd need more kerosene before long, she saw.

The large man was out of place down here, that was for certain. His head touched the ceiling and he had to duck under the few beams that remained. He looked around the room in wonder, then his gray gaze landed on Bertie and pinned her as hard as he'd pinned Jacko in the dock.

"Are ye mad, lass?" he asked. "You stay down *here*? This ceiling could fall upon you any second."

Bertie shivered as his rumbling, delicious voice filled the space. "Hasn't in sixteen years," she said stoutly. "And probably stood up a long time before that. Solid houses in this part of London."

"Whichever part it is," Mr. McBride said, half to himself. "Why'd you save me from those lads, woman, when ye'd led me to them in the first place? Why not let them beat me to a bloody pulp?"

Bertie folded her arms, spending a moment letting his Scottish consonants and vowels flow over her. "Well, you were supposed to run away, weren't you?" she asked. "You thought you could take on eight street toughs by yourself? You have to be daft as a brick."

"No, I wanted my watch." Anger flared anew in his eyes, never mind that he was down here at Bertie's mercy with no idea where he was, no help at hand. But *he* was the one in command, Bertie knew. Not her.

Mr. McBride pointed a strong finger at her. "Which you stole, right out of my waistcoat while I stood gawping. Give it back to me, and I'll say nothing."

———

SINCLAIR WATCHED the young woman's face flush in the candlelight, her guilt pure and simple. She swallowed and took a step back, rubbing her arms. She still wore the hat with the absurd violets, which was now hanging half over her right ear.

"Give me the watch, and I'll leave you be," Sinclair said, trying to gentle his voice. "No constables, no dock, though you are a bloody little tea leaf."

She didn't look impressed he knew rhyming cant: *Tea leaf —thief.*

"Why'd ya help Ruthie?" she asked.

Sinclair had difficulty catching his breath. It was close down here, the biting wind shut out. It took him a moment to realize that by *Ruthie* she meant Ruth Baxter, the kitchen maid who'd stood in the dock at the Old Bailey not an hour ago. Already the details of the trial were fading, a trial that would be put down as a loss to him, but Sinclair didn't care.

"Miss Baxter was innocent," he said. "Why should she go down for it?"

"Cause you're a barrister, hand-in-glove with the judges."

This young woman had a lot to learn about the common courts. Old Monty and Sinclair had been butting heads since Sinclair had first put on a wig. "Miss Baxter couldn't afford a defense. I knew she was innocent when I looked at her, and I knew Mr. Small was guilty. What does this have to do with my watch?"

"Well, Ruthie's a pal of mine, ain't she?" The young woman's eyes were deep blue in the candlelight. "Thank you."

"So, you decided to show your gratitude by pinching my watch and leading me into the arms of your ruffian friends?" He made a noise of disbelief. "If that's your method of thanking a man, I'd hate so see ye when you're annoyed with him."

She didn't smile. "I told ya, you were supposed to run. They'd have gutted you. What were you thinking? You should have just let it go."

His temper splintered. "Why the hell should I? It's *my* watch. My wife gave it to me."

The young woman took a step back as Sinclair's voice rose. "Yeah? You're a rich bloke. Have her buy you another one."

"I cannae, can I?"

"Why not?"

"Because she's *dead*!"

The words rang against the low ceiling and the uncaring stones, and suddenly, Sinclair couldn't breathe at all.

He'd never, not even the day she'd slipped away, declared flatly that Daisy was dead. Sinclair shied from the word. He'd said *passed, left him, was gone*. *Dead* meant too much finality, it meant dust and no return.

Sinclair struggled for air. "She's . . ."

He felt wetness on his face. Bloody hell. He hadn't wept either. Not really. To weep for her meant she was never coming back.

"She's . . ."

The world rushed around him, spiraling down into a single point, stifling. Blackness filled his vision, a pressure in his ears grinding out his strength. His knees were bending, and a void opened to pull him inside . . .

He blinked and found himself half lying, half sitting across the cushions piled on the floor. The young woman sat beside him, her hat gone to reveal rich dark hair, worry on her face.

"You all right, mister?"

This was the second time she'd asked him that tonight, as though sweetly concerned. She was a thief, had murdering friends, had brought him to this hole only God knew where to do God only knew what, and yet she asked with anxiety whether he was well. She'd dragged him to this sofa, he realized. Sinclair must have fallen nose-first on the floor, and she'd pulled him to the cushions and made sure he woke up.

"Damn it, woman." Sinclair put his arm behind his head and glared at her. "What am I to do with you?"

She stared at him in wide-eyed contemplation for another second or two, then she leaned swiftly to him and kissed him on the mouth.

A MACKENZIE CLAN GATHERING

CHARACTERS

Once again, as in *Mackenzie Family Christmas: The Perfect Gift*, we have an ensemble cast, but the most important characters are:

Ian Mackenzie
Beth Mackenzie
Lloyd Fellows
Jamie Mackenzie
John Ackerley (brother of Beth's first husband)

Important Secondary Characters

Belle Mackenzie
Megan Mackenzie
Hart and Eleanor, Duke and Duchess of Kilmorgan
Alec Mackenzie (Hart's son and heir)
Sergeant Pierce
Lord Halsey

I came up with the title "A Mackenzie Clan Gathering" long before I wrote the story, and my publisher instantly set it in stone (i.e., put it on their schedule and advertised it). Unfortunately, I couldn't come up with an exact story that far in advance (this was about a year and a half prior to publication), and the story that eventually came to me was no longer strictly about a clan gathering. However, by the time I had the plot, it was far too late to change the title. So I had to go with it. (More whackiness of the publishing world.)

The story is essentially a mystery—who broke into Hart Mackenzie's house and stole his collection of paintings? Ian is on the case, along with Lloyd Fellows, who in the meantime has been promoted to Chief Inspector.

The "clan gathering" became Hart's birthday, and in the end, they all did get there, but this story focused on Ian and his family.

I love catching up with the Mackenzies (which is why I wrote *Mackenzie Family Christmas*) and this was no different. In this gathering, all the brothers, Daniel, and the McBrides already have their HEAs, so it was nice to reunite them.

Ian also has to do some soul searching in this one. Beth's well-meaning brother-in-law (brother of her deceased husband), has become fascinated by Ian and wants to "help" him. I felt kind of sorry for John Ackerley, who is a bit clueless, but he has a good heart. In the end, both he and Ian realize that Ian is fine the way he is! (We and Beth already knew that).

I wrote this after I'd written *Stolen Mackenzie Bride*, and I decided to tie the past to the present through a descendent of the man from whom "Old" Malcolm Mackenzie had stolen his bride.

I also set up the idea of Ian compiling his family's history, which led to the next set of Mackenzie books, which takes us back to the days of Culloden.

SYNOPSIS

SCOTLAND 1892

IAN MACKENZIE IS AWAKENED AT KILMORGAN CASTLE ONE NIGHT to find robbers stealing the priceless art collection of his oldest brother, Hart. Since Ian and Beth are the only ones in resident at Kilmorgan at the moment, Ian decides he must find the art and the culprits before the family shows up for Hart's birthday gathering. With Inspector Fellows and Beth, he investigates, though Ian is somewhat worried by Beth's late husband's brother, a retired missionary, who decides to visit. Does John Ackerley hold the "cure" to Ian's madness? And can Ian discover what has happened to Hart's treasures, and who is targeting the Mackenzies before the enemy strikes again?

Return to Kilmorgan Castle to visit the Victorian branch of the Mackenzie family, and catch up on the brothers and friends, their children, and their lives.

EXCERPT: A MACKENZIE CLAN GATHERING

SCOTLAND, SEPTEMBER 1892

SOMETHING WOKE IAN MACKENZIE DEEP IN THE NIGHT. HE LAY motionlessly, on his side, eyes open and staring at darkness.

A dozen years ago, awakening to total darkness would have sent Ian into a crazed panic, ending up with him on his feet, roaring at the top of his voice in English, Gaelic, and French. Servants would have rushed in, restoring lights some foolish footman had put out, to find Ian standing up beside his bed, swearing in rage and fear.

Now, he lay calmly, absorbing the soft quiet of the darkness.

The reason for his calm lay behind him on the bed—his Beth, curled against him in a nest of warmth.

Whatever change in the huge house had alerted Ian had been too subtle to wake Beth. She slept on, her breathing even, one hand soft against his bare back.

Ian's mind rapidly churned through possibilities of what had dragged him from his dreams. His children—Jamie, Belle, and Megan—were fast asleep in their nursery. Ian knew whenever one of them was wakeful, knew it in his bones. They were shut behind the door of the large nursery at the end of the hall. Safe.

He let his senses expand to every tiny sound of the night.

This was Scotland in the autumn, and winds flowed down the mountains to swirl around Kilmorgan with the shrieking of a dozen banshees.

The vast house itself, built a century and a half ago, was usually alive with noise. Creaking of pipes Hart had installed to bring running water to the bedchambers. The crackle of Daniel's electrics experiments, the tinny sounds of the interior telephone system nephew Daniel had also created.

At the moment, all those noises, except the wind, were silenced. All except the *snick* of a window somewhere in the darkness of the house.

Ian and Beth were the only residents at Kilmorgan Castle, the vast mansion that stood north of Inverness. Hart, the Duke of Kilmorgan and master of the house, was in Edinburgh with Eleanor and his two children—they'd be here in the next day or so. His other brothers, Mac and Cameron, were at their respective country homes with their families, not due to arrive at Kilmorgan until a few days after Hart.

Ian knew the exact location of each house of his brothers, and how long it would take the families to travel to Kilmorgan to celebrate Hart's birthday next week. None of them could have arrived early, in the middle of this night, without Ian knowing about it.

Kilmorgan was quite empty for now, except for Ian's family, the skeleton staff needed to run the place, and three of the dogs.

Dogs . . . They were in the stables, guarding the prize racehorses. They weren't barking or making a fuss.

But Ian knew, without understanding how he knew, that someone who shouldn't be there was inside the house.

He slid out of bed, moving smoothly enough not to wake Beth. He stood a moment at the bedside, strong toes curling on the soft carpet, cool air brushing his bare skin. His valet, Curry, had dropped a nightshirt over Ian's head as Ian had headed to bed, but later, when Beth had joined him, the nightshirt had been quickly tossed away.

Ian moved past the shirt, a pale smudge on the carpet, to reach for the long folds of plaid Curry had laid across a chair to warm before the fire. Ian wrapped the kilt around his large frame, tucking the excess folds in around his waist. He then moved to the chest of drawers, opened the top one, and slid out a Webley pistol.

Ian never kept loaded guns in the house. Far too dangerous with children around. All shotguns were locked into cabinets in the steward's house near the stables; any personal handguns were kept unloaded, ammunition locked away in a separate place. Ian had made this a firm rule, and Hart had agreed.

Ian moved from the bedroom to his connecting dressing room, unlocked a cubbyhole within a cabinet, and pulled bullets from a box there. He lined up six in a perfect row, returned the box and locked the cabinet, and slid the bullets into their chambers with precision.

He left the dressing room through the door that led to the corridor, paused long enough to click the pistol's barrel into place, and strode swiftly and silently down the hall toward the gallery at the end.

Clouds covered the moon tonight, but a gaslight near the staircase illuminated a long stretch of corridor lined with windows. This was the front of the house, overlooking the drive that led to Kilmorgan. From the outside, the row of floor-to-ceiling windows was part of the grand façade created by Malcolm Mackenzie, the ancestor who'd first turned Kilmorgan from a cold castle into a home.

Ian saw no one in the upper hall, no furtive movement in the shadows, nothing out of place. He crept toward the staircase, his bare feet making no noise on the carpet.

Lights on the landings were kept burning all night, so that members of the household who wandered about wouldn't fall headlong down the stairs. Tonight, no one but Ian was in sight as he quickly descended.

Not until he turned along the ground-floor gallery that ran toward Hart's wing of the house did Ian find anything wrong.

A flurry of movement at the far end of the gallery caught his eye. Ian took in what he saw, assessed it all quickly, then pushed the conclusions to the back of his mind as he sprinted toward the half dozen men in dark clothes trying to exit through the garden door.

Ian could move swiftly and in silence, and he was upon them before they realized. He heard muffled curses in several languages, saw the bulk of bodies and what they carried. Several of the men made it out before Ian wordlessly landed amongst them.

The man Ian caught by the back of the neck expertly broke from him, swung around, and jammed a short cudgel toward Ian's stomach. Ian, who'd learned about dirty fighting both from his brothers and on the streets of Paris, avoided the cudgel and grabbed the arm that wielded it.

He swung the man around and into another, then Ian shoved his pistol into the second man's face.

In the next moment, both men crashed themselves into Ian, fighting for the gun. One man got his hand around it, but Ian yanked hard, and the pistol fell, skittering across the floor into darkness, out of sight, out of reach.

The toughs were good, but so was Ian. They had layers of clothes hampering them, while he fought like his ancestors, in kilt and bare feet.

The first man grunted as Ian ripped the cudgel out of his hand and bashed it into his abdomen. The second man's fist came at Ian's face. Ian caught the fist with his big hand, then the second man punched Ian right in the gut.

Ian spun away, fighting pain. The man he'd cudgeled was

doubled over, and Ian spun back to the second man, battling until he got him into a headlock.

The first man, holding his stomach, went for the pistol. A growl escaped Ian's throat. He slammed the second man away from him and went after the first.

The second man dashed out the garden door, but Ian didn't care. The first man, seeming to recover at every step, ran to where the pistol had fallen and scooped it up. Instead of turning to shoot Ian, he raced along the gallery toward the main stairs.

Ian went ice-cold. Beth was up there. Ian had heard the echo of their bedroom door closing as he'd fought—the galleries and staircase let sound carry in an almost magical way. He knew Beth would have made her way to the stairs and started down, as Ian had, to see what was going on.

This thug with a pistol was running directly toward her.

Ian sprinted after him, kilt flying up over his thighs as he put on a burst of speed. Ian knew this gallery, and the thug didn't— where the bare spaces between carpets lay, where tables had been placed in the middle of the floor so a piece of sculpture could be viewed from all sides. Ian dodged these and leapt from rug to rug, gaining on the man before he reached the stairs.

Ian tackled him. He heard Beth give a sharp scream as the thug went down under Ian's body.

Ian felt the cold pistol touch his ribs. In the next second, he'd be dead.

He used that second to roll, grab, and twist. The pistol came away from the man's hand and went off, the bullet striking somewhere in the vast ceiling.

Beth's scream came again, and then her shouts for help.

Ian hauled the thug around and punched him full in the face. The thug, instead of fighting back, wrenched himself out of Ian's grip, charged for the front door, yanked it open, and ran out into the darkness. Ian heard the man's boots crunching on gravel, and then nothing.

Ian dashed out after him, but the tough was gone, swallowed by night and swirling mists. Dogs were barking now, and men carrying lanterns were hurrying from the stables.

Ian closed the door. The thugs didn't matter anymore. The safety of Beth and his children was all to him.

Beth ran down the stairs, her dressing gown floating behind her. "Ian, are you all right? *Ian?*"

Ian caught her as she came off the staircase. He lifted her from her feet and crushed her to him. The feeling of her soft body came to him, the vibrancy that was the woman he loved.

If the man had reached Beth . . . The thug was the sort to grab a woman and use her as a shield, and then shoot her when she was no longer useful.

If Ian had been a few seconds too slow . . .

He buried his face in Beth's neck, inhaling the warm scent of her. She was beautiful, and well, and in his arms. Safe.

People brushed past him—the household servants coming see what was wrong. Lights flickered and grew brighter. Men came into the house through the front and garden doors, exclaiming, making sounds of disbelief and dismay.

Ian wanted them go away, to leave him with Beth alone in this bubble of peace he found in her arms, a place where the world couldn't touch him.

But it wasn't to be. His valet, Curry, once a London street villain, clattered down the stairs on swift feet. *"Bleedin' 'ell!"*

Beth tried to lift away. "Ian—love—I'm all right. We must see what is happening."

She was correct, of course. Ian had learned in this first decade of his marriage—ten beautiful, sparkling years—that he could not withdraw from the world. Once in a while, yes, with Beth and privacy, and maybe a lick of honey, but not always. He'd grown used to facing immediate situations without panic, without having to bolt.

Letting out a long breath, Ian raised his head. Beth gave him a little smile and tucked his kilt, which had come awry while he'd chased the thug, more securely around his waist.

The little gesture made Ian's heart beat swiftly. To hell with facing the world. Ian would take Beth back upstairs and let her unwrap him, so she could enjoy whatever she found in whichever way she wanted to enjoy it.

Beth, catching the look in his eyes, let her smile grow wider, but she shook her head. *Not yet,* she meant. *But later . . .*

Ian would be sure to take her up on the unspoken promise. Resolved, he twined his fingers though Beth's and let her lead him the rest of the way down the stairs.

The entire gallery glowed with light. The servants had turned up every lamp in the place.

Beth gasped in shock. Ian had seen and noted everything out of place as he'd run past in the dark, but he'd pushed the vision aside so it wouldn't distract him in his pursuit of the intruders. Now he faced the gallery and the truth of what he'd observed.

Most of the tables that had held sculptures were empty, and almost every painting from the garden end of the gallery was gone. These pictures had been painted by famous artists through the centuries, plus a precious handful by Ian's brother Mac. Only those that had been hung high, out of easy reach, remained. A few paintings lay piled on the floor, half ripped from frames, the frames broken. Ruined.

Hart Mackenzie's priceless art collection had just been ravaged and stolen, the thieves fleeing with the loot into the night.

THE STOLEN MACKENZIE BRIDE

CHARACTERS

Malcolm Mackenzie

MALCOLM! KNOWN TO IAN MACKENZIE'S FAMILY AS "OLD Malcolm," and to his own family as "the Runt," Mal Mackenzie is the youngest of six (five living) brothers.

Mal, in theory, is the only Mackenzie to have survived the battle of Culloden, and carried on the line to the Victorian Mackenzies. But is he?

Malcolm has the obsession of Ian and the determination of Hart. He feels a deep need to take care of his family, no matter that they're all older than he is—and with good reason. The Mackenzies are reckless, brash, arrogant, and single-minded. One of their brothers, Magnus, died when he was younger, his heart never fully developed. Malcolm never forgot his grief when he found Magnus dead, and he's driven to make sure the rest of his family remains well.

Mal runs the distillery that makes Mackenzie malt with the same tenacity, interested in learning new techniques to render Mackenzie malt the best in Scotland. He foreshadows Daniel with his interest in machines and technology and pursuit of the newest science.

When Malcolm sees Mary Lennox, he fixes upon her with the same determination. Mal never saw himself as the marrying sort, but he knows when he spies Mary that she'd make him the perfect wife.

The trouble is, she's English, the daughter of an anti-Jacobite earl, and already engaged to another. These are trifles to Mal, whose resourcefulness will show him a way to win her.

Lady Mary Lennox

LADY MARY HAS LED A FAIRLY SHELTERED existence in her father's house, and likely will in the house of the man she will marry, who also an earl. She's not in love with this earl, but she is resigned.

Despite Mary's upbringing, she's not quite as innocent and naive as she could be. The aunt who stepped in and raised Mary after Mary's mother's death has been married several times and taken lovers, and is frank about it. Mary knows exactly what goes on in the bedchambers of husband and wife or lovers, and again is resigned.

She determines, though, that if she can't have romance and happiness, that her younger sister will. Mary becomes the go-between for her sister and the young man she's fallen in love with, and works to facilitate their elopement—the young man is of lesser status, and Mary knows her father will never condone the match.

When Mary meets Malcolm, it is as though a blindfold is ripped from her. She sees for the first time what life really is, and that the path chosen for her will be dreary and crush her.

Malcolm, sees this too, and sets about persuading her to break her chains.

The choice is difficult for Mary, though, because she's loyal and loves her family. Not only that but Malcolm, by trying to take care of his brothers, is pulled into the Jacobite Uprising, and so now is branded a traitor.

Mary only sees Malcolm, a man she can never forget, and makes her choice …

IMPORTANT SECONDARY CHARACTERS

Duke of Kilmorgan (Malcolm's father)

Duncan Mackenzie

Will Mackenzie

Angus Mackenzie

Alec Mackenzie

Audrey Lennox (Mary's sister)

Jeremy Drake (Audrey's beloved)

George Markham, Earl of Halsey (Mary's fiancé)

Earl of Wilfort (Mary's father)

Gair Murray (a smuggler)

Padruig (Gair's sidekick)

Ewan (boy servant faithful to Mary)

Naughton (the Mackenzie's retainer)

Aunt Danae

Captain Robert Ellis (British cavalryman, captured by Malcolm)

AUTHOR'S NOTES

I love Malcolm! I became interested in him when he was mentioned as "Old Malcolm" by the Victorian Mackenzies, and he was solidly on the Mackenzie family tree I'd drawn when I first started the series.

The family tree says that Malcolm was one of six brothers, and only he lived after the Battle of Culloden Field in 1746. He was pardoned (eventually) for his part in the Jacobite Uprising and allowed to carry on the title of Duke of Kilmorgan.

But was he really the only survivor? Who were these brothers of his, and what happened to them during this turbulent time in Scottish history?

I decided I needed to know! I stockpiled books on the Scottish Uprising, Bonnie Prince Charlie, and the entire rebellion, and went to work.

The research was heartbreaking. The Highlanders were divided—not all followed Charles when he came to Scotland wanting to win back the British crown for his father James (the Old Pretender). In fact, some Highlanders, when Charles arrived in the west of Scotland, advised him to go home.

Charles famously said, "I *am* home," and rallied Highlanders to follow him.

Families were divided. The Scotsmen who followed Charles suffered quite a lot and in the end died at Culloden or were killed soon after. The victories early in the war (at Prestonpans and the ease with which Charles entered Edinburgh), gave the Jacobites much confidence, but in the end, they were defeated and basically slaughtered. Charles fled in the middle of the battle and hid in the western Highlands until he found his way back to France.

I envisioned Malcolm, young and interested in the scientific advances of his time (the beginning of the Enlightenment), having no use for the Jacobite cause and any nostalgia for the past. He and his brothers (and especially his father) didn't like the British, but they pretty much ignored them and got on with what they wanted to do. Malcolm gets pulled into the Jacobite cause reluctantly, as do his brothers.

The exception is Mal's oldest brother, Duncan, a fanatic Jacobite. Mal goes to the battle at Prestonpans to make sure Duncan stays alive, and becomes a hero of the battle, quite unintentionally.

———

IN MOST OF MY BOOKS, the action takes place over a few weeks or at most a few months. For this one, I played it out over the entire Jacobite Uprising, from September 1745 to April 1746. This gave Mal and Mary time to get to know each other before bad things happened. I also wanted them working together to survive and make their marriage strong. The theme throughout is Malcolm's need to care for his family and remain with Mary.

This was a writing challenge for me—also a challenge to deal with the tragedy of the time without the book turning morose. This is a romance, and it needed a happily ever after!

It was also interesting for me to write the ancestors of the Mackenzies. The Victorian Mackenzies all have an obsessive nature (shown most vividly in Ian), but they inherited it from their Mackenzie forbears.

Malcolm's favorite brother, Alec, has an artistic skill, which will resurface in Mac. Duncan Mackenzie has the drive and need for control that we see in Hart. Will's uncanny ability to get himself into and out of all kinds of trouble shows up again in Daniel and the younger Cameron. Malcolm's obsessiveness and drive comes out again in Ian and also Daniel and Lloyd Fellows.

As I grew interested in the early brothers, I knew I couldn't let them all die. Some had to survive so I could write more about them! I am also interested in Captain Ellis, the cavalryman Malcolm captures at Prestonpans and takes with him to Kilmorgan, who becomes a friend to Malcolm and Mary. I think he deserves a happily ever after himself.

———

MOST OF ALL, I simply enjoyed this book for itself. It has history, action, romance, adventure, sweetness, sorrow, heat, love, and a happy ending. My kind of story!

SYNOPSIS

SCOTLAND 1745

Malcolm Mackenzie knows the moment he sees Lady Mary Lennox, daughter of an English earl, that she is the one for him. The trouble is, Highland clans are rising to join Charles Stuart, who has landed in Scotland and headed for Edinburgh where Mary's family is currently residing. Not only that, Mary's father is in thick with the English government, and certainly doesn't want his daughter anywhere near a Highland barbarian. Plus, Lady Mary is already engaged to another.

Malcolm, who considers himself neither Jacobite nor loyalist, wants only to build up his business, avoid the uncertain tempers of his father and oldest brother, and win the hand of the beautiful and lively Mary. He makes plans to sweep her away to his castle north of Inverness, but his four interfering brothers and father, not to mention this annoying uprising, keep getting in the way.

Mary Lennox believes she's happy. She is fine with going through with her arranged marriage to please her father, at the same time helping her sister to find romance.

That is, until she sees Malcolm Mackenzie, youngest of the Duke of Kilmorgan's five sons, lounging like a lazy wolf in the middle of a proper English soiree. It isn't only his kilt that makes him different from her English acquaintances in Scotland, but his predatory air, his golden eyes, and his casual arrogance.

Soon she finds herself under the scrutiny of this man, and of his entire Highland family. Her ideas of duty and happiness splinter and fall away, as Malcolm makes her face the truth about herself and her life.

The dark winds of change, however, are flowing around Malcolm and Mary. Scotland is drawn inexorably into the battle between the Jacobites and the armies sent by the English government to crush the rebellion. Scots fight Scots, loyalties shift, and Malcolm finds himself plunged into a fight he didn't want, one that will change his life and the Highlands of Scotland forever.

» Rea

EXCERPT: THE STOLEN MACKENZIE BRIDE

SCOTLAND 1745

Mm, what sweet morsel is *that*?"

Mal Mackenzie, youngest of five brothers, called at various times in his life Young Malcolm, the Devil Mackenzie, and would ye get out of it, ye pain in my arse—the last mostly by his father and oldest brother—voiced the words as the tedious gathering suddenly grew more interesting.

The morsel was a young woman. What else would it be, with Mal?

"Oh, aye," his brother Alec muttered as he leaned against the wall, in a foul temper. "Of course ye'd notice the prettiest lass in the room. The most untouchable as well."

The lady in question glided through the drawing room on the arm of a man who must be her father. She wore a gown of rich material much like those of other young women here, but she stood out among them like a fiery bloom among weeds.

They were paraded, these ladies, laced into bodices and tight stomachers that showed a soft enticement of bosom, skirts swaying as they moved. They walked with eyes downcast to indicate what demure creatures they were—suitable wives for the bachelors, young and old, who'd come to view them.

Malcolm's lady, in contrast, had her head up, smiling at all, though the smile was somewhat strained. Her thoughts were elsewhere.

She had red-gold hair that caught the candlelight as she passed beneath the chandeliers. Mal couldn't see the color of her eyes from where he stood, but he was certain they'd be clearest blue. Or green. Or gray.

She noted Malcolm staring at her and paused for the briefest moment, the smile fading. Mal, who'd been leaning next to Alec, pushed from the cold stone wall to stand up straight, fires weaving through his nerves.

The young woman took him in—a tall, rawboned Scotsman in a fine coat, dressed like an Englishman except for the plaid that covered his legs to his knees. Malcolm prided himself in not looking entirely like these English whelps—he'd pulled his thick brown-red hair into a queue instead of stuffing it under a powdered cocoon-like wig, and had tied his neckcloth in a loose knot.

The young woman's gaze met his, and the answering sparkle in her eyes woke every sense in Mal's body.

Then she turned her head, looking past him as she scanned the crowd for someone else.

The moment, as fleeting as it had been, reached out and wrapped itself around him. The tendrils of something inevitable entangled the being that was Malcolm Mackenzie, changing everything.

Malcolm all but shoved an elbow into Alec, who was pretending to be interested in the interaction of the English and Scottish elite. "Who is she?" Mal demanded.

Alec moodily studied the crowd. "The blond lass, you mean?"

"Her hair's not blond." Mal tilted his head as though that could help him look under her modest lace cap. "'Tis the color of sunshine, tinged with the fire of sunset."

"If you say so." Alec, two years older and one of a pair of twins, gave Mal a warning look. "She's not for you, runt."

Runt was another name for Malcolm, who'd begun life very small, but now topped most of his brothers and his father by at least an inch.

The words *not for you* never deterred Mal. "Why shouldn't she be?"

"Shall I run a list for ye?" Alec asked in irritation. "She is Lady Mary Lennox, daughter of the Earl of Wilfort. Wilfort has an estate as big as this city, more money than God, and power and influence in the cabinet. The family is one of the oldest in England—I think his ancestor fought alongside Henry the Fifth, or some such. All of which makes his daughter out of reach of the youngest son of a Scotsman with what the English claim is a trumped-up title. Not only that, she's engaged to another English lordship, so keep your large paws to yourself."

"Huh," Malcolm said, not worried in the least. "Poor little morsel."

Mal followed Lady Mary's progress through the room, noting the polite way she greeted her father's friends and the mothers of the other daughters. Correct, well trained—like a pedigreed horse brought in to demonstrate what a sweet-tempered creature it could be.

Malcolm saw more than that—the restless twitch of her eyes as she searched the room while pretending not to, the trembling of a ribbon on the red-gold curls at the back of her neck.

She was vibrancy contained, a creature of light and vigor straining at the tethers that held her. At any moment, the shell of her respectability would crack, and her incandescence would spill out.

Did no one but Mal see? Those around her smiled and spoke comfortably to her, as though they liked her, but their reactions were subdued, as were hers to them.

This was not her stage, not where she would shine. She

needed to be free of this place, these enclosing walls. Out on the open heather maybe, in the Highlands of Mal's home, Kilmorgan, in the north. Her vibrancy wouldn't be swallowed there, but allowed to glow.

And she'd be with him, the layers of her clothing coming off in his hands, the warmth of her body rising to him. This woman belonged in Mal Mackenzie's bed, and he intended to take her there.

It would be a grand challenge. Lady Mary was surrounded, protected. Her father and the matrons circled her like guard dogs, to keep wolves like Mal at bay.

Mal made a noise in his throat like a growl. If they considered him a wolf, so be it.

"What are you grumbling over?" Alec answered, not happy. He did not want to be here; he hated Englishmen, and only duty to their father kept him calm in the corner instead of racing around picking fights.

"At last, something interesting in this place, and you have no use for it," Malcolm said. Alec was his favorite brother—well, the one who drove him the least mad—but Alec had his own tribulations.

"Let her be, Malcolm," Alec said sternly. "I'm supposed to be watching after you. You go near her, and you'll stir up a world of trouble. I'll not be facing Da's fists because I could nae keep you out of it."

"I could put you in the way of Da's fists, and maybe have your neck broken, with a few words, and you know it," Malcolm reminded him. "But I don't, do I? Why? Because you're me best mate, and I don't want you dead. The least ye could do is help me meet yon beautiful lass."

"And I'm calling to mind the last time I did ye such a favor. I remember pulling your naked self out of a burning house, and taking shot in my upper arm, which still hurts of a rainy morning. All because ye had to go after what wasn't yours."

Malcolm flushed at the memory. "Aye, any husband should be angry to find a strapping lad like me in his place next to his bonny wife, but he had no cause to set the bed on fire. Nearly killed the poor woman. Not surprised she left him behind and went to the colonies with her mum."

"He's still looking for ye, Mal, so stay clear of him."

"Nah, Da put the fear of God in him, and it was three years ago. And that lass isn't married." He waved a hand in the direction of the delectable Lady Mary.

"No," Alec said. "It'll be her father's pistol ye'll have to dodge instead."

"So, you'll not help me?"

"Not a bit of it."

Malcolm fell silent. He would never betray Alec's secret to their father—to anyone in the family—and Alec knew it. No leverage there.

"Ah, well." Malcolm's slow smile spread across his face. "I'll have to solve this conundrum on me own."

"That's what I'm afraid of," Alec said darkly.

———

THE INNOCENCE OF IT, Mary was to reflect later, should be astonishing. That moment in time—she at Lady Bancroft's soiree in Edinburgh, her only worry her role of go-between in the forbidden liaison of her sister.

The simplicity of it; the nothingness . . . If Mary had left that night for home, if they'd reached Lincolnshire without her ever having seen the broad-shouldered Scotsman who gazed at her with such intensity, Mary would have lived the rest of her life in peace, moved out of the way like a chess piece, sheltered from the rest of the board.

That night, she stepped into the wrong square at the wrong time. A storm had kept them in Edinburgh, and her father and aunt had decided they might as well accept the invitation to Lady Bancroft's fashionable gathering.

Malcolm would not have been there either, if his father hadn't sent his brother Alec to spy for him. Alec had brought Malcolm along for camouflage, and also because Alec didn't trust Mal alone on the streets of Edinburgh—for very good reason.

Mary's life would have been so very different . . .

For the moment, Lady Mary Lennox existed in a bubble of safety, sure in her betrothal to Lord Halsey, and more worried about her shy little sister than herself.

Tonight's gathering was a decidedly political one. Lady Bancroft had invited prominent Scotsmen to her soiree to reassure those in Edinburgh that rumblings of the Jacobite rising were just that—rumblings. Never mind that Charles Stuart had landed somewhere in the west, never mind he was trying to raise an army. He'd never succeed, and they all knew it.

Highlanders were harmless, Lady Bancroft was implying, thoroughly adapted to civilized living—enlightened men of science. They blended effortlessly with the English aristocracy, did they not?

In that case, Lady Bancroft ought not to have invited the two young Scotsmen warming themselves near the great fireplace at the end of the hall. Mary saw them as she scanned the room for the Honorable Jeremy Drake, the note from Audrey to him burning inside her stomacher.

The Scotsmen looked much alike, brothers obviously. But civilized, they were not.

They'd dressed in waist-length frock coats with many buttons, linen shirts, neat stockings, and leather shoes. Instead of breeches, they wore kilts, loose plaid garments wrapped about their waists.

Other Scotsmen here, in knee breeches and wigs, were indistinguishable from their English counterparts, and moved quietly among the company. These two, on the other hand, looked as though they'd risen from the heather, rubbed the blue paint from their faces, put on coats, and stormed down to Edinburgh.

They wore their dark red hair pulled back into loose queues —no wigs—and lounged with a restlessness that spoke of hunting in long, cold winters, bonfires on the hills, and the wild ruthlessness of their Pictish and Norse ancestors.

Though the two stood calmly, their stances relaxed, they watched. Eyes that missed nothing picked out every person in the room. Wolves, invited to stand among the sheep.

When Mary's scanning gaze passed that of the younger one, his eyes sparked, and she paused.

In that moment, Mary smelled the sweetness of heather under sharp wind, felt the heat of sun in a broad sky. She'd been to the northern Highlands once, and she'd never forgotten the raw beauty of it, the terrifying emptiness and incredible wonder.

This Scotsman embodied all of that, sweeping her to the place and time, under the never-setting sun, when she'd felt afraid and free in the same breath.

The moment passed, and Mary turned away . . .

To find her life completely changed. One tick of the clock ago, she'd been serene about the path she'd agreed to, ready to fulfill her duty to her father and her betrothed. At the next tick, she felt herself plunging into a long, dark pit, and she'd consented to step off the edge.

Mary shook off the sensation with effort. She had a mission to fulfill, no time for idle thoughts.

She drew a deep breath and said vehemently, "Frogs and toadstools!"

A few ladies jumped, but her aunt Danae, used to Mary's epithets, turned to her calmly. "What is it, my dear?"

"My fan," Mary said, making a show of patting the folds of

her skirts. "I've left the aggravating thing in the withdrawing room."

Aunt Danae, a plump partridge in a too-tight gown, put a soothing hand on Mary's. "Never mind, dear. Call for Whitman, and have her fetch it for you."

Their hostess, Lady Bancroft, who stood near, began to signal for one of her many footmen. Mary, who'd hidden the fan for the express purpose of going after it, said, "No need. Won't be a moment," and ran off before anyone could object.

Mary's fan was safely in a pocket under her skirt, so she quickly passed the withdrawing room and made for the stairs that led to the upper reaches of the house. Lady Bancroft was not spendthrift enough to waste candles lighting staircases, and Mary groped her way upward in the dark, only the moonlight through undraped windows to light her way.

Jeremy hadn't been in the vast drawing room below, nor had he been in any of the anterooms, so he must be waiting in his chambers above. Likely languishing there, distraught that Lord Wilfort had forbidden the match between him and Audrey. No matter, Mary would soon cheer him with Audrey's letter.

She made it to the upper landing, out of breath, and turned the corner for the wing that would take her to Jeremy.

A tall man stepped out of the shadows and into her path. Moonlight fell on a light-colored frock coat that topped a kilt of blue plaid.

He was one of the Highlanders from below, the younger one, who'd caught and held her with the heat in his eyes.

Primal fear brushed her. To be confronted by this man, a Highlander, in the dark, in this deserted part of the house was . . . exhilarating.

Mary also was touched with curiosity, wonder that such a being existed and was standing less than a foot from her. A warmth began in Mary's breastbone, spreading downward to her fingertips, and up into her face.

The man did not move. He was a hunter, motionless in the dark, sizing up his prey. At the moment, that prey was Mary.

Fanciful nonsense, Mary tried to tell herself. Likely he was staying in the house, perhaps on his way to his bedchamber.

Where he'd pull off his coat, unlace his shirt, lie back before the fire in casual undress . . .

Mary's throat went dry. She'd been listening too hard to Aunt Danae's tales of her conquests when she'd been a young woman. Aunt Danae had lived on passion and desire, but Mary was far too practical to want such things for herself. *Wasn't she?*

"I beg your pardon, sir," she said, trying to keep her voice steady. "My destination lies beyond you."

She spoke with the right note of haughtiness—after all, the Scots were a lesser people, drawn into civilization by the English. Or so her father claimed. Not that Mary truly believed in the natural superiority of Englishmen; she'd met too many Englishmen who were decidedly inferior.

The man said nothing, only stood in place, caught by moonlight.

The touch of fear began to rise. Mary was alone and unprotected, and he was a creature of the uncivilized Highlands. The clansmen raided each other's lands, it was said, stealing cattle, women . . .

"No matter," Mary said when he did not speak. "I will simply go 'round the other way." The house was built in four wings that surrounded a courtyard below. "Good evening, sir."

She swung away but had taken only a step before the Scotsman pushed past her and stood in front of her once more.

Her heart beating rapidly now, Mary swung around again, ready to make a dash for Jeremy's chamber. Jeremy was not a small man—he could clout this Highlander about the head for frightening the woman he hoped would become his sister-in-law.

Mary stumbled and nearly fell as the Scotsman put himself

in front of her again. A large hand on her shoulder pushed her back onto her feet.

"Steady, lass." His voice was a deep rumble, starting from somewhere in his belly and emerging as a warm vibration.

The hand on Mary's shoulder remained. No gentleman should touch a lady thus. He could grip her hand, but only when meeting her, dancing with her, or assisting her. The Highlander had stopped her from falling, yes, but he should withdraw now that she was upright again. Instead, he kept his hand on her, the appendage so large she was surprised his gloves fit him.

He stood close enough that Mary got a good look into his eyes. They were unusual, to say the least. Not blue or green as a red-haired man's might be—they were tawny, like a lion's. The sensible side of her told her they must be hazel, but the gleam of gold held her in place as securely as the hand on her shoulder.

"Please let me pass, sir," Mary said, trying to sound severe, but she sounded about as severe as a kitten. In his opinion as well, because he smiled.

The smile transformed him. From a forbidding, terrifying giant, the Highlander became nearly human. The warmth in the smile reached all the way to his eyes, crinkling them at the corners.

"I will," he said in a voice that wrapped her in heat. "As soon as ye tell me where you're going, and who ye intend to meet."

ALEC MACKENZIE'S ART OF SEDUCTION

CHARACTERS

Alec Mackenzie

ALEC MACKENZIE IS ONE OF A PAIR OF TWINS, THE SECOND youngest in the family. Alec and Angus were never the closest of twins—Alec gravitated toward Malcolm and his sense of adventure, while Angus retained a sense of responsibility to his home and father. When their mother dies, it is Angus their ducal father turns to, all but ignoring his other sons in his grief.

Alec is happy Angus is there to look after their father while he and Mal enjoy themselves traveling and reveling. When Malcolm begins running the distillery, Alec pursues his dream of painting and studies art in Paris, Rome, and Venice.

His adventuring comes to an end when the Jacobite Uprising begins. Months before this, Alec had on impulse eloped with an opera dancer from Paris, who then died bearing his child. Stricken with grief, Alec returns to Paris to rescue his child and make sure she's looked after.

Alec suffers much loss during the Uprising, including his twin, Angus. The loss makes him as determined as Malcolm to keep the family together, no matter what it takes.

Before he returns to England in search of Will at the beginning of his book, Alec had become an art tutor to Louis XV's of France's children, legitimate and illegitimate, and well known in France. He's listed as dead at Culloden so decides to make the best of his exile, but he also helps Malcolm design the gardens of Kilmorgan, to which he and Mal hope someday to return.

Meanwhile, he'll raise his daughter the best he can, making sure the world she grows up in is a safe one.

Lady Celia Fotheringhay

LADY CELIA WAS RAISED to be dutiful, and fully expects she'll marry a man that will bolster her father's career. Her father, the Duke of Crenshaw, is the leader of the Whig party, who backs and funds MPs running for office, hosts gatherings at his house to discuss politics, and raises regiments to fight for king and country.

One regiment he funds fought at Culloden against the Scots, and contained his son, Edward. Celia loves her brother, who always returned her affection, until Celia refused to marry the man her mother wants to pair her with.

Celia has a sense of duty, but she refuses to martyr herself in misery for the good of the Whig party. When she turns down the proposal, she is ostracized not only in her own family but in society as well. Celia tells herself she doesn't mind—she'll stay at home with her father and learn to paint, but her restlessness can't be contained.

She's not certain what life will have in store for her now— she will likely rusticate at her father's estate, but she wants so much more. Unfortunately, in her day, women were confined to a sphere—home, charity work, chapel, and social places like theaters and assembly rooms, but a woman in disgrace was more confined than most. Celia feels trapped by this life and ready to break free …

Celia is well read, having sat in on all lessons with her brother, and also took to art. She finds her escape reading and discussing books with her father, and also in art, loving to draw the spread of a cityscape before her from her studio at the top of her father's house. High above the world, she can be free of its pettiness.

She knows much about the battles of the Jacobite Uprising, from her brothers' stories, and can't help pity the Scots who'd lost everything, no matter that others portray them as bloodthirsty and vicious fighters.

Celia never dreams she'll face a Highland warrior herself, until she goes to Alec Mackenzie studio for art lessons, and walks in on him, slumbering with a babe in his arms …

———

Important Secondary Characters
　　Jenny Mackenzie (Alec's baby daughter)
　　Will Mackenzie (Alec's adventuring / spy brother)
　　Lady Flora (Formidable, i.e., scary, mentor to Celia)
　　Duke of Crenshaw (Celia's loving father)
　　Duchess of Crenshaw (Celia's mother, even scarier than Lady Flora)
　　Edward Fotheringhay (Celia's brother)
　　Mrs. Reynolds (Lady Flora's companion)
　　Josette Oswald (friend of Will's who runs a boardinghouse and place of safety)
　　Glenna Oswald (Josette's daughter)
　　Stuart Cameron (friend to Will and Alec, fellow Scotsman in danger)

AUTHOR'S NOTES

Author's Notes

I HAD DECIDED WHILE WRITING MALCOLM'S BOOK THAT ALEC AND Will needed stories of their own, and I really wanted to get to them.

But—Malcolm's book (*The Stolen Mackenzie Bride*) was my last contracted one at Berkley. That was fine with me at the time, because I was already contracted to write more books in my paranormal series, Shifters Unbound, which were coming out back to back.

When I was ready to write Mackenzies again, my publisher told me they weren't interested in more historical romances from me. I said "fine," because happily I can now publish books myself.

However, in my contracts, I have to at least submit a proposal for a new book to my publisher, and then they can either turn it down, or I can turn down the offer. So, in the spring of 2016, I wrote the proposal and first four chapters of Alec's book and sent it to my editor.

It takes time for editors to respond, even for routine submissions, so I waited a long time to hear back. When I did, my editor said she really liked the story, so she was going to try to get the publisher to take it.

The publisher did make me an offer, but a half-hearted one. There was no guarantee they'd take another book after Alec, and—the clincher for me—they weren't going to publish Alec's book until 2019, four years after Malcolm's book!

This is what made me say a firm, "No" and go indie with the Mackenzies.

This was about the middle of 2016. I had about seven or so other books to write (a couple in the Shifters series, plus I had also just sold the Kat Holloway mysteries; and I needed to keep up with my Captain Lacey and Riding Hard series—lots of work!). I put Alec on my schedule and finally was able to get to him in the summer of 2017 for a fall release.

Yay! I sweated this release, fearing no one would have any interest (or even remember the series), or wouldn't find it because it's not in bookstores (though bookstores can special order it), but I was pleasantly surprised! *Alec Mackenzie's Art of Seduction* did very well (in all languages) and continues to be one of my constant sellers.

———

Alec's book is a bit different from Malcolm's. Alec is stuck in London, searching for his brother Will. Only the Duke of Crenshaw, a powerful supporter of King George II, might know where Will is. Alec can't risk exposing himself to the duke, who would arrest him as a traitor, but the duke has a daughter ...

Celia was refreshing for me. She is another sheltered miss, like Mary, Malcolm's heroine, but eighteenth-century women were a bit more aware of the vulgarity of life, less hidden away than their Regency and Victorian counterparts. In the eighteenth century, for example, women could take part in politics

—while they couldn't hold office, they could campaign for candidates, and often held salons or dinners where they participated robustly in political debates.

While eighteenth-century women had fewer legal rights than women in the nineteenth century, these eighteenth-century ladies were able to speak more openly, and they weren't expected to be uninterested in sex—young unmarried women still had to be of spotless virtue, yes, but sex was not the taboo subject it later became.

The eighteenth century was also the time when what we consider "modern" living began. Many of the scientific discoveries of physics, chemistry, botany, and astronomy happened then, as well as global voyages made for scientific reasons, proving the world was a real place full of real people, no magic lands or hidden continents or magical people inhabiting the globe. Map making was improved, and the Prime Meridian was established at Greenwich as a way of calculating longitude (which had long eluded seafaring Europe).

For my master's degree in English literature, I extensively studied the eighteenth century (from Defoe to Jonathan Swift, to Richardson's Clarissa, to Henry Fielding, Fanny Burney, and on into the early nineteenth century with Jane Austen). It was an interesting time, both elegant and violent.

If you want a look into the life of a young debutante in the eighteenth century, from that debutante's point of view, I highly recommend Fanny Burney's *Evelina*. One of my favorite novels of the past!

SYNOPSIS

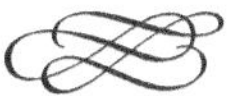

LONDON 1746

ALEC MACKENZIE KNOWS THAT LADY CELIA IS KEY TO FINDING his missing brother. The trouble is, Alec is supposed to be dead, and he needs the world to keep believing he is.

Alec will do anything to find his brother, Will, including pretend to be a penniless drawing master to London aristocrats. The one man who might know where his brother is being held is a powerful duke, and that duke has daughter who needs art lessons ...

Lady Celia is intrigued by the Scotsman, so obviously a warrior, who pretends he is not. She is also intrigued by his instruction on painting the human form, something no young lady should take an interest in. But Celia, ruined by The Disaster and already beyond hope, dares to let the Highlander teach her all he knows ...

EXCERPT: ALEC MACKENZIE'S ART OF SEDUCTION

The Attic of Kilmorgan Castle, June 1892

IAN MACKENZIE HEARD HIS NAME LIKE MUSIC ON THE AIR. HE didn't look away from the task he'd set himself, laying each page in its neat stack on the desk, exactly where it needed to go. He knew Beth would come to him the same as he knew when his next breath would be.

She entered the attic with a rustle of skirts, pausing in the open doorway to push a strand of hair from her face. Ian did not have to glance up at her to follow her every move.

"Ian? What on earth are you doing?"

Ian did not reply until he'd laid another page in its stack and squared it to match the notebook next to it. Beth liked him to answer, but Ian wanted to think out the sentences in his head beforehand so he could respond to her satisfaction. What *he* considered the most important part of an explanation was not always what others did.

"Reading," he said after a moment. "About the family."

"Oh?" Beth moved to him, the faint cinnamon scent that clung to her distracting. "You mean your family history?"

Ian had divided the surface of the large kneehole desk, left over from a century ago, into sections, one for every generation of the Mackenzie family. Those sections were divided into immediate members of that family. Papers, letters, ledgers, and notebooks had their own piles in each section, and they were stacked chronologically.

He laid his broad hand on the leftmost pile. "Old Malcolm." Malcolm's wife Mary's journal had provided entertainment for many a winter night with tales of Malcolm's exploits.

"Alec Mackenzie." Ian rested his hand on the next pile then the one after that. "And Will."

"You found their papers?" Beth asked in surprise. "I thought Alec and Will Mackenzie fled into exile after Culloden, when the entire family was listed as dead."

Ian shrugged. "All is here." He didn't speculate on how the letters and journals of Will, Alec, and their families had arrived at Kilmorgan—he only cared that they had.

"Have you read them?" Beth looked over the neat stacks, a little smile on her lips. Ian had come to learn this expression meant she was interested.

Ian didn't answer. He'd of course read each paper, each notebook, before deciding into which stack it should go.

Alec Mackenzie had left sketchbooks full of drawings of his children, his wife, his brothers, his sisters-in-law, his father. Another portfolio held sketches of the skylines of London and of Paris, and of the lands around Kilmorgan, as well as portraits of Alec Mackenzie himself, some of them intimate, Alec only a kilt, a wicked glint in his eye.

Ian opened one of the sketchbooks and pushed it toward Beth. This was of Alec as a young man, dressed in the manner of the early eighteenth century. His pale shirt had cotton lace at the cuffs, his long hair was pulled into a queue, and a strong face laughed out of the picture at them.

"Intriguing." Beth's breath was warm on Ian's cheek. "He was the artistic one, I gather, like Mac." She touched the paper. "But who drew this? Was his wife an artist too?"

"Celia." Ian turned over a page to show a young woman with dark curls under a small lacy cap, a round face, and a rather impish smile. "She drew the cities."

"Oh." Beth clasped her hands as Ian revealed a stretch of London as it had been in 1746. Rooftops marched through the fog—she recognized the view from Grosvenor Square toward Piccadilly and Green Park, but gaps existed where houses were now. "That must be the sketch for the painting that hangs in Mac's wing. How exciting." She looked at Ian with shining eyes. "Tell me about them." Her smile widened. "I know you remember every word of these." She touched the cover of a journal.

For a moment, Ian's interest in his ancestors faded as he lost himself in Beth's blue eyes. Beth was beauty, she was silence, she was the peace in his heart.

She was also stubborn in her own quiet way. She grasped his sleeve and towed him to a dusty settee, one gilded and uphol-stered in petit point, which had come to Kilmorgan straight from Versailles.

Beth nestled into Ian's side and drew her feet up under her, a further distraction from deeds of the remote past. "Go on," she said. "Tell me their story. All the details. I'll let you know which bits to leave out when you tell it again to the children."

Ian pictured the two of them gathering with Jamie, Belle, and Megan in one of their cozy chambers in Ian's wing of the house, plus his son's and daughters' antics and blurted questions as Ian tried to tell them a straightforward tale. Jamie and Belle especially constantly interrupted him, and stories rarely got finished the way Ian planned them. He looked forward to it.

For now, Beth was warm at his side, her hair soft beneath his lips.

"Once upon a time," he began—Beth had explained that all stories should begin with *Once upon a time*.

"A few months after the Battle of Culloden," Ian continued, "Alec Mackenzie left Paris and returned to England, in search of Will, who'd vanished for too long a while. Will's contacts hadn't seen him, rumor had it he might have been arrested, and the family was worried.

"The last place Will had been reported was London, so Alec packed his things, took his daughter, assumed a false name, and went to London ..."

———

LONDON, 1746

The screaming wove through Alec Mackenzie's dreams and jerked him from sleep.

For a breath he was back on the battlefield, men keening as they died. Soldiers shoved swords into his clansmen, his friends—never mind they were injured and begging for mercy.

Another breath, and the noise resolved itself into the wail of a child who didn't understand the pain of new teeth.

Alec wrenched himself out of bed, his nightshirt slipping from one large shoulder, his dark red hair tumbling into his eyes. He righted the nightshirt and stumbled into the chilly hall, not worried about trivial things like dressing gown and slippers.

No one stirred in the upper floors of the dark house on Grosvenor Square. This was one of the square's larger mansions, six stories high, four rooms wide, and several rooms deep. Alec's chamber was one floor down from the attic, his hostess pretending that Alec's position wasn't *quite* that of a servant.

Alec's daughter, Jenny, on the other hand, had to keep to a room in the attics, lest his hostess' guests, the cream of London's intellectual society and patrons of the arts, discover that a *child* actually stayed in the house.

One-year-old Jenny didn't care where she slept, but the positioning of the rooms made it a job to rush to Jenny's side when she needed her da'.

Alec shouldered his way to the back stairs and hurried up a flight. His feet, hardened from running over Highland hills, never felt the roughness of the wooden stairs.

He bolted into Jenny's nursery, cursing when he didn't see the nursemaid Lady Flora had hired. The poor woman needed to sleep, of course, but she was snoring in the next room through Jenny's screams, which were winding up to a pure Highlander howl. Alec's youngest brother, Mal, had screeched like that.

"All right, wee one," Alec whispered in Erse as he lifted his daughter into his arms, her soft warmth against his cheek. "Papa's here."

Jenny continued to cry, but she turned to Alec's shoulder and snuggled down, recognizing her father. Alec held her close, snatching up the bottle of medicine the nursemaid had concocted for Jenny's teething. Swore by it, the woman did.

Alec worked off the cork one-handed and flinched when the acrid stench of pure gin curled into his nose.

"Bloody hell." Alec threw the bottle into the smoldering fire, where it splintered, sending a spurt of blue flame up the chimney. "Well, lass, we'll have to find ye another nursemaid in the morning, won't we? One who won't poison ye with this filth."

In the meantime, there was nothing to soothe Jenny's pain, no other food, drink, or medicine near.

The room was cold as well. The small fire was here at Alec's insistence—Lady Flora's austere housekeeper saw no reason to waste fuel on a babe.

Alec lifted Jenny's blankets from her cot, wrapped her up, and carried her down the stairs to his own bedchamber. He laid her in the bed and then folded his big frame into a chair that he dragged next to it, not wanting to take the chance of rolling on her in his sleep. She was so tiny, and Alec was a bloody great Highlander.

Jenny warmed and calmed, Alec's big hand on her back, and she slept. Alec watched her, knowing that if anyone found Jenny here, he'd be standing before his hostess while she lifted her nose in the air and reminded him exactly how dangerous was his mission and that he should have left his child in France.

His daughter was silent now, sleeping in innocent happiness. Alec pulled a quilt over himself and drifted off, his slumber not quite so innocent and in no way happy.

But Jenny was safe, all that mattered for the moment. Now to make sure the rest of his family was as well.

———

"YOU'RE LATE," Lady Flora, Dowager Marchioness of Ellesmere, said as Lady Celia Fotheringhay hastened into Lady Flora's private salon, Celia's portfolio sliding dangerously from under her arm.

Celia had never been in this room before. Whenever she called upon Lady Flora, she was only allowed into the grand salon, which was two stories high, gilded and painted within an inch of its life, and stuffed with important people.

The *right* important people, Celia amended—the intellectuals and high-minded of the *ton* who supported the Whigs in their power and glory.

Celia had also never been inside this house without her mother, the formidable Duchess of Crenshaw. Lady Flora was said to eat innocent young ladies for breakfast, and so an older, stronger woman was a necessary guard.

For this visit, Celia was on her own and shown into a compact, sunny room on the first floor. This chamber was no less ostentatious than the grand salon, albeit on a smaller scale. The audience took place, alarmingly, at breakfast, and for an entirely different reason than Celia's previous visits.

Lady Flora was forty but her slim body and unlined face compared to a woman of twenty. She wore her golden hair pulled back into a simple knot, and her light blue eyes held as much chill as her voice.

She looked up at Celia from the remains of a repast. Her empty plate was whisked away by a silent footman, while another equally silent footman placed a cup by her elbow. Lady Flora poured thick coffee into it, the trickle of liquid breaking the delicate hush.

Celia's portfolio chose that moment to slip to the floor with a clatter. The clasp broke, and drawings of misty hills, vases of flowers, and Celia's family cat floated across the carpet.

"Drat," Celia said under her breath. The portfolio was awkward—she was always dropping the blasted thing.

To Lady Flora's exasperated sigh, Celia fell to her knees, her striped skirts billowing, to collect the drawings. She heard Lady Flora sigh again, and the two footmen appeared next to Celia, collecting the pages with deft, gloved hands.

The footmen restored the drawings neatly and efficiently to the portfolio and laid the large thing at the end of the table. A maid appeared out of nowhere for the sole purpose of helping Celia to her feet, then vanished.

"You're late," Lady Flora repeated.

The gilded clock on the mantelpiece gently announced it was quarter past eight. "Mother was in a bit of a state this morning," Celia said quickly as she brushed off her skirts. "There's an important debate today, you see, and Papa was wavering on what he wanted to say ..." Her mother's opinion on his vacillation had rung through the house.

Celia trailed off under Lady Flora's glare. Lady Flora obviously had no interest in the Duchess of Crenshaw's machinations regarding Parliamentary debates, at least not at the moment.

"The drawing master I've engaged is celebrated the length and breadth of France," Lady Flora said coolly. "He is instructing you as a favor to me, and to your mama."

Celia knew good and well how obligated she was to her mother and Lady Flora. She'd been told so at least seventy-two times a day for the past several weeks, ever since the Disaster. Drawing lessons with a professional artist was only one idea about what to do with the problem of Celia.

Celia was still astonished that her mother had consented to let her have the lessons at all, but her father had for once squared his shoulders and taken Celia's side against his wife. Then again, when Lady Flora explained that Celia could learn to paint portraits of the great and good of the Whig party, contributing to the cause of making Britain a world power, the duchess had capitulated.

Lady Flora's glare strengthened as Celia stood mutely. The woman was quite beautiful, in a brittle sort of way, which made her more daunting. Celia knew she ought to pity Lady Flora, who'd been devastated when her grown daughter had died a few years ago, but any grief had long since frosted over.

"Well, go on up," Lady Flora said impatiently. "A gaping mouth only lets in flies, so pray, keep it closed."

Celia popped her mouth shut, made a polite curtsy, and said, "Yes, Lady Flora."

As Celia turned to take up her portfolio, Lady Flora said witheringly, "No, no. A *servant* will carry it upstairs."

Celia snatched her hands back from the portfolio and hastened to the door, eager to remove herself from Lady Flora's presence. Before she could leave, however, she had to turn back.

"Um, where *is* the studio?"

Another heavy sigh. "Fourth floor, in the front, near the staircase. The footman will show you."

Lady Flora waved a hand in dismissal—like the empress of a proud Oriental country, Celia reflected as she hurried away. She bit back a laugh picturing Lady Flora in flowing Chinese garments, flicking her fingers while hundreds of lackeys bowed to her on their knees.

Celia lost her smile quickly. The image was far too close to the mark.

She followed the footman in satin breeches and powdered wig out of the room and up three more flights of stairs. Celia was gasping by the time they reached the top, but the footman breathed as calmly as he would after a lazy stroll in a garden.

He opened a door and indicated, with an elegant gloved hand, that she should go inside. Celia scurried past him, and the footman bowed and withdrew, closing the door behind him, the latch catching with a faint *click*.

Celia found herself in a quiet room flooded with sunshine. The chamber held a few chairs and a recamier draped with red cloth, an easel, a table filled with jars and brushes, and another table strewn with square frames of wood, folds of canvas, and a sheaf of drawing paper.

A fire crackled in the hearth, but except for Celia, the room was empty. No artist's assistant bustled about preparing canvases or mixing paints, no artist looked up to comment on her tardiness.

Celia had met portrait painters, including the celebrated Mr. Hogarth, when they'd come to paint her mother, father, brother, and herself, and she knew what artists looked like. Her instructor would either be thin and nervous with a wife and five children to feed, or elderly, fussy, and set in his ways, with a habit of making inelegant noises.

Lady Flora had said the artist was celebrated in France, so Celia pictured a small, dark-haired man with a turned-up nose and a thick accent, who'd click his tongue against his teeth when he regarded Celia's meager efforts.

Celia explored the room and the artist's accoutrements as she waited, hoping to find an example of the drawing master's work, but she saw none.

After a few moments, another footman discreetly glided in and laid Celia's portfolio on a table then glided back out again.

Celia hastened after him to ask if he'd fetch the drawing master, but the footman had gone by the time she reached the hall. Lady Flora's servants were trained to come and go like ghosts.

She hesitated in the stairwell, which was dim after the bright room, the only light coming from a shaded window on the landing.

How long was she to wait? Did the drawing master keep erratic hours, coming and going as he pleased? Was he a famous Frenchman quite annoyed he had to teach the likes of Lady Celia Fotheringhay, an English duke's spoiled daughter? Had he drowned his frustration in wine and now snored away the morning?

Well, he could cease being rude about it. Celia started down the stairs, determined to find another servant to fetch this haughty drawing master. If he lay in bed in a drunken stupor, it would be his own fault when the footman burst in to roust him.

A faint cry made Celia pause. The sound had come from somewhere within the house, behind one of the doors on the very floor she'd left.

Another whimper came to her, muffled but unmistakable. Somewhere down the hall, a baby was crying.

A baby in this refined house was as out of place as a weed that dared show itself in her mother's garden. Celia couldn't imagine Lady Flora letting any of her servants do anything so human as have children, nor allowing a friend's child to visit. Lady Flora's acquaintances kept their children well hidden from the world, in any case, not bringing them to London until they were old enough to be out in society.

Celia rustled back up the stairs and to the nearest door, opened it, found that room empty, and went to the next one. She tried a few more doors, seeing only elegant furnishings in the chambers behind them, all the while the fretful cry continued.

The chamber three down from the studio held the warmth of a bright fire and was filled with sunlight, a beam slanting from the window to touch the deep auburn hair of a man lying on a chair with his head back, fast asleep. A blue and white quilt covered his body, and in the clasp of one big arm was a tiny child with bright red hair. The babe snuggled into him, restless.

The man's face was slack with sleep, but it was strong, square and hard, the nose sharp, once broken. A brush of red whiskers covered his jaw, a brighter color than the hair that straggled across his cheek, and his mouth was a flat, grim line. He was large-boned, his body taking up the entire delicate-legged chair, the quilt drooping to reveal a wide spread of shoulders in a loose nightshirt. One bare foot protruded from the bottom end of the quilt.

Celia's gaze slid to the foot in fascination. She'd never seen a man unshod before. Even her brother, older by three years, hadn't gone barefoot when they'd played together in the grass-lands of Kent.

This foot was broad but well-shaped, the toes curled slightly in his sleep. The strength displayed in that appendage alone suggested that the rest of him would be as powerful. The blunt-fingered hand that cradled the child bore out Celia's observation.

He transfixed her. Celia had never encountered a man as basic, as *natural*, as this sleeping giant. He splayed formidably on the chair, like a lion at rest, not hunting at the moment, saving his strength for later.

Celia's gaze returned to his foot. Her too-vivid imagination pictured him opening his eyes, reaching out his hand to draw her near, sliding his strong foot up under her skirts along her calf. She could feel the warmth of the rough sole through her finely knit stocking, his leg twining hers as he pulled her closer. She'd tumble into his lap, and he'd stroke her hair with the same gentleness as he held the babe, and then he'd smile.

Fire seared Celia's chest. Her breath, which seemed to have left her, came rushing back with sudden sharpness.

She took a quick step back, but something about the man would not let her flee. His presence held her in place as unswervingly as Lady Flora's stares.

If *he* was the drawing master, he didn't look French at all, but Scottish, like those great Highlanders who'd invaded England this past winter. Celia saw no claymore or dirk lying about or any evidence of a tartan to confirm this theory, only a man in a nightshirt under a quilt, holding a tiny child.

Celia could fathom no reason for a Highlander to be here, unless Lady Flora had given him leave. Lady Flora was eccentric enough to do so—she gave sanction to all sorts of scandalous people, like poets and artists, actors and musicians. Lady Flora's lady's companion, Mrs. Reynolds, it was whispered, had once been a courtesan.

Not all Highlanders had tried to rebel, Celia's brother had told her. Half of them had fought for King George and Britain.

Even so, being in the presence of such a man was unnerving. *And,* Celia made herself be honest, *a little bit exciting.* Celia was never allowed to come anywhere near men who might be considered the least bit dangerous.

Celia could, of course, run back downstairs and ask Lady Flora who the man was and why he was here, but she didn't have the nerve to face the reptile in her den again. The lion in this one was less frightening.

She went to the man's side, disconcerted at how warm the air was next to him. The baby opened its eyes, looked up at Celia with complete trust, and said, *"Blurp."*

"Sir." Celia bent down as close as she dared, ready to dart back as she did when she woke her cat too quickly. "Sir."

The Highlander slept on, his lips parting to let out a snore. The snore wasn't loud, but it was deep and low-pitched, a sound only a man could make.

"Sir." Celia poked her finger into his shoulder.

Nothing. He was a lump of quilt-covered rock. His shoulder was hard as granite, her fingers not making a dent.

The baby gurgled at her encouragingly, but if the father would not wake up when his child moved, Celia doubted he'd respond to her soft taps.

Unfortunately for the Highlander, Celia had been raised by a mother who had no patience for anyone in her house, from the scullery maid to the duke himself, being a lie-abed. The Duchess of Crenshaw had all sorts of tricks to drag a person out of sweet slumber.

Celia moved around the bed to the washstand, lifted the delicate porcelain pitcher, brought it back to the chair, upended the pitcher, and poured a cascade of water over the exposed foot.

FIONA AND THE THREE WISE HIGHLANDERS

CHARACTERS

Stuart Cameron

Stuart Cameron was a close friend of Duncan Mackenzie, oldest brother of Malcolm in *The Stolen Mackenzie Bride*. He is captured after the battle of Culloden, along with Will Mackenzie, both imprisoned, where they are subject to cruel "experiments." He and Will are rescued by Alec Mackenzie in *Alec Mackenzie's Art of Seduction* and Cameron travels to France to recover.

Stuart has never forgotten Fiona Macdonald, the lady he'd loved but argued with the night before he left to join the Uprising. The memory of her sustained him through his dark days in prison, but he never thought he'd see her again.

Hungry for his home, he persuades Gair Murray, smuggler, and his sidekick Padruig, to get him back to Scotland and to the Cameron lands. Along the way, they pause for rest in a tavern, and there, Cameron beholds his beloved Fiona for the first time in a long while …

Fiona Macdonald

FIONA MACDONALD IS the sister of a man who decided that staying loyal to Hanoverian Britain during the Uprising of 1745 was the more prudent choice. Broc fought against his fellow Highlanders, then was wounded at Falkirk and had to sit out the rest of the rebellion.

Fiona adamantly disagreed with Broc, but she was also incensed at Stuart for rushing off to take up the cause, falling out with Broc and herself before he went.

After the war was over, when she thought she'd never see Stuart again, Fiona took to aiding the fleeing Highlanders whenever she could, though she risked her own freedom and life in doing so.

She's never forgotten Stuart, the only man she ever loved, but she's resigned to looking after her brother and surreptitiously helping out fugitives for the rest of her life.

Until Stuart walks into the tavern in which she chose to spend Christmas, and Fiona's world changes.

———

IMPORTANT SECONDARY CHARACTERS
　　Gair Murray (smuggler and rogue)
　　Padruig (Gair's partner, the more dangerous man)
　　Broc Macdonald (Fiona's brother)
　　Una (Fiona's redoubtable maid)
　　Neilan and Tavin Macdonald (Broc and Fiona's annoying cousins)

AUTHOR'S NOTES

I became interested in Stuart Cameron when I first met him in the pages of *A Stolen Mackenzie Bride.* I never know who will show up when I set out to write books, beyond the main characters. He was a close friend of Duncan Mackenzie (oldest brother to Malcolm), and Stuart's descendent, Elspeth Cameron, is the mother of Ian, Mac, Cam, and Hart.

When I was approached to contribute a story to a Scottish Christmas-themed anthology, I decided it was a great opportunity to write more about Stuart, and continue his history after Culloden. We see him again in *Alec Mackenzie's Art of Seduction,* and learn of his fate, but I wanted more. Where did he come from? What HEA was in store for him?

The one requirement for the anthology, beyond it being set in Scotland at Christmas, was that we used Balthazar's inn as part of the setting. I thought it a great place for Stuart to stumble across his former love, Fiona Macdonald.

I really like Fiona. She grieved Stuart, believing him dead, but she isn't a wilting weed. She runs around the Highlands on her own with her maid, doing what would be considered treasonous deeds.

She's in a hard place, because her brother, still nursing his injury sustained while fighting the army of Prince Charlie, is a dedicated Hanoverian (on the side of the British Crown.) But her heart is with the defeated Highlanders, so she is defying her brother by helping them. She also has no intention of being married off to the man her brother chooses.

The story also shows the plight of those in the immediate aftermath of the Uprising of 1745-46. It was a bleak and cruel time, which I tried to show while not making it too depressing for a Christmas story.

Also, I enjoyed bringing back Gair and Padruig, two reprobates who feature in the pages of the 18th-century Mackenzie tales. We first meet them as co-conspirators of Mal in *The Stolen Mackenzie Bride,* and they go on to play a role in *The Devilish Lord Will.*

Gair will do anything for cash, and so the fugitive Stuart persuades the pair to smuggle him back to Scotland from France, where he has been hiding and recuperating. He crosses Scotland disguised as Gair and Padruig's servant, and I could not resist calling them "The Three Wise Highlanders."

I have enjoyed starting off the 18th-century tales with a frame story—Ian Mackenzie relating the history of his family to his children.

If you have not picked Fiona and Cameron's story, I urge you to try it. It has become one of my favorites.

SYNOPSIS

NEAR INVERNESS, DECEMBER 1746

Stuart Cameron must fulfill a task to repay the reprobates Gair and Padruig, who have smuggled him across Scotland at Christmas in 1746. Fiona Macdonald, sister to his enemy, is the only one who can help.

Fiona is amazed that Stuart has returned from what she thought was certain death, but she's on a mission, and can't stop and fulfill her heart by hauling him into her arms. Stuart's plight is dangerous, and she has to choose between helping him and continuing her undertakings.

Padruig gives them no choice about Stuart's repayment, which involves a dangerous trek across a Scotland still teeming with British soldiers to the house of Fiona's brother, who has vowed to kill Stuart on sight.

This story takes place between the action in *Alec Mackenzie's Art of Seduction* and *The Devilish Lord Will*.

EXCERPT: FIONA AND THE THREE WISE HIGHLANDERS

THE THREE MEN WHO SWAGGERED INTO BALTHAZAR'S INN WERE bundled in drab thick coats, boots that must have squelched through every patch of mud from here to Aberdeen, and drenched hats pulled down to their ears.

Fiona Macdonald sat very still in the warm corner near the fireplace, feet buried in the straw on the floor. Beside her, Una, her maid, long-time companion, and fellow conspirator, stiffened, ready to become a guard dog in an instant. Una was not happy that Fiona had to rest in the common room, but the inn was crowded tonight, and a chamber was being readied for her by the innkeeper's daughter.

"We come bearing gifts," the smallest of the men sang out. He was a disreputable fellow, who removed his hat to reveal sun-bleached brown hair. His skin had the tough brown hue of old leather, but his smile was wide, his teeth whole if stained. "Is that not what ye do when ye see a star guiding ye to an inn at Christmastide? Is there a wee babe in the stables we should visit?"

The men in the smoky common room laughed. Through the din, the innkeeper, Balthazar, stroked his beard with his fingers. "There's already one wise man here, Gair Murray, and I'd not let ye within ten feet of a wee babe."

"Ye know me, then?" Gair's smile widened. "And ye bandy me name about, do ye? Worth a free jar, I'm thinking."

"Everyone knows ye, Gair. You're among friends here."

Not likely, Fiona thought as she wrapped her hands around her cooling mug of tea. Gair Murray, a smuggler, had no true friends, not really. He did favors for men up and down Scotland, but for pay, at the same time on the lookout for anything he could lift for himself.

His only friend in the world, if he could be called so, was the thin but much taller man next to him. Padruig looked out at the world with one gray eye, the other, lost in some long-ago battle, covered with a leather patch.

Both men wore cloaks over their coats, Padruig's black, Gair's brown with a stripe that made it appear suspiciously like an old tartan. Fiona hoped he wouldn't be caught wearing a forbidden plaid.

Padruig, as usual, said nothing as the more garrulous Gair bantered with the innkeeper.

Fiona regarded the third figure with growing tension. He was a huge bear of a man, a Highlander without doubt, his hair a strange shade of black. Soot, she realized as a streak of it came off when he removed his hat. He was trying to disguise the true color.

He was muffled to his ears in a plain gray scarf, he the only of the three not to have a cloak wrapped about him. He hunched his back as though trying to conceal his height, but he did a poor job of it. This was a man used to standing straight, proud, arrogant.

Perhaps his spirit had been broken, as so many of them had been. Fiona had once been a proud Highlander herself.

And still am. We are defeated, not gone.

The man had to pull down his scarf to drink the tankard of ale Balthazar shoved onto a table for the three men. More soot smeared from his hair, which shone like a streak of sudden flame.

Only one man had hair that brilliant shade of red. But he was dead, captured by the Hanoverians after Culloden, taken prisoner, vanished. Fiona's heart had died that day. He'd have been executed by now. Fiona's nightmares had showed her his death so many times in the last eight months that she was certain of it.

Until the man turned his head and looked at her.

Blue eyes like summer skies skewered her, and the firm mouth that had once kissed like fire pinched into a frown. He rose from the stool he'd just taken, as though unable to stop himself.

Stuart Cameron.

Her brother's enemy and the man who'd stolen her peace before he'd run off to join the doomed army of *Teàrlach mhic Seamas.*

———

PADRUIG EYED STUART IN CONCERN, though Gair continued telling the men next to them some tale he was inventing about their travels. Gair's constant banter kept people mollified until too late to recognize his perfidy.

Fiona Macdonald shouldn't be sitting in a wayside tavern in the middle of the Scottish Highlands with English soldiers hunting down any they even thought smelled like a Jacobite. She should have taken ship months ago to France or the Low Countries, or at least be home with her brother, anywhere she'd be safe. It was typical of her to decide not to flee or hide.

Stuart could not stop himself crossing the tavern to her. The room was crowded, so much so that none paid much attention to another weary traveler pushing through their midst.

The eagle-eyed maid, Una, glared up at Stuart as he approached. So she was still with Fiona. Loyal of her. Fiona sipped tea as though she noticed no one.

Stuart knew Fiona had seen him and recognized him. Best to corner her before she burst out with his true identity … not that the Fiona Macdonald he knew would do such a thing, although she might in her surprise. Or Una might, indignant at his return.

Stuart came to a halt next to Fiona, pretending to warm his hands at the fire. His heart thumped with Fiona's nearness, the flames before him nothing to the slow heat that churned through his body.

It had been so long since he'd seen her, touched her, simply enjoyed her presence. He'd dreamed of her, the image of her face, her smile, keeping him from the very bottom of despair.

"What are ye doing here, lass?" Stuart asked in a quiet voice.

"What are you?" Fiona's answer came as quietly. She rested her mug on her lap. "You're alive, I see."

"Aye. Barely."

"What happened to ye?"

"A guest of his majesty." Stuart shrugged, trying to maintain the stance of a servant who mooched along after Gair and Padruig. "Then France."

Fiona's eyes widened slightly. She had the loveliest eyes, green like jade in sunlight, which set off her very dark hair. He saw her realization that he'd been a prisoner—and she'd never know all of that horror if Stuart could help it. Escaped by the skin of his teeth—and with the help of the Mackenzie brothers —over the Channel to France. He'd rested and recovered there, but he'd soon longed to be back in Scotland, and so had hunted up the expert smugglers Gair and Padruig, and hired them to provide him passage.

"Ye should have stayed." Fiona's voice was barely above a whisper.

Did she mean in Paris or in prison? Stuart let the corner of his mouth pull into a half smile. "Missing home."

"Home isn't safe."

"Is it safe for you?" Stuart countered.

He saw the flinch Fiona tried to hide, though Una didn't bother to smother her scowl. Not much older than Fiona, Una had the flaxen hair of a Viking and the demeanor to match. She guarded Fiona like a lioness. For that, Stuart would forgive her scowls.

"Safe enough," Fiona said. "The soldiers don't always stop a woman."

"More fool they." The greatest fault the Hanoverians had was to underestimate Scotswomen. The English kept their own women so sheltered and subdued they assumed their northern neighbors did the same. "I thought ye'd be on a ship heading across the seas." *Without your waste of a brother,* he finished silently.

"Broc is ill," Fiona said, the gleam in her eyes telling Stuart she knew what he was thinking. "He never recovered after his injury at Falkirk."

"Does he still claim it was me who shot him?" Stuart allowed the smile to form.

Broc Macdonald, who'd stubbornly thrown in his lot with King Geordie, had suffered a leg wound at the Battle of Falkirk and had been carried, wailing, from the field. So Stuart had been told. He hadn't witnessed the injury.

"Yes." Fiona's own smile flashed then vanished. "Though I told him ye couldn't have."

"Loyal woman."

"'Tisn't loyalty. I know the truth."

Stuart barely heard her. Fiona's smile transcended her drab garments, shawl, and the faded cap she wore under a broad-brimmed hat. The ensemble made her look like an ordinary farm woman, instead of the laird's sister she was. Her beauty was like a breath of air in this musty place, returning the memory of her laughter, her quick wit, her sparkling eyes.

He recalled dancing with her in her brother's house not long before Prince Teàrlach marched on Edinburgh, her warm hand in his, her lithe grace as they moved in the patterns of the reel.

He recalled her red lips that neared his as they turned, hand in hand, then moved tantalizingly out of reach. The kiss on the terrace after that, when he'd wrapped his plaid around her and warmed them both, had been a fine end to the evening.

"Still," Stuart made himself say, "kind of ye to put in a word for me."

"You didn't shoot him because you were keeping Duncan Mackenzie alive." Fiona's sudden frown almost matched Una's in severity. She hadn't liked Duncan's recklessness and had feared he'd be Stuart's death. Duncan had perished on Culloden Moor, the poor man. He'd had all the arrogance but not the quick thinking of his younger brothers.

"For my sins." Stuart leaned closer, returning to the pretense of warming his hands. "But what are ye doing *here*, lass? In the middle of nowhere the day before Christmas Eve?"

Fiona glanced behind Stuart and folded her lips. *Hmm.* She didn't want to say in front of anyone who might hear. He saw none but Highlanders in the room, but one couldn't be certain which way any man's loyalty lay.

If she were any other lady, Stuart would shrug and not pursue it. But this was Fiona Macdonald, and she never did anything not worth learning about. He'd have the secret out of her. Perhaps later, in a dark chamber, with the door locked …

A distinct presence made itself felt—or smelled—at his side. Both women winced, and even Stuart took a step away. Gair rarely bathed, and the heat of the close room made him ripe.

"The question I ought to ask," Fiona said, pretending to ignore Gair. "Is why are you in such disreputable company?"

"Ah, she breaks me heart," Gair said with a dry chuckle. "We're saving his life, lass, is the answer. Spiriting him across the land to his home."

"Spiriting?" Una wrinkled her nose. "Ye couldn't spirit anything but whisky, Gair Murray. From the smell of things, ye've had a lot of it."

Gair laughed without malice. One thing Stuart liked about the man was that he knew exactly who he was and had no aspiration to be anything else.

"A fine reunion ye're having," Gair said. "But it's time to pay the piper. Not that I play the pipes. Can't abide the things."

Stuart straightened in puzzlement. "I paid ye, Gair. In advance. Every bit of silver I had. Ye insisted, I remember." He still felt the sting of handing over the last coins he had in his sporran. He hoped the king's armies hadn't stolen the rest of what he'd stashed at home.

"Aye." Gair returned the look without shame. "That was *my* payment. Now for Padruig."

Bloody man. Stuart had always known he couldn't trust Gair. To smuggle Stuart into Scotland and across the country without betraying him, yes. With his money? No.

"Ye don't share your take with Padruig?" Stuart asked, as though surprised. "I'd reconsider, Gair. He's a dangerous man."

He and Gair glanced as one at Padruig. The man leaned his left elbow on the table near a large tankard of ale, while he amused himself twirling a dagger in his right hand. His lank and long hair, worn leather eyepatch, and the concentration in his good eye did not lend reassurance.

Gair's humor didn't fade. "Oh, he's happy with what I give him. This is something special, he tells me."

The innkeeper had vanished, tending to whatever innkeepers tend to, but the common room remained crowded.

A few lads ran about serving the loud Highlanders, while the window grew dark with the cold midwinter night.

Stuart smothered a sigh and gave Fiona and Una a truncated bow. "Excuse me, ladies."

Gair guffawed and followed Stuart across the room to the table. Padruig flipped the blade through competent fingers and let it land, point down on the table's surface, buried a half inch into the wood.

"The landlord won't be happy with that," Stuart remarked as he slid onto a stool.

Padruig said nothing. Where Gair could talk the hind leg off a mule, Padruig was silence itself.

"What do you want?" Stuart asked him. "I'll have no more money until I reach home, and even then I might have nothing. The bloody English will have confiscated everything." Possibly not the cache of jewels he'd hidden well before he'd left to join the Jacobite army, but Stuart wasn't fool enough to mention jewels in front of Gair. "Take your share out of Gair's hide."

Gair went off into gales of hilarity, but Padruig's face remained impassive.

"'Tis nae coin I want."

Padruig so rarely spoke, that when he did, he drew attention. Even Gair ceased his laughter. Padruig opened the tankard and took a loud sip of ale.

"What then?" Stuart asked impatiently.

Padruig sipped again, set down the tankard, and wiped his mouth on his sleeve.

"A *sgian dubh.*"

Stuart's brows climbed. "A knife? Is that all? Cumberland's men might have taken all of those from my home as well, but likely I can find one stashed somewhere."

"No." Padruig's harsh word dried up Stuart's relief. "One particular *sgian dubh,* lost at Culloden Moor. Bring me that, and your debt to me will be paid."

THE DEVILISH LORD WILL

CHARACTERS

Will Mackenzie

WILL MACKENZIE IS THE SECOND SON OF THE 18TH-CENTURY Duke of Kilmorgan. The death of his older brother, Duncan, in 1746, makes Will the heir, which is the last thing he wants.

Will is a spy and an adventurer, roaming the world, learning secrets and diffusing dangerous situations. On one of these missions, in about 1734, he meets Josette Oswald, who is earning money to support her daughter by being an artist's model for Will's brother, Alec. The attraction is instant, and Will spends the next dozen years in an on-again, off-again relationship with Josette.

When Will is pulled into the events of the Jacobite Uprising, he is reportedly killed at the Battle of Culloden Moor, when in truth, he is captured and imprisoned, along with his brother's close friend, Stuart Cameron. (Stuart's story is told in *Fiona and the Three Wise Highlanders*.) Alec (also presumed dead) comes to Will's rescue in *Alec Mackenzie's Art of Seduction*.

After this, Will returns to his world of intrigue and espionage. On one of these covert missions, in 1746, he contrives to get himself captured in order to learn secrets of the British Army in remote Scotland, and is amazed when Josette glides through the door to rescue him.

Josette's reasons and Will's plans conflict but make Will realize just what he must do to make his life worth living.

Josette Oswald

JOSETTE OSWALD, born in France, lived an ordinary life of in lower-middle-class family in Paris, until she was seduced by a British Army officer, who deserted her once he'd gotten her with child.

Devastated, Josette learned to live on her wits, doing everything in her power to keep her daughter, Glenna, safe and fed. She meets Alec Mackenzie, a Scotsman who journeys often to France, who asks her to become his artist's model. Josette never considered herself a beauty, but she agrees, for money to keep her daughter. Alec is an honorable man, with no designs on Josette, and pays her fairly, for which she is ever grateful.

While posing for Alec one day, his older brother Will pops in for a visit. Josette takes one look at Will and knows he's trouble, but she can't help falling for him.

Will flits from place to place, never staying long, and his life is wrapped in intrigue and danger. Josette gets caught up in some of his adventures, helping him expose thieves and conspirators. She realizes before long that as exhilarating as it is to be with him, Will's life is mired in peril, and Josette fears her daughter will be endangered if she stays with him.

Josette is used to pushing Will away when things grow too intense, but she also can't help being glad when she sees him again.

She ends up in London, running a boarding house, which is

a staid but respectable job and keeps herself and her daughter safe. (We meet her there in *Alec Mackenzie's Art of Seduction*.)

When Josette needs help, she knows the only person she can turn to is Will. Even when he's listed as dead on the rolls from Culloden Moor, Josette sets off to find him, knowing that if anyone can thwart death, it is Will Mackenzie.

Important Secondary Characters

GLENNA OSWALD (JOSETTE's 16-year-old daughter)

Bhreac Douglas (old friend / foe of Will's)

Beitris (a very large Irish wolfhound)

Lillias McIver and Mysie Forster (women Josette wants to help)

Sir Harmon Bentley (an English squire, in Scotland to live high and avoid his creditors)

Lady Bentley (his very bored wife)

Clennan Macdonald (Old rival of the Mackenzies)

Henri (an angry young man, works for Sir Harmon)

Captain Robert Ellis (cavalryman in the British army, once in love with Will's brother's wife)

Lord Wilfort (father to Lady Mary in *The Stolen Mackenzie Bride*)

Naughton (retainer to the Mackenzie family)

Ewan (boy who works for the Mackenzies, played a role in *The Stolen Mackenzie Bride*.

AUTHOR'S NOTES

WILL MACKENZIE IS SUCH FUN! HE'S THE MACKENZIE BROTHER from the 18th-century Mackenzies who is a spy and adventurer, taking on missions to help his family and his fellow Scotsmen. He's not necessarily on the side of the Jacobites, but he certainly wasn't a Hanoverian either. Will Mackenzie plays his own game.

When I originally conceived of the ancestors of Ian Mackenzie, I had in mind that the entire family would be destroyed at Culloden Moor, except for Will's youngest brother, Malcolm, who lived to carry on the family and build the large house that Ian and his brothers inhabit in the Victorian and Edwardian eras.

However, when I started putting together the family and fleshing out their characters, I could not lose Will or Alec to tragedy. Plus I didn't want Mal to be too broken by what happens during the 1745 Uprising.

Authors are supposed to ruthlessly torture their characters, but I never can. I want these guys to be happy.

Therefore, Will and Alec would survive. I had to come up with a way for Mal to inherit the dukedom, as the youngest brother when his older brothers were still alive, but trust Will, the schemer, to work it out.

Will also has a softer side: He's an accomplished musician and often played the piano-forte his mother purchased before her death. Once she was gone, Will's father hid it in the cellars, but Will often crept downstairs and practiced on it.

Will's skill with music emerges again in Ian and also in Ian's daughter, Megan.

JOSETTE WAS a different sort of heroine from others I've written. She wasn't a sheltered miss from an aristocratic or even genteel family. She's a Parisian who has been around the block a few times and has had to figure out how to survive as a single mother with no support (her own family passed away when she was younger).

By the time of Will's story, Josette is in her thirties with a teenage daughter, and she's running a boarding house in London, which Will had obtained for her so she could make a living. This is where Josette is when she's introduced in *Alec Mackenzie's Art of Seduction.*

In that book, she's put out with Will, who is missing and presumed dead. She has loved him since she met him, when she was Alex's model, but theirs is a stormy relationship. Will comes and goes, putting himself into deadly danger, and Josette isn't certain she wants to 1) break her heart over him again and again, and 2) put her daughter in danger from his missions.

Josette is good at intrigue herself and in the past has helped Will in his spy missions. She pretended to be his wife in one, which tested her resistance to him.

Josette is also courageous enough to walk into a British Army camp, right into an interrogation room where Will is held prisoner, and take him out again under his captors' noses. I have to admire her!

Because the Victorian-era Mackenzies were always surrounded by dogs, I introduced a dog into Will and Josette's story. Not just any dog, but a giant, wiry-haired Irish wolfhound who takes to Will, Josette, and Glenna, Josette's daughter. Beitris is a sweetheart.

Returning to the 18th century and exploring more of the history of Scotland and the aftermath of the Jacobite Uprising was enjoyable as well.

Will and Josette have children of their own, and down the decades, one of their descendants turns up to the Victorian Mackenzies.

SYNOPSIS

JUNE 1747

When Josette needs help finding a trove of gold believed lost in the Highlands, she turns to Will Mackenzie, the most cunning, devious, and clever man she knows. But trusting Will with her secrets is akin to trusting the devil himself.

They've worked together in the past, pretending to be man and wife to ferret out information, and the venture did not end well. Will is dangerous, and so is his life, and danger is not what Josette needs.

But she knows the real reason she's avoided him is because he's Will Mackenzie, the golden-eyed, red-haired, unpredictable man with warm hands that bring her to life. Will has more secrets than Josette ever can fathom, and the most dangerous thing of all is that he's already stolen her heart.

EXCERPT: THE DEVILISH LORD WILL

June 1747

Scotsman." The cool English voice cut through the darkened room like an icy wind ruining a fine summer morning. "Speak to us, and I will ensure that your death is less agonizing."

Lord Will Mackenzie opened his eyes.

Nothing had changed. He remained seated on a stool in the cavern of an old kitchen, hands bound behind him, ankles also roped. No fire filled the hearth in the freezing room, and the only light came from windows high in the ceiling.

That light fell upon a major in the British army who sat on a hard chair, legs crossed, the man elegant in the dark red and silver braid uniform of an infantry officer. His hair had been tamed into a sleek queue, and his polished boots bore no speck of the mud that lay six inches thick around the makeshift army camp.

Major Haworth, a highborn gentleman, would let nothing, not even interrogating a stubborn Scottish traitor in the middle of nowhere, lower his standards.

The captain at his side was another matter. A hothead—a man who'd clawed his way up the ranks and instantly despised anyone his commanders pointed out as the enemy. Red-faced and foul-mouthed, the captain lounged against the stone wall with coat unbuttoned, his light brown hair straggling from the tail he'd pulled it into.

Will looked straight into Major Haworth's blue eyes and said in Erse, *If you think I even know anything to tell you, you're a gobshite idiot.*

The major and captain didn't understand a word. Haworth knew Greek and Latin and spoke perfect French, but Erse was a barbaric language, in his opinion, that needed to be stamped out. He'd expressed this sentiment more than once during the interrogation.

The captain's cheeks grew redder. "Speak a civil tongue, ye bloody Scots pig."

He drew back his hand to deliver a blow, but Haworth's cool voice stopped him.

"As you were, Captain."

The captain glared at the major but let his hand fall and dropped himself onto a wooden stool.

Will found it interesting that while the captain vented his frustrations with violence—demonstrated by the many bruises on Will's face and neck—the collected major was the more dangerous man in this room. Except for Will himself, of course.

Major Haworth reached long fingers to a silver bell on the rustic kitchen table. "Perhaps a light repast."

The furniture in this room, plainly made chairs and stools, matched the table. The bell was an incongruity, cast by a master silversmith, with a crest etched on one side, its handle fashioned of entwined silver snakes. The major had brought the bell with him.

He rang it now, its sound more appropriate for an elegant drawing room than an abandoned crofter's cottage.

"Woman!" the captain bellowed. "Bring us ale and be quick about it."

Footsteps sounded, and the wooden door swung open. The maidservant on the threshold bore a tray that held a delicate porcelain cup and saucer and tall silver pot—more of the major's belongings—and a dented tankard that obviously came with the house.

In the cant of a Londoner born and bred, the woman said, "I guessed ye might be thirsty, sir. It's hot work with these Scots, innit?"

Dark eyes swept over Will Mackenzie, and he did his damnedest not to react.

She wore the garb of a farm woman, a simple chemise covered by a laced overdress in drab homespun. Will had seen her in these kinds of clothes before, but he'd also known her in the sumptuous silks of a lady, her hair in soft curls, her bosom bedecked with jewels.

Beneath today's shapeless clothes lay the lush body he'd first seen in his brother's studio, when Alec Mackenzie had been scowling around his canvas at his newest artist's model, admonishing her not to move.

Will had been the one frozen as he'd beheld beauty lying before him, her scarlet drape covering very little.

In a sultry voice that had fired Will's blood, she'd said to Alec in her French-accented English, "*You* press your bum to cold marble for an hour, my lord, and see how much *you* squirm."

She was supposed to be in London. Supposed to be safe in the boarding house where Will had left her, looking after her daughter. Alec and Celia had said she was in London.

What on earth was Josette Oswald doing in the middle of Scotland in an army camp full of murderous British soldiers?

The major examined her in suspicion—clearly he'd expected someone else. "Who are you, madam?"

Josette poured a stream of dark liquid—drinking chocolate

by the smell of it—into the porcelain cup. She handed the cup to the major before depositing the tankard for the captain on the kitchen table.

"Mrs. Smith," she said glibly. "Me man runs the tavern in the village yonder. Sent to offer the best ale to the lads here, bless them. Nice to see Englishmen in this back of beyond."

The captain grabbed the tankard, took a greedy gulp, and then spat out the liquid. "Ye call this the *best* ale? Horse swill will do for a name, madam."

"I'm certain it's the finest they have," Major Haworth said quietly. The captain subsided and took another sip, which he swallowed. Then another. He'd decided not to let it go to waste, Will saw.

"Thank you, good lady," the major said. "And thank your husband."

Josette curtsied, but instead of beetling off, she turned her thoughtful gaze to Will. Her cheeks were as round and pink as they'd been nearly a dozen years ago when she'd portrayed Helen of Troy rising from her bed the morning after she'd eloped with Paris. Alec had been full of grandiose ideas for paintings in those days.

"He don't look like much," Josette said critically. "You sure this was one what gave you so much trouble at Culloden?"

"Appearances are deceptive, madam," Major Haworth said. "He is tamed for now, but believe me, these Highlanders are the very devil. The sooner they are all hanged and their ways stamped out, the better." He took a sip of chocolate. "Ah, well prepared. Thank you. If you'd brought your own supplies, Captain, you wouldn't have to rely on village goods."

The captain snorted but he continued drinking the ale. Josette lingered while Major Haworth took several more slow sips of his chocolate, as though she would take away pot and cup as soon as all were empty.

"Now then, sir," Major Haworth said to Will, clicking his cup to his saucer. "Let us start again. My patience is wearing thin, and I will give you over to my men soon if you do not speak. Please tell me all you know. Or be drawn and quartered—alive—for raise … raising … arms against your … your rightful king."

His words began to tangle on his tongue, and he shook his head as though trying to clear it. Behind him Josette quietly closed the door and drew a bolt across it.

The captain took another long gulp of ale, and choked. The major turned to him, his movements too slow. The captain fell from his chair to his knees and then did a prolonged topple to the floor, landing on his face.

The major rose jerkily, drawing a long knife that hung at his side. He stumbled as he rushed at Josette, and his cup fell to the floor in a porcelain smash.

"Damn you." Haworth glared at her. "That was a gift from my mother."

The major might be prissy, but Will had seen that he was a deadly fighter. Josette quickly sidestepped as the major struck, but she would not be fast enough.

Will sprang from the stool, still bound, and slammed his body into Major Haworth's. The major swung the blade at him, but only caught Will's loose shirt as whatever potion Josette had put into the chocolate gripped him.

The knife went slack, and the major, all six foot three of him, tumbled to the dirt floor in a heap of long limbs.

Josette snatched the knife from his hand and had Will's bonds cut in seconds.

"God's balls, woman." Will kept his voice a whisper, but it rang with rage. "What the devil are you—"

"Shout at me later," Josette said softly but fiercely, the London accent dropping away. "Follow me now."

Will growled as Josette caught his numb hand and pulled him to the back of the kitchen, making for an alcove near the fireplace he'd already spied as a potential way out.

Before Josette could duck into it, Will caught her around the waist, pulled her to him, and kissed her hard on the mouth.

Josette started, then her lips parted and her hands landed on his chest, her mouth softening to kiss him back. Her body warmed his, moving the blood that had been cut off by the ropes. Will's limbs burned as her fire swept through him.

The kiss grew stronger, memories pouring in with it: Josette's shy look as she, as Helen of Troy in Alec's studio, sent Will a tiny smile. Will had winked at her, hiding his sudden and overwhelming longing.

Seeing her weeks later in regal finery at a salon held in Alec's honor by the cardinal who'd commissioned the painting. Josette's ready acceptance to help Will uncover the cardinal's secrets—for money, of course. Josette had been raising a daughter and was always in need of funds.

Years later in Salisbury, when she and Will had posed as man and wife to discover the plans of a certain high-placed English lord who could expose a Highland plot. Josette had been a fine actress, playing a slightly dim but devoted wife smitten with her husband.

Their nights in bed, when they'd forgotten about playacting and spying, and simply enjoyed each other, knowing their time together would soon be over.

The Salisbury ploy had been the last, and had ended stormily. The boarding house in London had been Will's gift to her, a safe place for her to make a living and raise the irrepressible Glenna.

Will tasted Josette's heat in this drafty farmhouse kitchen with his captors lying senseless on the other side of the room. She'd done that—for him.

Why?

He abruptly broke the kiss. Josette gazed up at him, her fists on his chest. She was a dozen years older than when she and Will had first met, but the passing time had turned the desperate young woman into a beautiful and capable lady. Josette's face was as soft as he remembered, her dark eyes as glowing, her hair as sleek, her lips as ripe.

The kiss and their locked gazes lasted only a few seconds, though time seemed to slow to a trickle.

But they had to escape before the major and captain awoke. Will seized Josette's hand and pulled her through the narrow door beside the fireplace to the tunnel beyond.

Josette shook off his grasp and slid past Will to guide him through the darkness with confidence. The cords had cut off blood to Will's feet, but at least the captain hadn't taken away the old shoes Will had found to complete his guise as a poor farmer.

Josette warned him of a short flight of stairs that delved into the earth before he fell down them. This must be a smuggler's tunnel, built to let the farmer who'd lived here move whisky, brandy, and even men—anything those in the village wished to hide from soldiers and the excise men.

Josette had obviously explored the tunnel, because she led Will unerringly through twists and turns, down more stairs, then up another flight.

When at last she pushed open a gate—hinges oiled and silent —and began to step into the cool Scottish night, Will stopped her.

"They'll be scouring these hills once they find me gone. Best we hide a bit."

"I've got transport," Josette said, her voice a bare whisper. Her breath warmed his cheek. "It will take us to safety."

In the darkness, Will squeezed her hand. The late evening air felt heavenly, but he had no intention of diving out into it, his red hair like a beacon to all those searching for dangerous High-landers.

"We wait until dark," Will said. "I know a place where we can go to ground while they search. They'll give up after a time. The major is not one for living rough."

Once in hiding, Will would interrogate Josette as to what she was doing here, where she'd left her daughter, and why she'd been on hand to rescue him. The interrogation would be thorough and intense and might involve a night together, the pair of them wrapped in shared blankets.

"We go now," Josette said. "My transport won't wait forever."

"Then let him go. We'll compensate him later if need be."

"No, Will." Josette's voice turned hard. "Ye need to come with me. *Now*."

Will blinked at her. In the half light, her face was set, eyes determined.

"Josette?"

"I'm sorry, Willie."

He knew there was someone behind him, stepping out from shadows before he could register the danger. He noted a flurry of movement and turned in astonishment before a single, very hard blow rendered him senseless.

A ROGUE MEETS A SCANDALOUS LADY

CHARACTERS

David Fleming

DAVID FLEMING. HART MACKENZIE'S RIGHTHAND MAN AND BEST friend, the person who has stood with Hart through thick and thin. David manipulates things (and people) behind the scenes, allowing Hart to win the glory for whatever they manage to accomplish.

David is distantly related to the Mackenzies. His great-great-great aunt, Donnag Fleming, marries Angus Mackenzie, the son of Malcolm and Mary (*The Stolen Mackenzie Bride*). Donnag's brother was David's direct ancestor, which is how he retains the Fleming name down the centuries.

When Hart Mackenzie meets and falls for Eleanor Ramsay, David falls for her as well. Hart's idea of marrying Eleanor at first is to make a dynastic marriage of convenience (see *The Duke's Perfect Wife*), which of course, Eleanor denies him.

David, angry at Hart's treatment of Eleanor, confesses his love for her and asks her to marry *him*. Eleanor, being the wise young woman she is, turns him down. David grieves for a while but realizes she was right. When Hart decides to woo Eleanor again, David does all he can to help the two find happiness.

This leaves David alone and despondent, sliding deeper into decadence.

The day he hits rock bottom, he knows that there is only one place he can go for refuge. He drags himself to Shropshire, to the home of his friend and mentor, the vicar, Dr. Pierson.

Little does he know that Dr. Pierson's niece, the beautiful Sophie Tierney, has also sought refuge there …

Sophie Tierney

SOPHIE, sweet Sophie. She's no fool, having studied ancient history and archaeology under her uncle Lucas (Dr. Pierson), and enjoying searching for his ruins of Roman Britain alongside him. She made the unfortunate and naive mistake of marrying a man (the Earl of Devonport) who, after running through her dowry and blaming Sophie for not producing an heir, takes the drastic step of divorcing her.

Sophie's husband has decided upon the tactic of ruining her thoroughly, bribing and cajoling his friends to allege that they had adulterous affairs with her. Sophie, who would never dream of betraying her husband, even after she'd fallen out of love with him, is bewildered and heartbroken.

Her reputation in tatters, she flees to Shropshire to lose herself digging up the nearby fields with her uncle in search of his Roman villa.

At breakfast one morning, she is surprised when a hungover, half dressed man falls into the dining room begging for coffee. She looked into Davids gray-blue (and bloodshot) eyes, and is lost.

———

Important Secondary Characters

DR. LUCAS PIERSON (UNCLE LUCAS): Vicar of a parish in Shropshire and good friend to David, obsessed with finding a buried Roman villa.

Laurie Whitfield, the Earl of Devonport (Lackwit Laurie, Sophie's erstwhile husband)

Sinclair McBride: Genius barrister

Hart and Eleanor: Duke and Duchess of Kilmorgan

Dr. Howard Gaspar: Archaeologist friend to Uncle Lucas

Oliver Griffin (Griff): Man bringing suit against David

Other Mackenzies and McBrides

AUTHOR'S NOTES

I LOVE DAVID FLEMING. THE MAN WHO SCHEMES AND CONNIVES on Hart's behalf, who's not above a little conning and manipulation to get the job done. He's sardonic and self-deprecating, and is shamed only when facing Eleanor Ramsay.

He's mad for Eleanor when we first meet him, but unfortunately for David, Eleanor doesn't return his love and has eyes only for Hart.

Poor David! I knew I had to give him a happy ending from the moment he appeared in *The Duke's Perfect Wife*. He was so deliciously dark-hearted and roguish that of course I had to write about him.

I have to confess that this is one of my favorite books of the series. David lives in such a dark place, thinking no one will ever be for him. And then he meets Sophie.

The scene of him waking from a drunken stupor to find the sweet Sophie Tierney looking back at him had been in my head for years, and I was happy to finally be able to write it all down.

I'm fond of what's called the grumpy / sunshine trope, though I like my sunshine heroines (or heroes) to have a bit of fight in them. Sophie does, as she has fallen into scandal through no fault of her own.

At the time (late Victorian England), divorce was a terrible scandal, often ruining both parties and sometimes rendering them unable to marry again, at least in the Anglican church (this was one of the problems Princess Margaret had when she wanted to marry Peter Townsend). Sophie's reputation is being trashed at the beginning of the story, so that her husband (with whom she's separated) can divorce her.

David, of course, has all kinds of schemes up his sleeves to free her and make her blameless. He comes to love her enough to do it without expectation of anything from her in return.

I also enjoyed the archeological aspect of the story. I'm very interested in ancient history, particularly that of Rome (though Egypt is also truly fascinating). So much so that I write a mystery series set in Ancient Rome (the Leonidas the Gladiator mysteries as Ashley Gardner).

Late Roman villas and artifacts can be found all over England, as the Romans settled there for quite some time. I thought a nice tiled floor in a villa would be fun for Sophie and David to help Sophie's uncle find.

I adore Eleanor, and it was a delight to let her take the stage again. Her rattling speeches cover a mind as bright and devious as David's own. Bringing Sinclair back for a speaking role was nice as well. He might be my favorite McBride, though Elliot is close competition.

I was so pleased to give David his happy ending. He deserved it, and so did Sophie.

David appears in a few other books, such as *A Mackenzie Family Christmas, The Perfect Gift*, helping Hart find a Ming bowl for Ian. He uses Uncle Lucas (Dr. Pierson) to help him in that caper.

He and Sophie return again in *A Mackenzie Yuletide*.

SYNOPSIS

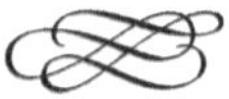

SHROPSHIRE, FEBRUARY 1893

DAVID FLEMING, HART MACKENZIE'S RIGHT-HAND MAN, SEEKS refuge with his vicar friend in Shropshire, only to find that the vicar's beautiful niece, Sophie, Lady Devonport, is seeking refuge as well.

Tongues are wagging all over London about Sophie, and she finds that the only gentleman sympathetic to her plight is the reprobate David.

David and Sophie match wits as they help her uncle dig up the countryside searching for a villa from Roman Britain, and David decides to use his conniving ways to fix all Sophie's problems.

In the quiet spaces of the countryside, David finds some peace from his reprobate existence but now faces a new problem—he's falling for Sophie, a woman far out of his reach.

EXCERPT: A ROGUE MEETS A SCANDALOUS LADY

February 1893

As jails went, it was not too bad, David decided. The lockup on Marylebone Road consisted of one small room where the arrests of the night waited for the magistrate's decisions in the morning. David had commandeered a place by the wall, bribing the inhabitants to not steal every piece of clothing on his body by parting with all the coins in his purse. His watch would be next. A man with only one eye kept that eye on it.

The place stank and was filthy, the bodies of sleeping men heaped on the floor. Vermin scratched in dark corners. But at least there was a window, high above, that let them know the sun had fully risen.

Any request that word be taken to David's solicitor, his valet, his very good friend the Duke of Kilmorgan—or even a random person in the street—had been ignored. The constables who'd dragged him from the park had pushed David in with the other arrests of the night and left him. Now here he lay.

Did the bottom of the slope feel like this?

David's head pounded, his throat was on fire, and his

stomach roiled. All he wanted was more whisky to soothe the pain. That and a soft bed, a beautiful woman, and perhaps a cigar.

No, the thought of smoke brought on more nausea. He'd leave the cigar until he felt better.

The door creaked. "Mr. Fleming!" The turnkey bellowed the name without interest.

David climbed painfully to his feet. "Here I am, my good fellow. Have you brought my breakfast?"

A few of the inmates guffawed. "Aye, fetch me a mess of bangers and a bucket of coffee," one croaked.

The turnkey ignored them, his balefulness all for David. "Come on, you."

A bit early to see the magistrate, David mused, though perhaps the man wanted to make a start on his cases for the day. Thieves of apples, handkerchiefs, and children's clothes; ladies selling favors; and David.

He followed the turnkey through a dank passage to a larger room that was empty but for a table and chair. A burly constable joined them and pushed David into the seat.

"Thank you, sir," David said to the turnkey. "Kind of you to show me to my parlor."

"Shut it," the constable said as the turnkey growled and left them. "When the Super comes, you be respectful."

"Superintendent, is he?" David said. "My, I am moving in high circles now."

The constable hit him. A blow across the mouth, not hard enough to draw blood, but enough to make David's head rock back. "I *said*, shut it."

David heaved an aggrieved sigh. He held up his hands as the constable bunched his fist again, and made the motion of turning a key over his lips.

The door opened once more to admit a tall man. David's first instinct was to rise, because the gentleman who entered was one of distinction, but the constable's warning glare kept him to his seat.

Hazel eyes in a hard face met David's, hair that was just touched with red glinted in the bad light. He had the height, the build, and the manner of Hart Mackenzie, the Duke of Kilmorgan, but he wasn't Hart. It was his half-brother, Detective Superintendent Lloyd Fellows.

David relaxed in relief until he saw the frost in Fellows's gaze.

"Oh, come now," David said, giving him his most charming smile. "You don't truly believe I was trying to shoot a man in Regent's Park, no matter how much he goaded me. If you examine my pistol, you'll find it fully loaded and un-fired."

Fellows's face remained granite hard. "Griffin has brought charges of assault and attempted murder on you, and his earl uncle is calling for your blood."

"For pity's sake." David pointed to the bruises on his face. He was plastered with mud, still a bit drunk, and spattered with dried blood. "Does *this* look like I assaulted myself? A solicitor would be a fine thing, Detective Super."

"I have recommended that the magistrate let you return home until this is sorted. He does not like the idea, but he bows to the might of the Duke of Kilmorgan."

David heaved a sigh of gratitude. God himself would bow to the might of Hart Mackenzie.

He rose. "Good old Hart. Thank you, Fellows."

"Sit down." Fellows pointed at the hard chair. David obediently sat, wincing from his bruises.

"It's a serious accusation, Fleming. One that could get you hanged, or at the very least, sent to Dartmoor. Doesn't matter who your connections are—you're not a peer, so you'll be tried at the Old Bailey with everyone else."

"Griff has to prove it," David said. "I do know that much about the laws of jolly England. Innocent until a jury says I'm guilty." He spread his hands on the unclean table. "I did not discharge my pistol, I promise you. I ducked when Griffin discharged *his* at *me*. I don't know why I bothered—he's a rotten shot."

"I convinced the magistrate there was no immediate evidence to suggest you tried to kill Mr. Griffin. However, many witnessed the ensuing fight. You can bring counter charges against him, of course."

"Bugger that." David once again surged to his feet. "If I'm not being charged, I believe I am free to leave."

Fellows gave him a nod, but a grim one. "Don't flee to the Continent. I have a friend in the Sûreté, and he'd find you, but you'd rather he didn't. I hear you have an estate in Hertfordshire. Perhaps lying low there for a time is a good idea."

David shuddered. His ancestral home—Moreland Park—held too many foul memories. "I will retreat to my London house, pour coffee down my throat, soak in a bath, and sleep for a week. With that satisfy the magistrate?"

"I doubt it." The dry tone in Fellows's voice was something he shared with Hart—that edge that told its recipient he was a damned fool. "Before you withdraw from the world, the duchess requests that you call upon her."

David sank to the chair again, his strength gone. "She does, does she?"

Fellows, David could spar with. Hart Mackenzie, he could face. Hart's wife, Eleanor … that was another matter entirely.

"Please tell her I am suddenly stricken with a dire disease and must quarantine myself in my house with a cask of whisky."

Fellows regarded him in some pity. "Tell her yourself." He tapped the table once, turned, and walked out.

"Heaven help me," David muttered. It was some time before he made himself rise and follow the impatient constable out.

———

DAVID KEPT a stash of Mackenzie malt in his carriage for emergencies. He imbibed a little now to clear his head as his coachman took him to Grosvenor Square.

The Duke of Kilmorgan owned a tall house on one side of the square, which dominated all others around it. The house had been in the family since the late eighteenth century, when the Mackenzie family had begun to prosper once more. The Battle of Culloden, in which they'd fought on the side of the Jacobites, had nearly wiped them out. But the canny Mackenzies had managed to regain their title taken from them as traitors to the crown and recover their fortune. They'd bought the house that had been owned by the Marquess of Ellesmere, and swarmed in.

David was distantly related to the family through his ancestor aunt who had married Angus Mackenzie, a son of the glorious Malcolm Mackenzie and his English wife, Mary.

The distance was everything, David thought as he stared up at the house. Hart was a duke, and his brothers had courtesy titles, large houses, and plenty of money. David, the shirttail relative, was still in his evening dress from the night before, thoroughly coated with mud, and coming tamely to the house when sent for.

Eleanor would be waiting in her parlor, rustling in some silken gown Hart would have bought her. Her red hair would glisten, and she'd have a secret smile on her face that betrayed she was a woman in love—with Hart, of course. There had never been anyone else for Eleanor.

She'd gaze at David with her cornflower blue eyes and ask bluntly what sort of scrape he'd gotten himself into now.

David wouldn't mind, except that once upon a time, he'd been madly in love with the dratted woman. He'd asked her to marry him, and she'd turned him down with a speed that had made his head spin.

He still cared for her, but the burning passion had subsided.

Eleanor and Hart belonged together, and no one could tear them asunder. So be it.

David took another gulp of whisky, which burned to his empty stomach.

He held up the flask in salute. "Apologies, dear El, but you are the one thing I cannot face today." He rapped his stick on the roof. "Hinch!"

A tiny trap door opened, and the eye of his large coachman blinked at him. "Yes, guv?"

"Change of plans. Take me …" Home? No. His valet, Fortescue, would fuss, and his housekeeper would try to bring him soup, like an invalid. Someone would send word to Hart, and Eleanor would corner him. Or his solicitor would pop by to discuss the grave charges, or Griffin would send his solicitors to threaten David.

London wouldn't do, and neither would Hertfordshire. Scotland? No, too many Mackenzies in Scotland.

There was only one place in the world David could think to go, and he wasn't certain of his welcome even there.

"To Shropshire," he finished.

Hinch's eye widened. "Guv? Ye want me to drive you all the way to Shropshire?"

"Yes. If we make a start, we'll arrive early tomorrow morning."

"But it's me wife's birthday." The red-rimmed eye held pleading.

David heaved a sigh. "You're right, Hinchie. I'm being selfish. Take me to a station and get me on a train heading west. Then do as you please."

"Thank ye, guv." Hinch vanished. The carriage jerked forward, nearly dislodging David from the seat, and made at a swift pace for Euston Station.

———

DAVID HAD little recollection of the journey. He swayed in the first class carriage alone, finishing off his flask before a waiter helpfully brought him champagne. He had little to eat, as he doubted his ability to keep anything down.

The Shropshire hamlet he aimed for lay well south of Shrewsbury. David had to change trains several times, assisted onto the last, small chugging train by a stationmaster who more or less hoisted him aboard and dropped him into a seat.

By the time they reached the village three miles from David's destination, he was well inebriated and mostly asleep. He vaguely remembered being escorted from the train and pushed onto a dogcart as he mumbled the direction.

The jolting, sickening cart finally halted then listed as the driver climbed down. "You're here, guv."

Here was very, very dark, and utterly cold. David had no recollection of what he was doing or where he'd been trying to reach.

Light shone in his face, and David cringed. The driver and another man who'd joined them hauled David out of the cart and to his feet, but David promptly collapsed as soon as they let him go.

He fell on wet paving stones with grass between them. The boots in front of him drew back, and a face bent toward him. The head was shaggy and a white noose encircled its neck. David flung up his hands, crying out.

"Good heavens," a rumbling voice said, and the face resolved into one of comforting familiarity. The white noose, David realized, was the collar of a country vicar.

"Sanctuary," David whispered.

The vicar stared at David for a time before he let out a sigh. "Help me get him inside," he said to the driver.

———

THE NEXT MEMORY David had after that was light.

Far too much light, pounding through his eyelids and searing at his temples. He groaned.

The sound was loud, and David cut it off. He lay for a long time in dire misery before he realized he was in a bed piled high with quilts, a rather comfortable one at that.

The bedroom was tiny, with whitewashed walls, the ceiling sloping abruptly down to the eaves. David discovered this fact when he sat up and banged his head on a roof beam. A window about four feet square let in the dazzling sunlight.

His coat and waistcoat had been removed, but not his trousers. He tried very hard to remember where he was and why he'd come here, but at the moment, all was a blur.

When he at last dragged himself from the bed, David couldn't find his coat, but a dressing gown had been draped over a chair. Ah, well, the inhabitants of this house would have to take David as he came.

David struggled with the dressing gown, only managing to get one arm inside before he found the door to the bedroom and opened it. This led onto a landing, no other doors around it. If he hadn't hesitated on the threshold, he'd have plunged straight down the stairs.

Recollection about where he was grew as he went down the staircase, its wood dark with time. At the bottom lay a white-washed passage that ran the length of the cottage. If David remembered aright, *this* door led to a dining room. He didn't particularly want food, but Dr. Pierson would have thick, strong coffee, and at the moment, it was all David craved.

He chose the correct door, stumbled into the room, and collapsed onto a chair on one side of the table, eyes closing. He slumped forward, forehead resting on the polished table, and let out another groan.

A hot beverage slid toward him. David could tell by the scent that curled into his nose that it was tea.

"Coffee," he mumbled. "For the love of God."

"Tea might be a wee bit better in your condition," a light voice said. "I've read books on the matter."

The speaker was not Dr. Pierson, David's longtime friend and sometime mentor, a burly man with a beard and a rumbling voice. This voice held a clarity that slid through David's stupor and touched something deep inside him.

He raised his head—carefully.

And beheld the most beautiful woman in the world. She sat across the table from him, surrounded by a halo of light, and gazed at him with unblinking green eyes.

A MACKENZIE YULETIDE

CHARACTERS

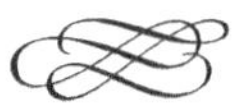

As in *A Mackenzie Family Christmas* and *A Mackenzie Clan Gathering*, this story has an ensemble cast, but the most important characters are:

Ian Mackenzie
Beth Mackenzie
Jamie Mackenzie
Gavina Mackenzie
Megan Mackenzie
Curry
Violet and Daniel Mackenzie

Important Secondary Characters

Cornelius Pemberton (a collector)
Mr. Magill (an archeologist)
Mac and Isabella Mackenzie
Belle Mackenzie
Hart and Eleanor, Duke and Duchess of Kilmorgan
Ainsley and Cameron Mackenzie
Lloyd Fellows

David and Sophie Fleming
Stuart Mackenzie (son of Cameron and Ainsley)
Robbie Mackenzie (son of Mac and Isabella)
Andrew McBride
Magdala
The Ghost

AUTHOR'S NOTES

WHEN MY PUBLISHER WANTED TO PUT *A MACKENZIE CLAN Gathering* in print, they decided it was too short for a mass market paperback and asked me to write a Mackenzie Christmas story to bundle with it. It took me about twenty seconds to decide I wanted to write another Christmas story (I'd had it in the back of my mind already).

This one would take place after the main books, once the four brothers, plus Daniel, David, and Lloyd all had their happy endings. I wanted to introduce the next generation as young adults, almost ready for books of their own. All of the Mackenzie children are now in their teens, except for those born to Daniel, David, and Lloyd.

The story has two prongs—First, Mac Mackenzie late one night swears he sees a ghost. When he reports this the next morning at breakfast, the family divides in the two camps: Those who think it's a real ghost and speculate on which ancestor it will be (Megan, Jamie, and Mac), and those who don't believe in hauntings (Gavina, Belle, and Ian). Nevertheless, the family immediately schemes to catch it, one was or another.

The second prong of the story involves Ian, who once again

"

wants to find the perfect Hogmanay gift for Beth. He is scouring the land for it, coming up against obstacle after obstacle.

Jamie Mackenzie, who is ever trying to impress his genius father, also wants to give his parents a gift, one that will delight them and earn their praise. Gavina, sensing he's up to something, joins him, while Megan becomes Ian's assistant in his task.

I enjoy revisiting the Mackenzies and writing about their real lives beyond their initial romance (though there is plenty of romance going on). This book let me explore the personalities of the next generation: Megan the musician and dreamer, Belle the pragmatic scientist, Jamie uncertain on the cusp of adulthood, Gavina the madcap who breaks the restrictions on young women.

All four feature in the following book, *The Sinful Ways of Jamie Mackenzie*, as do more of their cousins.

I also introduced another Mackenzie, this one a descendent of Will and Josette from *The Devilish Lord Will*. We'll see more of this character in future books.

A Mackenzie Yuletide leaves the family celebrating a festive Christmas and Hogmanay, and Ian, who has the last word, is amazed at the happy life he's found.

A MACKENZIE YULETIDE is available in e-book form as a standalone, and in print in **A Mackenzie Clan Christmas** anthology (with *A Mackenzie Clan Gathering*). See Links to the Series for more information.

SYNOPSIS

DECEMBER, 1898

THE MACKENZIES GATHER FOR ANOTHER FAMILY CELEBRATION OF Christmas and Hogmanay. It will be a full house with all the Mackenzies and McBrides and their offspring, as well as friends and their families.

The house party gets off to an interesting start when Mac, painting in his studio late one night, swears he sees a ghost. The younger Mackenzies, aided by the Duchess of Kilmorgan, go on a ghost hunt.

Ian Mackenzie, who knows there are no ghosts, pursues a problem of his own–obtaining the perfect Hogmanay gift for Beth. But there are obstacles to his quest plus rivals for the priceless object who might get to it first.

EXCERPT: A MACKENZIE YULETIDE

December 1898

Mac Mackenzie paused, his paintbrush dripping, at the soft sound from the end of the corridor.

The skylights in his room at the top of Kilmorgan Castle, the vast Mackenzie manor house, were dark. Mac didn't remember night falling, but when he became deeply immersed in painting, time passed swiftly.

It was also cold, his fire having died to a glow of coals. Lamps glowed softly, which meant his valet, Bellamy, must have entered and lit them.

Mac pulled himself out of the painting of a Scottish landscape and restored himself to the here and now. It was mid-December, at two in the morning, and his wife and children were snugly asleep in the floors below. Mac's brothers and their families slept in their wings of the vast house, all awaiting the celebrations at Christmas and Hogmanay.

No one should be up near the studio at this hour, but that did not mean his son, Robert, hadn't climbed restlessly out of bed to roam the halls. Or that Robert and his cousins Jamie and

Alec hadn't gathered for a stolen smoke or nip of whisky they didn't think their fathers knew about.

Mac wiped his brush and dropped it into his jar of oil of turpentine. He mopped at his hands, which never stayed clean, but didn't bother trying to scrub off his face. Nor did he remove the kerchief that kept his hair more or less free of paint. Once he found the source of the noise, he'd return and finish the shadowing that was challenging him.

He shrugged on his shirt, now noticing the cold. Painting with fervor heated his body, so he usually ended up in only his kilt and shoes.

Mac stepped into the cold, silent hall. It ran narrowly before him, ending in a T—one direction led to Ian's wing, the other to Cameron's. He saw a flutter of white in the shadows, heard again the quiet rustle that had cut through his painting haze.

"Iz?" Mac called softly.

He started down the corridor. If Isabella, his darling wife, had come up to entice him to bed, he'd play along. The studio had a wide, comfortable sofa, and he could build up the fire to keep them warm while they bared more skin . . .

Another flutter, then silence.

Mac began to grin. Isabella had a teasing streak, and when she turned playful, life became splendid. Mac's blood warmed, and he forgot all about painting.

"Izzy, love." He started after her, anticipation building. What game would she play this time? And how would Mac turn the tables, as he loved to do?

He reached the split in the corridor. Stairs led down from here to the floors below, or he could turn to one of his brothers' wings. Years ago, the sons and daughters of the Mackenzies had slept in nurseries on these top floors, but they had long since moved to larger bedchambers below.

That fact was in one way sad, but then again, the older children would be marrying in a few short years, and nurseries would fill again. Mac's adopted daughter, Aimee, was nineteen now, and so beautiful.

Which was very worrying. Mac found himself snarling like a bear at gentlemen she danced with at the balls Isabella had carefully selected since Aimee's debut.

An icy draft poured over him as he tried to decide which way to turn. The wind cut, making him shiver. Who had left a blasted window open?

He thought the chill came from Cam's wing, and he quietly moved that direction. The short hall beyond was empty and dark.

"What the devil are you doing, love?" he said, a bit louder. "It's freezing. Let's go to the studio and make it cozy."

Another rustle. Mac followed the noise around the corner to the longer corridor. At its end was a flash of white, then nothing.

Mac gave up stealth and sprinted down the corridor. He'd catch Isabella and she'd laugh, then he'd carry her to where they could tear off what little clothing Mac wore and enjoy themselves.

A window lay at the end of the hall—open, Mac saw as he reached it. As he'd suspected. Mac slammed it closed.

He heard a whisper of sound and spun around. Behind him, where he'd just come from, stood a lady in white. A chance moonbeam caught on her red hair.

In that instant, Mac knew this wasn't Isabella. Different stance, different height, and Isabella was . . . alive.

Why he thought this woman wasn't, Mac didn't know. Maybe because the moonlight made her skin deathly pale, or because the white dress floated, though the draft had gone. Mac couldn't see every detail of her, but she seemed to have no hands or feet.

Mac's heart beat faster, but he felt no fear. Kilmorgan was an old place—this could be any lady, from any era.

"Good evening," he said softly. "I'm Mac. But you probably know that. What's *your* name, lass? Which one are you?"

The apparition was utterly silent. Mac took a step forward, wondering what would happen when he reached her. Could he walk straight through her? And would that be impolite?

He was halfway down the hall to the hovering lady when she vanished, abruptly and utterly.

Clouds slid over the moon. Mac was left in the freezing cold and dark, alone, disappointed, and suddenly tired.

He moved quickly back to his own wing, doused the lights in the studio, and fled downstairs to his bedchamber, which was warm and inviting. His wife was fast asleep in their bed, and never moved when Mac climbed in with her, spooning close to her in their heated nest.

"I saw a ghost last night," Mac announced at the breakfast table.

Ian Mackenzie took a moment to decide whether this declaration was interesting enough for him to look up from the letter and photographs that had arrived in the morning's post. Mac liked to spin yarns, and Ian had learned to ignore most of them.

He glanced at Mac, who slid into a place at the long table, his plate loaded with eggs, sausages, ham, and scones dripping with butter. A few rivulets of butter trickled over the edge of the plate to make perfect round pools on the tablecloth.

Their nephew Daniel laughed. "Did you, Uncle Mac?"

"I did," Mac answered without worry. "Vanished before my eyes."

Violet, Daniel's wife, made sure their seven-year-old daughter, Fleur, wasn't giving too many bits of toast to the dogs, and leaned forward eagerly. "Interesting. Where did you see it?"

"My wing. Then it floated to Cam's wing and disappeared." Mac shoved most of a scone into his mouth and chewed noisily.

Ian had difficulty knowing when Mac was teasing or serious. Hart and Cameron were straightforward with their speeches—sometimes loudly so—but Mac made up stories or played with words, bursting out laughing in the middle of them. Ian had learned to wait until Mac wound down to judge whether what he spoke was truth or exaggeration. He returned to his letter and let the others at the table play it out.

Breakfast at Kilmorgan was an informal meal, with food placed on the sideboard for all to enjoy. Some days the ladies indulged in breakfast in bed, but most mornings they made their way to the dining room to eat with the family. The younger Mackenzies were welcome—no banishment because they had not yet reached a specific age. The four brothers had made that decision years ago.

Ian liked the breakfast gatherings. He read his letters or newspapers while various Mackenzies chattered around him. At the house he shared with Beth and his three children, breakfast could be intimate or rowdy, the five of them crammed around the table.

As soon as Mac ceased speaking and began to eat, Ian's daughters, Belle and Megan, entered and helped themselves at the sideboard.

Megan finished filling her plate first and took a seat next to Ian. Megan was thirteen now, and becoming so beautiful. Ian lost himself in looking at her eyes, so like her mother's, and her hair that was glossy brown with a touch of red.

Belle, her plate heaped almost as much as Mac's, sat on the other side of her sister. Ian noted they kept to the placement that was usual at home—they knew he preferred it if everyone sat in the same seats day after day.

"Good morning, ladies," Daniel boomed at them. "Uncle Mac has seen a ghost at the top of Kilmorgan Castle. What awful specter haunts our midst? A Highlander of old, calling to his clan? Great-great-great-grandfather Malcolm bellowing for his whisky? A lady waiting for her lover to return from one of our many rebellions?"

"Papa." Fleur shook her head at him. Like Violet, she was a skeptic.

Megan shivered. "I hope it's not the lonely lady."

Belle scoffed. "There are no ghosts. They are seen only by people who are drunk or mad." She caught Mac's grin and flushed. "Not that I mean you are mad, Uncle Mac. Or drunk. But it has been shown that oil of turpentine and the components of paints can make one's brain behave as though it is intoxicated. You might have breathed in too much last night."

Mac winked at her. "An excellent theory. Very scientific. I assure you, dear niece, I keep plenty of air flowing through my studio and avoid a buildup of fumes. I truly did see a ghost. Kilmorgan is quite haunted."

"Poppycock," Belle said, but Megan shivered again. "There has been absolutely no proven existence of ghosts and spirits," Belle went on. "Those who pretend to have gathered evidence are frauds. Oh, I beg your pardon, Cousin Violet."

"No need, sweetheart," Violet answered calmly. "I know all about frauds and hoaxes. Do not worry, Megan. Whatever your uncle Mac saw, it wasn't a ghost."

"If you say so," Mac said before he fell to devouring the rest of his breakfast.

Megan did not return the smile, from which Ian deduced she was not reassured. He reached over and squeezed her hand.

"There are no ghosts," he said firmly. "They do not exist."

"Quite right," Belle said on Megan's far side.

Belle looked for rational and scientific explanations for everything, from a flower pushing through the earth to how far away the stars were, to how rain clouds formed. Her inquisitive and eager mind had worked through most of the books in Ian's library, and she'd quickly absorbed everything her brother's tutors had taught them.

Jamie, Ian's oldest, had gone off to Harrow, leaving his sisters behind, but Ian had insisted they hire another tutor, one who could keep up with Belle's swift mind. She was determined to go to university, to study to be a doctor. Ian saw no reason why she should not—Belle was brilliant and ought to be allowed to do anything she wanted.

Beth tried to explain to Ian and Belle that education for a woman was very difficult, but Belle only furrowed her brow and said she'd do it. Ian knew she would, and he'd certainly use all his might as a Mackenzie to ensure that she found a university that would take her.

Megan was no less intelligent, but in a different way. She was highly imaginative, constructing entire worlds in her mind and acting them out with her dolls or the dogs. Where Belle made her way through scientific journals, Megan read fairy tales and lengthy novels. Megan was also quite musical, able, like Ian, to learn a piece of music by hearing others play it through once. Unlike Ian, though, Megan could play it back with feeling, often ending up sobbing by the close of the piece.

Megan was compassionate; Belle a force to be reckoned with. Beth expressed surprise that the two got along so well, but Belle was Megan's defender, and Megan's gentleness eased Belle when she grew frustrated and impatient.

"What is this talk of ghosts?" Isabella Mackenzie floated into the room, her red hair drawn up in the latest fashion, which Ian privately thought resembled a giant pincushion. Isabella changed her hair nearly every week.

Mac rose from the table, wiped his mouth, and kissed his wife soundly on the lips. "Saw one. Upstairs last night."

"How exciting." Isabella helped herself to toast and tea from the sideboard, sat down, and raised her cup to her lips. "Tell me all about it."

Mac launched into his tale once more, and Ian returned to his letter. He'd written to a man in London, asking for particulars on what was in the photographs and line drawings—an antique necklace with intricately worked loops of gold and hung with emeralds and lapis lazuli. It was ancient, Roman, and had purportedly belonged to a Roman consul's wife, though Ian was skeptical about that. Somehow it had ended up in the treasury of a church in Norwich, and when the parish needed to raise money, they'd decided to sell it, as it was non-ecclesiastical and had been hidden away for a rainy day.

They'd sold it to a small museum in London that hadn't really been able to afford it, and the necklace hadn't proved a great attraction, giant fossil bones being more interesting to the museum's patrons. The museum had quietly sold it on to a collector in Paris.

Ian had decided the necklace would look perfect on Beth, and wanted it for her Hogmanay present.

There was a problem, however. The necklace had disappeared after the sale, and no one knew where it was. Ian, with the determination Belle had inherited from him, set out to find it.

The letter, from a London acquaintance who'd photographed the piece when it had lain in the museum, confessed he did not know where the necklace had ended up. The Frenchman who'd purchased it claimed it had never reached his Parisian mansion. Somewhere between London and Paris, the necklace had vanished.

Ian read the words, studied the man's photographs and drawings of the necklace, and made up his mind that nothing would deter him.

"Excellent," Isabella said. "Once we trap it, we'll know whether it is a true ghost or someone playing tricks on poor, sleepless Mac."

Ian looked up. "Trap it?"

"Yes indeed." Isabella's green eyes sparkled as she gave Ian her wide smile. "We're off to catch a ghost."

"Poor thing," Megan said, her mouth turning down.

"It's only someone playing tricks," Belle said. "You'll see. We'll catch them and give them a good talking-to."

"Poor thing," Megan repeated.

Ian squeezed Megan's hand again and slid one of the photographs toward her. "I'm going to find this for your mama," he said. "Will you help me?"

THE SINFUL WAYS OF JAMIE MACKENZIE

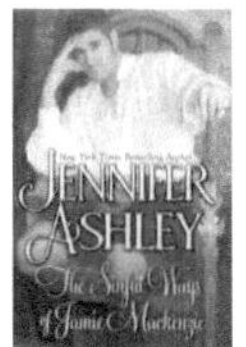

CHARACTERS

Jamie Mackenzie

What can I say about Jamie Mackenzie? He is Ian Mackenzie's oldest son, the recognized leader of the younger Mackenzies, and has inherited Ian's knack for solving other people's problems without them realizing it.

Jamie had to grow into his self-assuredness and his ability to take command. He is the son of a man people either believe is either a genius or mad, and Jamie feels the weight of those who judge him accordingly.

However, he did grow up in a loving family and household, and is very close to his parents. His sisters and cousins drive him distracted, but he loves them very much and will do anything for them.

From his older cousin, Daniel (Cameron's son), Jamie gained a fondness for mechanics, loving to tinker with motorcars, aeroplanes, and any other machines that catch his attention. His restlessness had taken him around the world, to race cars, fly planes, and rescue friends from dire situations.

Jamie knows he's searching for something different, some

more fulfilling than his wandering life, but he's not certain what.

Until a young lady from his past bangs into him in the middle of a crowded dock in Southampton ...

Evie McKnight

I HAD to search a long time to find the counterpart to Jamie, which was similar to the search for Beth for Ian (I interviewed and dismissed at least five heroines for Ian before Beth came along. As soon as the did, the whole story clicked).

The same thing happened with Evie. I toyed with the idea of Jamie falling for Miss Carmichael, an overly sheltered American heiress he sees disembarking in Southampton, while he's waiting for Daniel and Violet and family. But she wasn't right for him. (However, she will be right for another Mackenzie cousin.)

Evie came out of the blue while Jamie's attention was elsewhere, and I knew—this was his lady! She has a past with him (if a brief one), she's lively and adventurous, she won't let him order her about, and she has her own problems to attend to.

Evie, like Jamie, comes from a close and loving family (I love her younger sisters, and they might reappear). She has a tragedy in her past, which has led her to decisions she starts to regret, namely, being engaged to an affable and wealthy man when she re-encounters Jamie.

(I had a bit of fun creating her fiancé, Atherton, who's kind of a dweeb, but he's not overtly awful. Covertly, yes.)

Evie has no idea why meeting Jamie again sends her into such a turmoil of indecision, and tries to distract herself with the task of helping her old friend from her university rowing team rob the British Museum (for very good reasons).

But Jamie pushes in there, as well ...

IMPORTANT SECONDARY CHARACTERS
Hayden Atherton: Evie's fiancé
Iris Georgiou: Friend of Evie from university
Imogen Carmichael: American heiress
Ian and Beth Mackenzie
Alec Mackenzie (Hart's son and heir)
Mal Mackenzie (Hart's second son)
Gavina Mackenzie (daughter of Cameron and Ainsley)
Belle Mackenzie (Jamie's younger sister)
Megan Mackenzie (Jamie's youngest sister)
Andrew McBride (son of Sinclair McBride and now a junior barrister in his own right)
Eleanor and Hart
Ainsley and Cameron
Isabella and Mac
Adeline and Gayle Hodgkinson (flatmates of Gavina and Belle)
Curry: Still taking care of the Mackenzie family
Other Mackenzie cousins
Various dogs

AUTHOR'S NOTES

I DEBATED A LONG TIME ABOUT WRITING BOOKS ON THE NEXT generation of Mackenzies, but I had so many reader requests, and I so enjoyed getting to know Jamie, his sisters, and cousins in the novellas, that I decided to let their stories be told.

Jamie was a natural place to start, as he is the oldest of the younger cousins (except for Daniel, of course).

I still had reservations, because Ian Mackenzie is one of my most popular characters of all time, and how could I do justice to a book about his son?

I realized that Jamie too would have these questions about how to live up to his father, and the way he deals with them shaped his character. I also had to come up with a heroine to match him, which took some time.

The book is the romance between Jamie and Evie, but it also gives a look at what has happened to the other Mackenzies. I couldn't spend time on every single one of them (I'd still be writing …), so I focused on a few, who play roles in the story. Others will feature more prominently in future books. But I made the decision that Jamie's book would not only be a romance, but a catch-up on the family.

This part of the Mackenzie series takes us forward in time, to 1908, when most of the younger generation are becoming (or have become) adults.

The Edwardian age was different from the Victorian, a time of great change. Technology was rapidly advancing, as was opportunities for women (more slowly). The ladies of the family can all go to university and think about careers. Belle, for instance, longs to go into medicine or science, Megan wants a career in music, and Belle's flatmates work in an astronomy lab.

I did realize that the ages of the next generation Mackenzies would make them in their twenties and thirties during WWI, and that is something I can't ignore.

However, I made the decision that none of the Mackenzies would lose their lives during the war. This is a romance and a family saga, not a tragedy. They will have to deal with the war, of course (it affected everyone), but the Mackenzies will make it through. These will always be tales of happily ever after.

I enjoyed getting to know the younger Mackenzies. Alec, Hart's oldest son, has a fiery temper and is under much pressure as heir to the dukedom of Kilmorgan. His younger brother, Mal, is more fun-loving, comfortable in his role as the spare. Both of these brothers are extremely eligible bachelors, but in Jamie's story, they each set their eyes on ladies that leave them floored.

Gavina has become such a wonderful character to write. She inherited the impetuousness and charm of her mother, Ainsley, and the determination of her father, Cameron. She's a young lady who will let nothing in the world stop her, though she'd not quite certain what she wants out of life. I have a special story in mind for her.

I have heroes for Belle and Megan as well, as they venture out into the world in pursuit of their futures.

See the Mackenzie / McBride Family tree at the end of this book to keep all the Mackenzies straight!

Much more to come.

SYNOPSIS

APRIL 1908

WHEN IN TROUBLE, SEEK A HIGHLANDER ...

Even if you pushed him into a river ten years ago ...

When Evie McKnight slams into Jamie Mackenzie on a quay on Southampton, she flashes back to the day she accidentally knocked him into the river Cam. When she fished him out again, he shocked her with a searing, bold kiss before walking away in dripping wet shirt and kilt.

Evie has no business reveling in memories of Jamie then and the nearness of him now—she is betrothed to a respectable man from a respectable and wealthy family. But Jamie appears everywhere in London, assisting Evie and her sisters, becoming friends with her fiancé, and agreeing to be drawn into the heist Evie has planned in order to save her best friend's father from ruin.

The son and heir of Ian Mackenzie, Jamie has roamed the world encountering adventure after adventure, and now he's back home to settle down as he promised his family. But Jamie is restless, searching for something he can't seem to find, trying to live up to his potential as the son of a genius.

When he sees Evie again, he knows what he's been striving

for, and he is not going to let the trivial matter of her betrothal to a dull stick and the fact that she wants to break into the British Museum put him off. Jamie is Ian Mackenzie's son all right—he'll use all the Mackenzie determination and adroitness to prove that she is for him, and he for her.

EXCERPT: THE SINFUL WAYS OF JAMIE MACKENZIE

April 1908

JAMIE MACKENZIE STOOD AT THE RAIL AT THE SOUTHAMPTON docks and craned his head for a better view of the young woman who strolled down the gangplank of the massive ship moored before him.

The lady was surrounded by chaperones, the tall man and harried-looking woman probably her parents, the other two matronly women likely aunts or a former governess or two.

The liner, the *Baltic*, the largest in the world, blocked any view of the ocean with its vast, dark bulk. A large opening in its hull disgorged passengers onto the open pier, more than two thousand of them, into the blustery late April day.

The young woman stood out, not only because she wore a gown of soft yellow—not the most practical choice for the sooty pier—but because she carried herself with a grace that set her apart. Golden hair peeped from under a white hat—again a questionable choice of attire for the docks, but perhaps her family had instructed her on what to wear.

A black-clad man with a large photographic apparatus

bumped past Jamie. "Sorry, guv," he said cheerfully. "Almost missed her."

He set up his tripod, unfolded his camera, pointed his long lens at the young woman, and began snapping away.

"Who is she?" Jamie asked.

Click ... click ... click. "You don't know? Imogen Carmichael, American heiress, richest woman in the world—so I'm told—come to these shores to land herself a titled husband."

"Title, eh?" Aristocratic monikers held glamour and romance for Americans, and not only for *them*, Jamie reflected. So many, even in this country, were entranced by a *Lord This* or *Marquess of That.*

As the nephew of a duke and cousin to the duke's heirs, Jamie knew the true worth of titled gentlemen.

He leaned on the rail, wind tugging at the Mackenzie plaid kilt around his hips. "She is a beauty."

"She's fair enough." The photographer shrugged. "Whether I like her or not, my instructions are to get as many photographs of the lovely lady so those what put pen to paper can write all sorts of guff about her."

Miss Carmichael turned slightly, and Jamie swore she stared directly at him. He inclined his head, rewarded by a slight flush to the lady's cheeks. Or maybe that was the sudden wind that streaked down the dock, an icy, briny blast from the Channel.

Never mind that Jamie himself wasn't titled. Mackenzie was an old name, a revered one—one spoken with awe and a little shiver. He could convince Miss Carmichael she didn't need a title. Persuade her to let him steal her away, as Old Dan Mackenzie had done with his bride so long ago—

Someone slammed into Jamie's back with the suddenness of a cannon ball, sending him hard against the railing. He slipped on an oily patch and felt his too-tall body begin to pitch over the side, gravity inevitably taking him down to the black water between ship and dock.

The young woman in drab brown who'd run into him dropped her portmanteau and seized handfuls of Jamie's coat, sucking in a lungful of air as she hauled him upright.

"Trying to drench yourself again, are you, Mackenzie?" she demanded breathlessly.

Jamie turned when she released him, meeting blue eyes the color of delphiniums. Those wide eyes had gazed at him another day, long ago, on the banks of the Cam, when she'd pulled him to safety as she'd done just now.

It couldn't be ...

She had hair like darkness, cheeks pink from the wind, and was bundled in a practical coat, her hat squashed down over her ears. The brown coat and hat were as dull as their surroundings, but her eyes emerged from them like bright sky after gloom.

Jamie hadn't seen her in half a dozen years, but her wry smile hadn't changed. The blasted woman had always laughed at him.

"Evie McKnight." Jamie took a step back from her, meeting the solid rail. "Trying to push me in again? At least you didn't bring your oar this time." He glanced behind her as though searching for it.

"Is that all you remember about me, Mackenzie?"

"It is burned upon m' memory, McKnight." Jamie's backside even now recalled the sharp *whap* from the oar that had inadvertently landed on it as Evie, on the lady's rowing team at her Cambridge college, had rushed with it to her scull.

"I didn't need it today," Evie said, eyes sparkling. "You were so lost in the famous Miss Carmichael that you could have gone straight into the drink without my help."

"No, lass, I was minding my own business when a lady barreled into me."

Evie flushed—she could never control her blushes. "Ogling women will be the death of you, Mackenzie. At Cambridge, it was your interest in girls in rowing costumes that was your undoing..."

"Not ogling," Jamie said with indignation. "I'd come to cheer on the team."

"Not what you said when you were climbing out of the river."

Jamie's language had burned the air. Evie's face had been beet red at her blunder, and her fellow teammates had laughed themselves sick.

Jamie Mackenzie, the arrogant Scotsman, up to his waist in muddy water, had cursed and floundered until Evie had lowered her oar to him and pulled him from the river. The mud had made a sucking sound as it disgorged him, which had thrown her teammates into further glee.

"I did apologize," Evie said.

"I know. Ye did it beautifully."

Evie's face went even more red, and Jamie knew why. His own was heating at the moment.

"Well, I am glad that is cleared up," Evie said briskly. "I recommend you don't fall in here. Far too dangerous."

Evie leaned to retrieve her portmanteau, but Jamie beat her to it and held the bag out to her. Her hand closed on the handle, half an inch from his.

"What are you doing here, anyway?" Jamie asked. "Besides trying to push me in ... *again*."

Evie dithered, her feet shifting as though ready to flee. She glanced at their hands, both still on the bag's handle. Jamie withdrew unhurriedly, but Evie moved the bag to her other side, as though worried he'd try to grasp it again.

"Returning home from a sojourn in New York with my mother and sisters. My sisters are all grown up now, and Clara is ready to marry. Hence the journey to New York, though both Clara and Marjorie have declared they prefer Englishmen." She spoke in a rush, the words pat, as though her thoughts roved far from the docks, the shock of running into Jamie diverting her only momentarily.

"I notice you're not speaking of *yourself* rushing to America to snare a husband," Jamie said. "Or did you? Engaged, are you?"

Evie jumped, returning her full attention to him. "I am, as a matter of fact."

Jamie's brows rose. "To an American magnate? Ready to bathe in goat's milk and honey, or whatever American magnates put into their baths?"

"Hardly." Evie's sunny smile blossomed. "He's a respectable Englishman and a gentleman. Mr. Hayden Atherton. We've been betrothed nearly a year now."

"Oh, yes?" Jamie feigned excitement then shook his head. "Never heard of him."

Evie laughed, her face lighting up and driving everything else from Jamie's thoughts. "No, of course, you haven't. He isn't one of your reprobate university friends. He is kind and genteel. Polite, cultured."

"Sounds a right dull stick." Jamie made a mollifying gesture when she puffed up like an indignant hen. "My apologies, McKnight. You know how to stir up my fractious side. Congratulations on your upcoming nuptials."

Even as he spoke, Jamie had a curiosity to meet this Mr. Atherton. Was he as polished and perfect as she implied? Good enough for the fiery Evie McKnight? Would Mr. Atherton tame her fire, or would she pry him from his boring stupor?

"Thank you." Evie's air of condescension was incongruous with the windblown curls trickling from under her hat. "What are *you* doing here? Besides ogling heiresses, I mean? I saw Miss Carmichael onboard. She's lovely, but a bit vague."

"I was *not* ogling …" Jamie growled. "Never mind. Here to meet my cousins—Danny and his wife and bairns. They were racing cars and risking their necks in America. I told him I'd assist in the unloading."

A gleam of interest lit her eye, but everyone was fascinated by motorcars. "Ah yes, I saw them during the voyage. I wasn't able to meet them—my mother kept us herded together. They seem a warm family. You at least have kind relations, Mackenzie."

"Ha. I wouldn't call any of them *kind*," Jamie retorted. "Some more interesting than others, maybe. Why have ye strayed then, from your herd?"

Evie darted her gaze about, as though debating what to tell him. He wondered very much what she'd been in a hurry to do when she'd nearly knocked him down.

"I saw an unusually tall Scotsman in danger of falling from the pier," she said glibly. "I thought I'd warn him."

Not at all true. She hadn't noticed Jamie until she'd run smack into him.

"Very amusing. Warn me? Or push me over?"

Evie rubbed her chin, leaving a smudge from her sooty glove. "Actually, I hadn't quite decided." She scanned the pier once more but this time, she grinned. "Oh, dear, Mackenzie. Your heiress has gone."

Jamie turned his head to see that, yes, the lovely Miss Carmichael had disappeared into the sea of brown and black coats, likely whisked off by her parents to a train or a posh hotel. Ah, well …

He abruptly realized that as soon as the radiance of Evie McKnight had entered his sphere, the pale beauty of Miss Carmichael had faded to nothing.

"There he is!" a voice floated to them. "There's Jamie!"

A straw boater hat on a young lady bobbed up and down in the morass of disembarking passengers, and a thin arm waved frantically.

"Your family at last," Evie said with a touch of relief. "I must dash. So nice to have caught up with you, Mackenzie. *Do* be careful while leering at young ladies near bodies of water."

She whirled in a flutter of practical wool and dashed down the pier. Jamie watched her go, in the opposite direction of the ship, white petticoats flashing around dark boots.

Who was she racing to meet? The fiancé? And if so, why had he not been at the foot of the gangway, ready to lift her into his arms? Jamie would have grabbed her the moment he saw her and smothered her in kisses.

But if not the fiancé, then who was she meeting? Jamie gazed after Evie until he lost her in the crowd, his curiosity aroused in a way it hadn't been in a long time.

The journalist, whose camera Jamie realized was now pointed his way, clicked one last frame then began folding up the apparatus.

"What the devil?" Jamie growled at him.

The journalist answered with a grin. "Mackenzies are always good for copy." He shouldered his camera and marched away, unmindful of Jamie's glower.

———

"Who was that delicious man you were speaking to, Evie?" Clara McKnight settled herself into the second-class train compartment amid boxes and bags that the ladies had not wanted to entrust to the porters. The porters, already burdened with the bulk of their baggage, had relinquished the extras with relief.

"Speaking to?" Marjorie repeated in delight. Evie's younger sisters, Marjorie and Clara, were seventeen and nineteen respectively, and held the energy of youth Evie fondly remembered in herself. "Evie was speaking to a man? What would Mr. Atherton say?"

Evie dropped into her seat across from her mother, who regarded her too shrewdly. Mrs. McKnight's soot-black hair was styled in a soft pompadour that suited her slender face, her body poised on her seat. Clara had inherited her looks, Clara who'd turned heads in the hotels and public spaces of New York. Evie's mother had turned plenty of heads in her day, so said their besotted father, and still did.

"Do tell, Evie," Mrs. McKnight said, her dark blue eyes watchful.

Evie found herself flustered. "He is an old friend. I met him at Cambridge."

"Cambridge?" Marjorie asked with interest. "Where you were locked into your ladies' college down the road and never spoke to the gentlemen?"

"We did see them from time to time." Why was Evie so disconcerted? Her encounter with Jamie today had been a harmless one, old acquaintances chatting about past times. Distracting, though, as she'd not been able to send the telegram to her friend Iris she'd hastened down the docks to do, before her mother and sisters had called her to them. "They came out to cheer our rowing team."

"I'm certain they did." Marjorie collapsed into mirth, sagging into the piled up bags at her side.

"What nonsense." Evie did her best to be haughty while Marjorie went off into gales, and even Clara, more composed than her younger sister, smiled knowingly.

"You haven't told us his name, dear," Mrs. McKnight said gently.

"Jamie Mackenzie." The words came out in a rush. "I mean, *Mr.* Mackenzie. He is nephew to the Duke of Kilmorgan."

"Duke, eh?" Marjorie crowed.

"Hush, darling." Mrs. McKnight could rebuke without raising her voice. Marjorie stifled her giggles, but her eyes danced. "I am certain the young man is perfectly respectable," Mrs. McKnight went on.

"He is," Evie answered with a straight face.

Had Jamie always been so tall? There'd been a hardness

about him he'd not had as a youth, his skin bronzed from a sun far from English shores. Evie was suddenly curious about where he'd been and what he'd done. Would he laugh as she'd seen him do, throwing back his head and roaring with abandon when he heard something hilarious?

His handsomeness was altogether different from her fiancé's. Jamie had a slightly crooked nose—from a scrap in his first year at Cambridge, she'd heard—red-brown hair, brilliant blue eyes, and as she'd observed, a hardness that lent him an air of danger.

Hayden Atherton, by contrast, had a chiseled face that any sculptor would wish to capture, a warm smile, golden blond hair, and fine brown eyes. He'd recently grown a trim beard that made him quite distinguished.

Ladies regarded Evie with envy whenever she appeared on Hayden's arm. General opinion was that Evie and Hayden would produce quite beautiful children.

Such statements made Evie contemplate the method for conceiving those children, and there her imagination went hazy. As much as she tried to picture her wedding night with Hayden, something inside her—modesty?—would not allow her to form a clear vision.

Today, however, a memory had thrust itself up into her thoughts, scattering all contemplation about Hayden.

Evie saw an angry Jamie charging at her out of the river, eyes flashing fury. Before Evie could dodge from him, large, wet hands cupped her face in a strong grip. She'd gazed up into steely blue eyes framed by damp red-brown lashes.

Before Evie could apologize or admonish Jamie for touching her—or say anything at all—his mouth had come down on hers, crushing a firm kiss to her parted lips.

Evie had tasted rage in the kiss, but also excitement and a hungry need she'd never before experienced. To her consternation, the same hungry need had stirred in *her*.

Jamie had kissed her thoroughly, his hands holding her steady, his wet coat damp against her rowing costume. He'd kissed her while her mates on the team had watched avidly, while Evie's knees had gone weak, and her breath had deserted her.

He'd kissed her until she'd gasped, then Jamie had released her, brushed a thumb across her now-wet lips, and turned and walked away from her. Even now, the image of his waterlogged kilt clinging to his backside, his bare thighs flashing as he strode from the river, came to her too vividly.

Her teammates, her closest friends in the world, had watched in shock and delight. The teasing Evie had endured since that day had been merciless.

She'd seen Jamie now and again in the next year until he left Cambridge, he talking or laughing with friends, wind blowing back his academic gown to reveal the kilt he insisted on wearing. He'd nodded at her when he'd seen her, sometimes flashing a bone-warming smile, sometimes feigning fear that she might have her oar with her, as he'd done today.

Today, when he'd gazed at the ship, wind tossing his hair, every line of him strong ...

The train bumped over a crossing, jerking Evie back to the present. Marjorie was watching her, her youngest sister too perceptive. Evie quickly turned her head and peered out the window at the passing countryside.

Evie was engaged to the handsome and eligible Hayden Atherton. She had no business thinking about Jamie Mackenzie, speculating on what sort of man he'd become. She especially had no business daydreaming about the astonishing kiss he'd given her years ago.

Absolutely no business at all.

FINAL NOTE

I am ending this guide with Jamie's book. The stories following his will feature in the next volume.

Books about Belle, Megan, Gavina, Alec, Mal, etc. will appear, as well as more stories about past Mackenzies and Mackenzie friends (Captain Ellis, Old Dan Mackenzie, and others).

The Mackenzies are like my own family to me, and it is no hardship to revisit them time and again.

See the Mackenzies / McBrides timeline for which books fit into which eras, and the Mackenzies / McBrides family trees for who is related to whom.

Thank you for reading and supporting the series. I hope you are enjoying spending time with my favorite family.

Best wishes,

Jennifer Ashley

MACKENZIES / MCBRIDES
SERIES TIMELINE

(**Note:** The chronological timeline is not necessarily the order in which the books were published)

Eighteenth-Century Mackenzies

The Stolen Mackenzie Bride
1745-1746
Malcolm Mackenzie and Mary Lennox
Children:
o To Alec: Jenny (Genevieve Allison Mary)

Alec Mackenzie's Art of Seduction
1746
Alec Mackenzie and Celia Fotheringhay
Children:
o Mary pregnant with Angus

Fiona and the Three Wise Highlanders
December 1746

Stuart Cameron and Fiona Macdonald

The Devilish Lord Will

June 1747
Will Mackenzie and Josette
Children:
• To Malcolm and Mary: Angus Roland
• To Alec and Celia: Magnus Edward

Late Nineteenth Century Mackenzies

The Madness of Lord Ian Mackenzie

Summer 1881
Ian and Beth

Lady Isabella's Scandalous Marriage

September 1881
Mac and Isabella
Children:
o To Mac and Isabella: Aimee (adopted)

The Many Sins of Lord Cameron

September 1882
Cameron and Ainsley
Children:
o To Ian and Beth: Jamie
o To Mac and Isabella: Eileen

The Duke's Perfect Wife

February 1884
Hart and Hart
Children:
o To Ian and Beth: Belle

o To Mac and Isabella: Robert

o To Cam and Ainsley: Gavina

The Seduction of Elliot McBride

April 1884

Elliot McBride and Juliana

Children:

o To Elliot from previous relationship: Priti

o Ainsley pregnant with Stuart

A Mackenzie Family Christmas: The Perfect Gift

December 1884

Ian, Mac, Cam, Hart, their wives and children, Daniel

Children:

o To Hart and Eleanor: Alec

The Untamed Mackenzie

June 1885

Lloyd Fellows and Louisa Scranton

Children:

o To Cam and Ainsley: Stuart

o To Ian and Beth: Megan

Scandal and the Duchess

November 1885

Steven McBride and Rose Barclay

Children:

o Louisa pregnant with daughter (Elizabeth)

Rules for a Proper Governess

December 1885

Sinclair McBride and Bertie

Children:

o To Sinclair (from previous marriage): Caitriona and Andrew

o Louisa pregnant with daughter (Elizabeth)

o To Elliot and Juliana: Gemma (b. 1885), Patrick (b. 1886)

The Wicked Deeds of Daniel Mackenzie

March 1890

Daniel Mackenzie and Violet

Children:

o To Sinclair and Bertie: Marcus (b. 1886), Elena (b. 1888)

o To Hart and Eleanor: Malcolm Ian (1887)

o To Lloyd and Louisa: Elizabeth (1886); William (1888); Matthew (1889)

A Mackenzie Clan Gathering

September 1892

Kilmorgan Castle, northern Scotland

All Mackenzie families.

Children:

o To Daniel and Violet: Fleur Mackenzie, born 1891

A Rogue Meets a Scandalous Lady

February 1893

David Fleming and Sophie Tierney

A Mackenzie Yuletide

December 1898

Kilmorgan Castle, northern Scotland

All Mackenzie families, McBride families, and David Fleming and family.

Children:

o To David and Sophie: Lucas Fleming, born 1894

Edwardian Era Mackenzies

The Sinful Ways of Jamie Mackenzie
April 1908
Jamie Mackenzie and Evie McKnight
Children:
o To Daniel and Violet: Dougal Mackenzie, born 1899

MACKENZIE FAMILY TREE

Ferdinand Daniel Mackenzie (Old Dan) 1330-1395
First Duke of Kilmorgan
= m. Lady Margaret Duncannon
|
Fourteen generations
|
Daniel William Mackenzie 1685-1746(?)
(9th Duke of Kilmorgan)
= m. Allison MacNab
|
6 sons
Daniel Duncannon Mackenzie (Duncan) (1710-1746)

William Ferdinand Mackenzie (1714-1746?)
=m. **Josette Oswald**
|
Glenna Oswald (stepdaughter, b. 1731)
Duncan Ian Mackenzie (1748-1836)
(Ancestor of Magdala Mackenzie)
Abby Anne Mackenzie (1750-1838)

Magnus Ian Mackenzie (1715-1734)
Angus William Mackenzie (1716-1746)

Alec William Ian Mackenzie (1716-1746?)
=m. Genevieve Millar (d. 1746)
|
Jenny (Genevieve Allison Mary) Mackenzie (1746-1837)

=m2. **Lady Celia Fotheringhay**
|
Magnus Edward Mackenzie (1747-1835)
Catherine Mary Mackenzie (1750-1836)

Malcolm Daniel Mackenzie (1720-1802)
(10th Duke of Kilmorgan from 1746)

= m. **Lady Mary Lennox**
|
Angus Roland Mackenzie 1747-1822
(11th Duke of Kilmorgan)
= m. Donnag Fleming
(ancestor of **David Fleming**)
|
William Ian Mackenzie (The Rake) 1780-1850
(12th Duke of Kilmorgan)
= m. Lady Elizabeth Ross
|
Daniel Mackenzie, 13th Duke of Kilmorgan (1824-1874)
(1st Duke of Kilmorgan, English from 1855)
= m. Elspeth Cameron (d. 1864)
(descendent of **Stuart Cameron**)
|

Hart Mackenzie (b. 1844)

14th Duke of Kilmorgan from 1874
(2nd Duke of Kilmorgan, English)
= m1. Lady Sarah Graham (d. 1876)
|
(Hart Graham Mackenzie, d. 1876)

= m2. **Lady Eleanor Ramsay**
|
Hart Alec Graham Mackenzie (b. 1885)
Malcolm Ian Mackenzie (b. 1887)

Cameron Mackenzie
= m1. Lady Elizabeth Cavendish (d. 1866)
|
Daniel Mackenzie = m. **Violet Devereaux**
|
Fleur Mackenzie (b. 1891)
Dougal Mackenzie (b. 1899)

Cameron Mackenzie = m2. **Ainsley Douglas**
|
Gavina Mackenzie (b. 1883)
Stuart Mackenzie (b. 1885)

"Mac" (Roland Ferdinand) Mackenzie
= m. **Lady Isabella Scranton**
|
Aimee Mackenzie (b. 1879, adopted 1881)
Eileen Mackenzie (b. 1882)
Robert Mackenzie (b. 1883)

Ian Mackenzie = m. Beth Ackerley
|
Jamie Mackenzie (b. 1882) = m. Evie McKnight

Isabella Elizabeth Mackenzie (Belle) (b. 1883)
Megan Mackenzie (b. 1885)

Lloyd Fellows = m. **Lady Louisa Scranton**
|
Elizabeth Fellows (b. 1886)
William Fellows (b. 1888)
Matthew Fellows (b. 1889)

McBride Family

Patrick McBride = m. Rona McDougal

Sinclair McBride = m.1 Margaret Davies (d. 1878)
|
Caitriona (b. 1875)
Andrew (b. 1877)

m.2 **Roberta "Bertie" Frasier**
|
Marcus (b. 1886)
Elena (b. 1888)

Elliot McBride = m. **Juliana St. John**
|
Priti McBride (b. 1881)
Gemma (b. 1885)
Patrick (b. 1886)

Ainsley McBride = m.1 John Douglas (d. 1879)
|
Gavina Douglas (d.)

= m.2 **Lord Cameron Mackenzie**

|

Gavina Mackenzie (b. 1883)
Stuart Mackenzie (b. 1885)

Steven McBride (Captain, Army)
= m. **Rose Barclay**
(Dowager Duchess of Southdown)

|

Helen Rona (b. 1887)

Related Stories

Stuart Cameron (1714-1794)
=m. **Fiona Macdonald** (1718-1808)

|

Alina (b 1747)
Stuart Michael (B 1749)
Broc (1751)
Innis (1754)

David Fleming = m. **Sophie Tierney**

|

Lucas Fleming (b. 1894)

Note: Names in **bold** indicate main characters in the Mackenzie
series

SERIES ISBNS

IN PUBLICATION ORDER

All books are available in e-book, print, and audio except where otherwise noted.
Also see "A Note on Availability" following this list.

Books are listed in publication order.

The Madness of Lord Ian Mackenzie
ISBN: 978-0425244463

Lady Isabella's Scandalous Marriage
ISBN: 978-0425235454

The Many Sins of Lord Cameron
ISBN: 978-0425240496

The Duke's Perfect Wife
ISBN: 978-0425247105

A Mackenzie Family Christmas: The Perfect Gift
ISBN: 978-1791502713

The Seduction of Elliot McBride
Print ISBN: 978-0425251133

The Untamed Mackenzie
(in print in The Scandalous Mackenzies)
ISBN: 978-0425266274

The Wicked Deeds of Daniel Mackenzie
ISBN: 978-0425253953

Scandal and the Duchess
(in print in The Scandalous Mackenzies)
ISBN: 978-0425266274

Rules for a Proper Governess
ISBN: 978-0425266038

The Stolen Mackenzie Bride
ISBN: 978-0425266021

A Mackenzie Clan Gathering
(in print in A Mackenzie Clan Christmas)
ISBN: 978-1984805584

Alec Mackenzie's Art of Seduction
ISBN: 978-1946455093

The Devilish Lord Will
ISBN: 978-1946455574

A Rogue Meets a Scandalous Lady
ISBN: 978-1946455826

A Mackenzie Yuletide
(in print in A Mackenzie Clan Christmas)
ISBN: 978-1984805584

Fiona and the Three Wise Highlanders
(in print in Tartan and Mistletoe)
ISBN: 978-1951041441

The Sinful Ways of Jamie Mackenzie
ISBN: 978-1951041632

A NOTE ON AVAILABILITY

The Mackenzies series began as traditionally published books at Dorchester, and then continued at another house (Berkley), when Dorchester went out of business.

Some of the books are indie published under my JA / AG Publishing imprint: *A Mackenzie Family Christmas*, and then *Alec Mackenzie's Art of Seduction* and all books after it.

All of the books are available in e-book, paperback, and audio.

What this means:

1) **E-books** are available online through all ebook vendors: Amazon, Barnes and Noble, Kobo, Google, and Apple, and directly from me via Jennifer Ashley's Web Store. The e-books are available **worldwide**.

2) **Print** books for the **traditionally published books** are on the shelves at or can be ordered from any bricks and mortar bookseller, and are also available online (Amazon, BN, etc). The English books should be available worldwide, and most of the books are available in translation in other countries. Print

books can be ordered by any bookstore via Ingrams (see Links to the Series for ISBNs).

3) **Print** books for the **indie published books** can be purchased online from Amazon, BN, and other booksellers internationally. They can also be purchased (US only) from me at Jennifer Ashley's Web Store.

All indie books in print can be special ordered by any bookstore. If they say they can't order it for you, argue! I have listed the ISBN numbers in the Links to the Series chapter in this guide to assist booksellers in getting you books. **Ingram** lists all my books in their catalog (booksellers can order directly from them).

4) **All audio books** are available from Audible, Apple, Chirp, Kobo, Google, Audiobooks.com, and many others, and the indie published ones are also sold on Jennifer Ashley's Web Store.

5) **Libraries:** All **traditionally published** books are available in libraries either in print or e-book. I have my **indie published** e-books on Overdrive and other library aggregators, and many libraries carry them. Always let your libraries know what books you want to see—they can order what they don't already have.

6) **Translations:** The Mackenzie books are currently available in many translations, mostly in **German, French,** and **Italian,** which are in e-book and paperback. They have been translated into many more languages—search online or in local book-stores. I list current translations on the Translations page on my website.

7) **Shorter books in Print**: The shorter books published by Intermix (Berkley's e-first imprint) have been gathered into print volumes. *The Untamed Mackenzie* and *Scandal and the*

Duchess can be found in **The Scandalous Mackenzies**, and *A Mackenzie Clan Gathering* and *A Mackenzie Yuletide* are in print in **A Mackenzie Clan Christmas**. The indie published *Fiona and the Three Wise Highlanders* is available in print in **Tartan and Mistletoe** (with *A First-Footer for Lady Jane,* a Regency Hogmanay story).

8) **Collections:** I have also gathered the books I have published under my JA / AG Publishing imprint into boxed sets / collections.

The 18th-century Mackenzies: *Alec Mackenzie's Art of Seduction, The Devilish Lord Will,* and *Fiona and the three Wise Highlanders* have been bundled into **Mackenzies: Lords of the Highlands.**

A Mackenzie Family Christmas, A Rogue Meets a Scandalous Lady, and *The Sinful Ways of Jamie Mackenzie,* have been bundled as **Mackenzies (Collection II): Scandals and Rogues**.

More sets will follow as the series continues.

If you have exhausted all the above resources and still can't find the books, please contact me through my website (www. jenniferashley.com), and I'll see how I can help you.

OTHER BOOKS BY JENNIFER ASHLEY

Regency Bon Bons

(short, sweet Regencies)

A First-Footer for Lady Jane

(In print in *Tartan and Mistletoe*)

Duke in Search of a Duchess

A Kiss for Luck

Along Came a Prince

(All three in print in *Regency Bon-Bons*)

Historical Mysteries

Kat Holloway "Below Stairs" Victorian Mysteries

A Soupçon of Poison

Death Below Stairs

Scandal Above Stairs

Death in Kew Gardens

Murder in the East End

Death at the Crystal Palace

The Secret of Bow Lane

The Price of Lemon Cake

(novella)

Mrs. Holloway's Christmas Pudding

(holiday novella)

Speculations in Sin

A Measure of Menace

(novella)

A Moveable Feast

(novella)

A Silence in Belgrave Square

Murder in Blackfriars

ABOUT THE AUTHOR

New York Times bestselling and award-winning author Jennifer Ashley has more than 120 published novels and novellas in mystery, romance, historical fiction, and urban fantasy under the names Jennifer Ashley, Allyson James, and Ashley Gardner. Jennifer's books have been translated into more than a dozen languages and have earned starred reviews in *Publisher's Weekly* and *Booklist*. When she isn't writing, Jennifer enjoys playing music (guitar, piano, flute), reading, hiking, cooking, and building dollhouse miniatures.

More about Jennifer's books can be found at
http://www.jenniferashley.com

To keep up to date on her new releases, join her newsletter here:
http://eepurl.com/47kLL